The
Forrester
Inheritance

Also by Daisy Vivian

Rose White, Rose Red

THE FORRESTER INHERITANCE

A REGENCY ENTERTAINMENT

Daisy Vivian

Walker and Company
New York

First published in the United States of America in 1985 by the Walker Publishing Company, Inc.

Published simultaneously in Canada by John Wiley & Sons Canada, Limited, Rexdale, Ontario.

Library of Congress Cataloging in Publication Data

Vivian, Daisy.
  The Forrester inheritance.

  I. Title.
PS3572.I86F6 1985   813'.54   84-25793
ISBN 0-8027-0838-2

Printed in the United States of America

10 9 8 7 6 5 4 3 2 1

To my mother,
D.V.M.D.T.,
and for my beloved friend
Irene Saro (1948–1984)

=1=

MARIANA LAID ASIDE her copy of *The Golden Wingéd Bird*, for Mme. de Grayne was in a talkative mood. It was no use scolding Papa for his casual air toward the sitters who supported them, though the fact was that while Papa was a very good painter, and really quite clever at taking a likeness, he simply could not afford to be so cavalier. Sheer practicality forbade it. And yet he did, and foolish women like Madame de Grayne waited in the parlour at his pleasure. And Mariana had to lay aside her book of poetry and entertain them. Not that Madame de Grayne needed much in the way of entertainment, for she prattled away in the Anglo-French accent that always seemed so charming until one had become surfeited from hearing too much of it. And Mariana had heard so much that it was sometimes a great temptation to simply drift away, to float off on wings supplied by Quentin Quartermain and his magnificent verse.

She awoke with a start, realizing from Madame's inflexion that a question had been posed.

"An' do you not agree weeth thees, Mees Mariana?"

Mechanically the girl nodded, having not the faintest idea to what she was agreeing. It made no difference to Madame, who continued with scarcely a pause, "An' then the valet . . . what was 'ees name? Sellees, *n'est-ce pas?*"

Mariana agreed once more. Yes, the man's name was Sellis, and now she knew where they were, for this particular scandal was one of Mme. de Grayne's favourites, an attempted murder and suicide in royal circles. It concerned the dreadful Duke of Cumberland, fifth son of the monarch, and the dramatic events a year past. Madame had been living in a London backwater just then, but you would think she was an habitué of the court from her command of the tattle.

"Thees man, Sellees, he creepy-creep into thee room wis' 'ee *coup de chou* . . . how you would say, 'cabbage chopper' . . . an' he strike!"

She made a hideous whistling sound with her teeth.

"*Formidable!* No? To wound a king's son!" But now she seemed to recollect her own precipitous flight from such attackers in France and conveniently added, "Steel, 'ee was a *canaille*, eh? Even eef the Duke *was* sleeping weeth ees wife!"

Mariana tried to look suitably horrified, but she had so many times heard the news of the Duke's amatory arrangements that they had little power to shock her. Besides, the Duke had recovered, though Sellis, in the long run, had not. She knew Madame would complete the details.

"But the valet, 'ee was the hound. They fin' heem weeth 'ees t'roat cut weeth the razor! Satisfactory, no?"

"But not very tidy, I'm afraid," Mariana interposed before the woman could go on. It stopped Madame in mid-breath, and disappointed her as well, for she was quite prepared to carry the recital on to the bitter end. Luckily, another visitor was announced.

"The Marquis is here, miss," Bridie said diffidently. "What should I do?" For the maid was well aware that Mariana's papa had forbidden his old friend to pay respects to Mariana.

The girl cast a significant and warning glance toward Madame. "I shall come directly, Bridie." The servant withdrew and Mariana made her apologies.

"*Chère* Madame," she began, hoping her use of the French would ease her departure, "a thousand pardons, but I really must speak to a gentleman who is an old friend of my father. You will excuse me, I hope?"

"An' I am to seet 'eer *alone* to await ze papa?" asked Madame crossly. "Eet 'as been an eternity already."

"I'm sure he won't be long," Mariana promised. "Let me just have a word with the gentleman and I will see what can be done."

It would be for her own sake as well as Madame's, for she was not sure she could listen to stale court gossip for the next quarter hour as she had for the last. The Marquis was patiently waiting in the hall. Mariana apologised.

"He still will not see me, then?" asked the Marquis.

"I am afraid not. He is quite adamant. Is there a message I can give him?"

The Marquis shook his head sadly. He was a handsome gentleman of middle years, upright and honourable. Mariana thought it a great shame that her father should treat him so, and for so trifling a matter.

"No, no message. Except, perhaps, that young Tyger Dobyn is said to be in Dublin."

Mariana racked her brain. "Tyger Dobyn? Ah, that would be . . ." Then light broke. "I have it! The so-called 'gentleman pugilist,' is he not? The man they say took Corinthianism a step too far?"

The Marquis assented with a chuckle, though holding up an admonitory finger. "But still a gentleman, Miss Mariana, still a gentleman. One of the favourites of the Prince."

Papa, she knew, would argue that such a distinction would bar the man from gentility forever, but then, Papa loathed the Hanovers with a passion she never quite understood.

"And will he be fighting here?" she asked, not for her own information but because she knew her father would be interested.

The Marquis pretended to be scandalised. "Fighting is illegal, Miss Mariana. Only the riff-raff patronise it." This the girl knew to be quite untrue. Illegal, perhaps, but it was patronised by many in very high places. "No," the Marquis continued, "I doubt that he will be fighting, but he is a great gambler, too, they say, and I expect we shall see him in the gaming rooms."

Mariana sighed. "I hope not, sir. You know my father's weakness. I should not like to put him in the way of temptation. But it was kind of you to call, even knowing that I could not receive you properly." The Marquis's sigh matched her own. He understood.

He took his leave then, and Mariana hurried back to the parlour. Madame de Grayne had been replaced and Papa sat in the chair by the window, perusing his morning mail. "I've put her in the studio and told Bridie to fetch her a pot of tea. That should hold her for a bit, if Bridie brings biscuits as well."

3

"What should hold her, dear Papa," said Mariana with a look of comic resignation, "is the sight of the artist at his easel. It is quite unpardonable how you treat your patrons."

"Oh, pshaw, patrons! Madame de Grayne comes here because she has nothing better to do. Couldn't afford to live in London and came here to Dublin. It ain't my fault, is it, if Dublin is dull?"

His daughter hardly had an answer. To one accustomed to the great city across the water, Dublin was, indeed, quiet. Actually she rather liked it, though Mr. Porter, her father, did not.

She glanced quickly at the post, discovered an envelope addressed to herself, and smiled to see who it was from.

Lucy's letter began well enough to have appeared in a copybook. Really, that was the first alarming thing that Mariana noticed about it, for Lucy had never been known to write a straightforward letter in her life. Notes dashed off at odd moments, bounded and compounded by blots and dashes, her epistles were invariably in a style that could at best be called an untidy scrawl. But now, instead of the usual mélange of vivid impressions and incomplete thoughts, the phrases of the letter were measured and the general tone disturbingly sedate.

Lucy had been Mariana's avowed best friend since their first day at Miss Pecksniff's exclusive school for young ladies. They had shared secrets and midnight treats, as well as hopes, triumphs, and tragedies in varying amounts, all through their young girlhood. If there was one regret at being away from London for Mariana, it was absence from her friend, though the letters, swift and chatty, regularly flew back and forth across the Irish sea. This one, however, was decidedly odd.

"Well, I'm demmed!" Lynval Porter cried from across the room as he perused *his* post.

"What is it, Papa?" asked Mariana mildly. She was used to his frequent outbursts.

"I am not only buzzled with the best, but knocked about, dizzled and dazzled! Flat out, my child! Flat out I am, indeed!"

Mariana looked up from Lucy's letter with a smile, but her papa's usually merry face had gone quite grave. Disturbingly so. She could not remember ever having seen him quite like this before. The sheet

4

he held in one aristocratic hand was visibly trembling, while with the other hand he steadied himself against a chairback.

Mariana stuffed her friend's letter in her pocket and sprang to her father's side. "Papa, what is it? Do sit down, you look quite unwell. What has happened?"

Lynval Porter was almost incoherent. "Unwell, you say? I look unwell? By Gad, I *am* unwell! He has gone and died on us!"

Mariana felt the touch of panic at her throat. This might be a severe blow indeed, for Papa's acquaintance had become sadly shrunken with their change of fortune, and the loss of even one friend could be momentous.

"Who is it, dearest? Who has died?"

Mr. Porter dropped his hands in a telling gesture of defeat. "Uncle Forrester has gone to his glory and left his fortune in other hands."

"No!" Mariana was as thunderstruck as her father. They had for years lived on expectations. Papa and Uncle Josiah Forrester had lately not been on the best of terms, certainly, but who would have thought it would come to this? As she often did in times of stress, Mariana searched the old man's portrait on the wall as if the unsmiling face would give up the secret of its interior meditation. She had scarcely known him; no clue presented itself.

"To whom did he leave it? Some charity, I suppose, Papa?"

"I don't know. Some ragtag scamp who got on his good side, I daresay. The solicitor don't tell me. There's plenty of family in the wife's connexion, I believe. He could have made it over to the Archbishop of C., for all I know or for all the difference it makes. It wasn't left to me—not to us—in any case." He shook his head blindly. "What shall we do, daughter? Penury stares us in the face. It seems there is no hope left."

"He left us nothing at all, Papa? I thought it was assured."

Porter waved the letter disparagingly. "Oh, yes, *something*. A paltry six hundred a year, as an insult. How can the two of us manage on that, eh? Canvas and paint alone cost a mint, even over here!"

Mariana could not help a little sigh of relief. Six hundred was certainly not the fortune they had expected, but it was more than the income they had recently been living on, after all. It was lucky her own needs were small; Papa's were another thing. In addition to the ever present need for paint and canvas, her papa's prime failing, if failing it could be, was that of an over-generous heart. Even in the palmy gaming days it had been clearly understood that he would as lief give away a new topcoat as yesterday's gazette. Once, long ago, he had even done so.

Here in Dublin they could live much more inexpensively than at home in London on a small competence from Papa's late mother, supplemented by an occasional commission from the local Anglo-Irish gentry or even a passing tourist, as travellers were nowadays called. Certainly even in exile they were far from lonely, for there was a colony of English people in similar circumstances who lived here in much the same way as they might have done in Calais had there been no difficulty with France. Though it was usually considered something of a way station for the financially embarrassed, it looked as if *they* might be destined to go on living here forever. Not that there was anything *wrong* with Dublin to Mariana's mind. As a city she adored it, but Papa would never be satisfied here. London was home and he was never happy far from Bow Bells.

The stern face of Uncle Forrester's portrait betrayed no humour. She could not remember if it was a true likeness, for he and Papa had had their great falling out before she was born and the opportunities since then had been rare. At the time of their rupture Uncle Forrester was a City merchant just reaching beyond prosperity toward riches, and Papa (having gambled away the most of his inheritance) was in his employ. Papa was young then, and his uncle was settled in his own ways. Each secretly thought he was doing a great good turn to the other, so much so that they rarely saw eye to eye on any matter. The break had come when the elder had the temerity to question the younger's wisdom in taking a wife with no fortune and absolutely no prospects. The outcome was a subdued (for they were both gentlemen) but serious quarrel that unhappily estranged them forever—unhappily, since the bond of affection had run deep and the loss was immense to each of them. Mariana, of course, thought Papa quite right in marrying, for otherwise she might not exist. It was a pity the marriage had gone astray.

On the bedside table in Papa's chamber was an exquisite miniature, which he looked at the last thing at night and the first thing in the morning. Sometimes, Mariana fancied, he even had quiet conversations with it, as she often did. It was all the girl knew of her mother, the picture of a young lady with a sweetly tremulous smile and large dark eyes that hinted at some secret unhappiness. The impression was quite possibly only an illusion fostered by the artist's fashionable romanticism. The painter had not been Papa, who was more at home on larger canvases, but a friend. Mariana knew she must have inherited her own fiercely practical streak from someone other than her father; perhaps Mama had been more sensible than the miniaturist had allowed himself to see.

She bent to retrieve the embroidery hoop and silks that had been knocked from the table in the flurry of excitement. The vivid colours made a brave display against the carpet and she found herself taking a little courage from their brightness. Lucy's letter, which she had quite forgotten, crinkled in her pocket but she left it for the moment. Much as she adored her friend, the matters at hand were of more importance than girlish gossip.

"Don't fret, dearest," she said comfortingly to her father. "I know that to you this amount seems *very* small, but it is better than nothing at all, is it not? I vow, you gave me quite a start. Just think, we managed by being careful with what little we had; now we have a little more to add to it. We've doubled our income! In a way we're quite rich."

He rallied enough to pat her hand. "Oh, I know well enough we're not skint, but close enough for my taste. I had such high hopes of taking you home, letting you come out among our own sort. What do we do now, eh? I imagine we have a mound of debts to take up the slack."

"For the moment, but something will turn up," she said firmly. "It always has. A great commission for you may be just around the corner, perhaps; or I shall marry the Marquis over your foolish objections; or you will find a rich and compliant widow who will not mind taking on a spinster as daughter, though, I must confess, I find that unlikely."

"Spinster, my foot!" her father chuckled, half out of his pet. "If you are on the shelf at twenty, I shudder to contemplate the case of some others. As for marrying, you know I believe you far too young

7

and pretty to waste yourself on the likes of Downsbury. The effrontery of that old raven, proposing to a gel young enough to be his daughter!"

But Mariana rose to this. "He is a kindly gentleman and your true and dearest friend, Papa. I shall not hear you ill use him when his motives come straight from the heart and are perfectly honourable. It is high time you made it up with him, you know. You two are very alike. You must miss him a great deal.

"Alike! Indeed! For one thing, he is years older than I. . . . And well off," he added gloomily, looking again at the letter he still clutched in his hand.

"He is two years *younger*, dear, and as sweet and generous as yourself."

Lynval looked at her sharply. "I say, you're not thinking of acceptin' him?"

"Over your objections?" Mariana asked smoothly. "I might, at that, you know. You and he would still be friends if he had not made such a chivalrous advance to me. It was quite flattering to you as well, after all."

"And not to you, I suppose? A marquis wanting to marry a mere chit?" His temper seemed much improved and Mariana pressed onward.

"Well, dear parent, he as much as said to me that securing *your* future meant as much to him as looking after mine. That *is* friendship, no matter how you look at it."

"Said that, did he?" Papa sounded pleased. "By Jove, quite quixotic, although I wager a young girl wouldn't think it very romantic. Worried about me, was he? Well, he has his good points, I suppose, the same as anyone else." He seemed to muse on that thought for a moment. Then, "But what are we to do about this?" He shook the letter. "Shall we contest the will?"

"If Uncle was as careful a man as you say, I am certain he will have assured himself that there are no loopholes whatsoever. Besides, Father, it was his own money, was it not? Fairly made by his own efforts, not inherited? Whatever your personal feelings about him, would you truly be happy with money he wished to be given to someone else?"

Her papa's eyes twinkled as he laid a finger aside his nose. "It may come as a sad shock to you, pet, but I should be very happy, indeed, though I don't suppose I'll have the opportunity to demonstrate it." Ruefully he shook his head. "As far as I can see, it appears that we shall have to settle in to the rigours of genteel poverty. It isn't by any means what I had in mind for you, but it seems to be my destiny."

She knelt and laid her head against his knee. "We shall have each other, you know," she said softly. "That is worth more than a fortune."

They sat in companionable silence for a few moments, then he grimaced. "I shall have to go to London, I suppose, and be lighted upon like a duck on a Junebug, for my worthy creditors will have had intelligence of this even before I."

She rose and kissed him tenderly on the forehead. "We're clever folk. We'll think of something. Meanwhile, you have a sitting. I think Madame de Grayne should have finished her tea by now, don't you? Mind you flatter her, she has been quite patient."

"I am always charming with female sitters; it is the secret of my great vogue. I love to flatter."

"On the *canvas*, Papa. Be flattering in the portrait too, and her friends will come in flocks."

"God forbid," murmured Mr. Porter prayerfully. "Like every portraitist I try to walk the fine line between truth and avarice." He rose from his chair. "Well, I can only do my best."

Straightening his cravat and settling his beautifully tailored coat about his shoulders, he went into the studio. "My dear Madame," Mariana heard him say dulcetly, "you are looking absolutely radiant today. We must capture you in just this light."

The crisis was averted, at least for the moment. But Papa had been correct in one thing. It was most disquieting to have one's dreams of a comfortable, if not lavish, future snatched from under one in such an abrupt way. The legacy would, as it stood, ease things a little, but not by very much. It was so tiresome to be always cutting corners and turning last year's hems. Scrimping. Perhaps the practical thing would be to marry the dear Marquis, but what self-respecting girl could accept a man merely because he wanted to provide for her father? Friendship was all very well, but it could be carried too far, in her view. If the Marquis had mentioned his desire to provide for his old friend as a secondary theme in his proposal, she reflected, she might have accepted him at once. To become a person of rank would be a pleasant alteration, after all. The fact that the Marquis was as old, or nearly, as her father did not disquiet her in the least, for older men quite often marry young girls (but older women and young men? Odd that that should be unacceptable) and he *was* quite handsome, in a ruined way; certainly distinguished. Still, to have been addressed in such a fashion was quite unthinkable.

The letter in her pocket rustled once more as she closed the door to the studio. She listened for a moment to be sure all was well inside, then sat in the window-seat to finish Lucy's news. At the top of the second page the style changed dramatically, reverting to the old slapdash tracks of Lucy at her most impatient.

> *Dearest heart [it said], I cannot go on any longer being proper. I must tell you my great good news and have done with it for I do not want you to think I have become a noodlehead without you here to set me an example. [Here there was a large blot that had been scraped, but to no avail. The letter continued beyond it.] I am in love! [Oh, Lud, thought Mariana, the third time this year!] I mean to say that I am truly [heavily underscored] in love for the first time. Oh, my dearest friend, I know you will love him as much as I do. On reflection, perhaps not quite so much. We are to be wed in but two months' time and I must [even more heavily underscored] have you and no one else as my bridal attendant. No one else will do! If you will not stand beside me in this time I swear I shall do something quite drastic! I don't know what. Run away to Gretna Green, perhaps, and become a scandal. Really, puss, you must do your best. More, for I will not have no for an answer!*

Mariana took a moment to ease the little pang in her breast, for she and Lucy had always been close—closer than sisters, they often said to each other—but now her dear closest confidante would become something quite different, a respectable married lady. This of sweet scatterbrain Lucy! It gave one such a turn!

Mariana, we have been friends ever since I caught you putting salt in the headmistress's sugar bowl and I feel I can say this next bit without giving offence. Dearest, I do not know what your present circumstances may be, but I imagine they cannot be the best in the world. The journey to London would undoubtedly put a strain on your pocket, but for the love you bear me [all underlined] do arrange it! My papa will bear all the cost and I truly cannot manage alone! You will be doing me a great injury if you let misguided pride [scored together, plus a small blot for emphasis] stand in the way of my complete happiness on this most important day!

Well, that was nonsense, of course. The household coffers were not exactly overflowing, but with a little managing something could be done. But oh, how lonely it would be in London *after* the nuptials. What could she do there all alone? Perhaps there would be enough so that Bridie, that pillar, that resourceful maid-of-all-work who had been with her since she could remember, might travel as companion. But what about Papa, in that case? He could not go, for if he so much as set foot in London his creditors would have a writ out and he would be detained. They were, she was sure, poised to pounce. But with Cook's help he could manage alone here for a fortnight, surely.

Bridie came into the room at that instant, as if the thought of London had summoned her. "If you please, Miss Mariana, there's a woman to see yez."

"A lady, Bridie?"

"A lady, indeed," snapped the imposing matron who swept through the doorway. Although it was unlikely she would see forty again, there was no question but that she was the epitome of elegance, from her tall hat of black velvet to her creamy yellow laced boots. The astrakhan-lined redingote of poison-green merino fitted her to perfection, and it was evident that she knew it. Hours had undoubtedly been passed assuring that it should be so. Mariana had never seen anyone so completely self-possessed.

"Lady Battledore, my girl, as the servant might have had the wit to inform you."

"Yes, madam, so she might," said Mariana, "had she been given the chance." She gave Bridie leave to go, then turned back to the unexpected visitor. "Won't you sit down? How may I serve you?"

"Battledore," repeated the woman, enunciating each syllable with frigid emphasis. "*Lady* Battledore," she said again as she took the proffered chair.

Mariana was not at all taken aback by this flummery. She did not, naturally, care to be rude, but really, enough was enough, and she had had her share of surprises today.

"I assure you, madam, my hearing is of good quality. I quite understood the name, but I fear it possesses no great significance for me."

Lady Battledore's eyebrows raised almost to her hairline. "You really don't know? The name means nothing to you?"

Mariana considered carefully. "There *was* a Eugenia Battledore at Miss Pecksniff's school, but I hardly . . ."

"My last husband's niece. Dreadful, simpering creature. Did she have that spotty complexion at school?"

"I am afraid so," Mariana answered, wondering where all this was leading.

"Still does! Stuffs herself with all manner of sweets, then tries to mend the damage with paint and layers of powder. Useless, of course."

"Of course," Mariana agreed.

Lady Battledore squinted at her. "You appear to have a good complexion. No sweets for you, I daresay?"

Mariana thought guiltily of her secret passion for marzipan. "I try to regulate them."

"Wise of you." Unexpectedly she thrust her face forward. "Still don't know, eh?"

"I'm very sorry," the girl answered, wishing heartily that this peculiar quizzing game might end. What *could* this tiresome (though titled) woman want of her?

"Sorry? Waste of time. Don't be. Never believe in being sorry. Every moment is precious. Mine *and* yours. Well, everyone knows me in London, not to mention Paris, Berlin, and Vienna. Or at least they *did*, until that Corsican madman began to implement his scheme of conquest. By the time he's done I shall be quite forgotten, I am sure." She looked about her in a disparaging fashion. "To think I am *reduced* to revelling in the fleshpots of Dublin."

Mariana, meanwhile, was racking her brain. "If it is a portrait you've come about . . ." she began, then saw that this was the wrong tack.

"Ah, still daubs, does he? Every gentleman needs a diversion. I expect he's too old for wicked women, ain't that so?" She cackled smartly at her own joke. "Too old for wicked women, I expect he *is*!"

"My father is in great demand, and rather far back in his work, Lady Battledore, though for a consideration he might consent to see you."

"Oh, might he? Charming, I'm sure."

"A preliminary consultation, you see."

"For a consideration? Clever gel, you know where the money is at, I see," said Lady Battledore with heavy irony.

"Because he is *so* very popular. His aptitude for catching a likeness is quite remarkable," said Mariana.

The older woman rapped her fingers smartly on the arm of her chair. "I pray, do not essay the art of puffery, my child. You haven't the guile. I can read you like a book. A book with *very* large print." But she said it kindly, as though they shared a confidence. "No, I have come to see your father on quite another matter. I will be much obliged if you will fetch him at once."

"Indeed, I cannot, Lady Battle . . . er . . . field?" said Mariana a little crossly, for she did not think herself as guileless as all that. "The person sitting to him is an important client and would rightly take it amiss. She has paid her guineas and should not be cheated."

Lady Battledore looked as if she had been struck. Her face became quite crimson and her mouth dropped a little. One or two seconds were required to regain her composure. "Do *not* presume to cross *me*, young woman! My time too is limited and valuable. Do as I say and fetch your father at once!"

"Certainly not!" cried Mariana. She was aghast that this perfect stranger should presume to issue orders to her, and in her own house, too.

Lady Battledore rose grandly and shook her umbrella. "Do as I say, and be quick!"

The studio door was flung open. "What on earth is this commotion?" demanded Mr. Porter. "How can I work, Mariana, if you insist on knocking up a row with every . . ." He stopped, quite thunderstruck at the sight of the belligerent woman in the middle of his parlour who was brandishing a raised umbrella for all the world as if she intended to strike his daughter.

"You will oblige me, madam," he said sternly, "by relinquishing your bellicose posture and proffering some explanation for this extraordinary behaviour."

Slowly she turned to face him.

"Good heavens!" he said rather weakly. "Emilia?"

"The same," Lady Battledore acknowledged condescendingly. "How have you kept, Lynval? Not so plump as I recall you. Exile seems to agree with some. For your age you look well."

"And your tongue, my dear, has not dulled a whit." He shook his head in disbelief. "But what on earth are you doing in Dublin?"

It elicited an earshattering chortle. "I came to see if you'd forgotten me!"

"Tush," Mariana's papa snorted. "Forgotten the bane of my young married life? Not likely. And to whom are you shackled these days? Not still old Fotheringay?"

"Lady Battledore," said Mariana, not sure how she should proceed in the face of this tender reunion, "since I apprehend that you and my father are already known to each other, perhaps I may offer you a dish of tea?"

"If it is China," said her ladyship, amiable now that the stormclouds were past, "none of that ghastly Indian brew."

"Never mind," interposed Mr. Porter smoothly, "I cannot imagine

14

that Lady . . . Battledore, is it now? . . . will have the leisure for refreshment. Her carriage must be waiting."

"Too quick by half, Porter," said her ladyship firmly. "I have yet to state my purpose, and I shall not be evicted until I do." She turned her attention back to Mariana. "Yes, my dear, China tea and milk. No sweetening."

Now from the studio came the disgruntled Madame de Grayne, exhibiting the woebegone look of the abandoned. She was a weedy woman with an unfortunate spot on her nose that Mariana privately hoped Papa had the chivalry to omit—the spot, not the nose. Her Gallic ire was somewhat eased by an introduction to a titled English-woman.

"*Enchantée, très enchantée, Madame Battledore*," she simpered. "I 'ave seen you many time in London." The red spot grew ever more carmine as Mariana eased her toward the door.

"Amazing," said Mr. Porter, "what any title, any title at all, will do. Despite her words, I imagine that woman has absolutely no idea who you are, never saw you in London, and hasn't the slightest notion if your title is true or false, and yet she trembled as if she had spoken to the Empress of the French at the very least."

"Perhaps she *may* have seen me," said her ladyship. "I opened my house there for a brief time last year. But fancy you comparing me to Josephine. You have grown quite gallant with age."

"You've met the Empress?" Mariana asked in awe.

"Oh yes—charming creature, Josephine, though she wears damp gauze, which is bad for the health. Always has a sniffle. Caribbean blood, I daresay. Accustomed to the heat."

"Lady Battledore will be leaving shortly, Mariana," said Mr. Porter. "See to the tea."

"In a moment, Papa. Let her ladyship finish."

The visitor smirked. "Caught your interest, have I? Not such an old harridan as you thought? Well, I daresay Josephine is well enough, for most purposes. A bit tedious after the first hour, since she has no conversation at all past the sort of flirtatious chatter that men seem to enjoy. Her sisters-in-law are no better. Worse, if anything. Damme, but it makes one long for the *ancien régime*. They

15

may have doused themselves with toilet water instead of using honest soap, but they never used the wrong fork and their conversation was brilliant. What posterity will say of this jumped-up lot, I don't know."

"The tea, Mariana," repeated her father testily, and Mariana made her escape to the kitchen, where Bridie was recounting her meeting with the quality.

"So I says to Miss Mariana, 'There is a lady to see you, Miss Mariana,' an' this old party pushed past me as if I was a bag of dirty clothes. 'La-ddd-y Battledore,' she says, grand as you please. Who she may be at home is a different thing, I'll wager."

"If you wants to know," said Cook, "she's been Lady Fotheringay, Lady Bast, Lady Cheltenham, the Countess of Dorrick, and Lady Sinden." She counted on her fingers. "Oh, and Lady Battledore, that's five."

"Six," said Bridie. "You can't count. What happened to 'em all?"

"May we have some tea, Cook?" asked Mariana. "Jasmine, I think, and some scones."

"Not the India tea," Bridie mocked. "That's all slop to her."

But Cook was more amenable. "Would you be wanting some cakes, miss? I have some lovely fairy-cakes just fresh today. I knew her ladyship in the old days, and I remember she allus liked them."

"Did she?" asked Mariana vaguely. "That would be very pleasant." She lingered to hear the end of the conversation, trying to look as if she were not eavesdropping on the servants' conversation.

"Oh, yes, I knew her well in the old days. When Mr. Porter was first married she was in and out of the house at all hours. She was allus the same as now, grand, but a good heart."

"Must to have had, with all them husbands. She must have liked a bit of change to have had six."

Cook busied herself at the hob. "Only five. I see where you went wrong, though. Lady Cheltenham *was* the Countess of Dorrick. Her private name, you know. And as for change, she never. They all died, poor things. I daresay she was too high-spirited for them."

Mariana was a little taken aback at such frankness below-stairs, but reflected that she shouldn't have been listening anyway. But how fascinating! Reluctantly she slipped out the door and returned to the parlour.

There she found that unfortunately the relationship between host and guest had markedly deteriorated. Lady Battledore's umbrella was once more in play and she pounded the floor for emphasis as she shouted at Papa, who was ignoring the ruckus completely. Perhaps he could not hear her, for he was shouting as loudly as she.

"Demmed imbecile!" trumpeted the enraged woman.

"Imbecile, am I?" cried Papa. "Silly old cat!"

"It was because he consorted with the likes of you that I lost poor Sinden in the first place! He couldn't stand your kind of life, and it killed him."

"Aye," Papa responded, "you lost him for another, and him for still another, and him for another still! What's *become* of old Fotheringay? Have you killed him off like the others?"

"Much *you* have to say," Lady Battledore retorted with annoying energy. "While my poor sister and I were sitting in the parlour counting stitches waiting for you to return from the clubs and dens you frequented . . ."

"Hoo! You never kept the poor girl company for a full evening in your life," scoffed Papa. "Gay as a goose in the gutter, you were, and I daresay you still are, for all you're on the wrong side of fifty!"

This shaft left Lady Battledore curiously unperturbed. "Tell it not in Gath, sir, for you are older than I!"

"I daresay that is true, my lady, if you have sunk to counting only eight of ten."

Quite unexpectedly they both broke into hearty laughter, which in turn brought tears to their eyes. It seemed to Mariana that they both had been struck by the identical fit of madness. Temporary, she hoped. It was as if they shared some fascinating, though slightly addled, secret. One that she could never take part in.

Seeing the tea and the cakes, they sat down at once like greedy schoolchildren, and betwixt gulps and nibbles exchanged tattle and reminiscence, ignoring Mariana completely. She slipped out of the room with a great deal of wasted discretion, for they hardly knew she had come and gone.

2

IT WAS FAR into the evening when Mariana heard Lady Battledore's carriage finally drive off. She could hear Papa closing the house for the night, locking the doors and quietly moving up the stair. Presently there was a gentle tapping at her door.

"Come in, Papa," she said softly.

"I only wanted to bid you a good night, my dear," he said as he entered. Then he peered at her closely. "You look rather drawn, Mariana. I fear you work too hard. Taking charge of the household and a crotchety old man may be too much for you, eh?"

"No, Papa, it's only the candlelight. I am quite well."

"Nevertheless, it is time you slept. The strain on those cornflower eyes will fade them, and we mustn't have that."

She wondered if he was thinking of her mother, whose eyes, as he had often told her, were exactly the shade of Mariana's own. Where was her mother now, she wondered? Whenever she had asked before, Papa had always put her off by saying merely that her mama lived in France with another gentleman. But surely she could not live there now? Perplexing. And what had Lady Battledore to do with all this?

As if he sensed that she was filled with questions, Papa laid his fingers across her lips. "Sleep now, pet."

"I'll go to sleep soon," she promised, "but Papa, what about Lady Battledore?"

He looked at her oddly, sharply, then smiled. "An agreeable old rattle, for all her faults. Part of me lurid past, you know."

She waited. Was he about to reveal something of those hidden years of which she knew nothing? But he only chuckled, perhaps recalling some past folly.

Just as he was about to close the door he turned and came back to her bedside. Then he seemed to hesitate and begin to turn away, and still again, with resolution, turned back and asked her hesitantly, "Mariana, my dear, have you missed your mother dreadfully all these years?"

She could not have been more surprised. "Why, no, Papa. I never knew her. Perhaps I should have done if I had been older, but she went away when I was so *young* . . ."

He nodded. "Exactly. You were so young. I have wondered sometimes if we did the right thing, she and I. It is always so hard to know who is the strongest in a marriage."

"Must there be a strong and a weak, Papa?"

"Perhaps not, perhaps not." He touched her cheek lovingly. "I fear I have been selfish all these years, keeping you to myself, but you see, I believed them when they all told me it was for the best." He kissed her again and moved toward the door. And once again looked back. "A holiday, that's what you need, my girl. Getting away for a bit is the ticket. We'll talk about it tomorrow." And he was gone.

She heard him still pottering about on the lower floor, then quietly let himself out of the house, carefully locking the door behind him. Now he would, she knew, head for his club, where he would play until the wee hours with friends who, like himself, could ill afford to part with a shilling; fellow exiles reaching back for a touch of their lost years. Mariana felt little alarm at this; exiles do not play for credit, since it has long since been exhausted. There would be some little profit or loss, nothing very considerable, only token amounts to lend point to the game. She turned her cheek to the pillow and slept easily.

And slept late, for some reason. Papa had not yet come down to breakfast by nine of the clock, and she ate alone. Meditatively sipping her tea, she thought of his curious conversation at her bedside. Now she reconsidered his question, and answered it in quite the same way: No, she had not missed her mother, because she had never known her mother. Papa and Cook and Bridie had been all the family she had ever needed. And at school she had had Lucy. She had never thought that anything or anyone was lacking.

Bridie marched into the breakfast room projecting disapproval before her. "Please, miss, she's come again. I rec-a-nize the carriage through the winder." Mariana looked out and thought that, certainly, that saucy barouche was unlikely to belong to anyone in this staid neighbourhood. The lady was not long in thrusting herself into the room.

"He's told you, I imagine," she said without preamble. "Quite a nice plan, is it not? We shall be happy together, you'll see. Now, now, don't gawk at me, gel. Lord, if you go all speechless at my generosity it will quite defeat my purpose. A companion, nay, a playmate is what is wanted, not a statue."

Mariana was quite speechless. She had no notion of what Lady Battledore was speaking, but the idea of being a playmate to this mature woman was a little daunting.

Her ladyship did not pause for an answer, instead she sniffed the air. "I say, is that the tea you served me yesterday? Quite extraordinary. The best I've had outside of London. Foreigners have simply no idea how to brew tea, have you noticed? What is it called again?"

"Darjeeling, ma'am," Mariana replied without the trace of a smile. Actually, she had no idea *what* it was, simply their usual breakfast blend brewed in the usual way. She did not even smile maliciously when she said, "We always say that it is the best tea to come out of India. I am so gratified that you agree." No, she was quite demure and dropped her eyes prettily.

Her visitor looked down her nose. "I believe I asked for China tea."

"I believe the China tea was all gone," Mariana said sweetly and watched Lady Battledore closely. In fact, her ladyship held her tongue admirably, though the strain must have been intense. She fidgeted, twitched her nose, wagged her head back and forth, and then allowed she might have just a sip.

As Mariana poured, Lady Battledore went on with the monologue with which she had made her entry. "He *did* tell you, did he not? It is *such* a capital idea, I wonder I had not thought of it before. How soon, do you think, before we can begin to set out?" Then, when Mariana failed to respond, this was followed by a slap on her thigh and a sharp, "Your father, my dear, is a *neddy!*"

Then, at Mariana's quick look this was amended somewhat. "Oh, I know he's your father, and blood *is* thicker than gin and all that, but you know, he *did* agree that it was his place as a father to tell it you. Such a neddy . . . and you must admit, I have *some* basis for comparison."

Mariana hardly knew what to say except, "Do you, madam?"

Lady Battledore's hand went to her temple in a gesture most certainly learned from Mrs. Siddons. It was effective, but a bit overdone in this instance. "Where is he? This is quite ridiculous. It must be settled now, for I haven't the patience for such folderol! I shall have a crisis, I know I shall! Let him be fetched at once. Please!" This was couched as a request, though there was no question but that it was an order; nay, a command. Striding into the hallway she trumpeted up the stairwell: "Porter! Porter! Where are you, you wretch? Come out and defend yourself, or I'll come looking, no matter where you are!"

And true to form, Papa was surprising. He appeared promptly. Something which, in his daughter's experience, he had never been known to do before.

The odd thing was that he came in through the front door.

And even odder, he was not alone.

From her vantage point in the breakfast room, Mariana could see the newcomer quite well. Indeed, for all his early morning pallor and a faintly dishevelled look common to men who have been gaming all the night long, he was strikingly handsome. He was quite tall, perhaps past six foot; he was masterfully tailored so that his extremely broad shoulders and powerful chest did not appear at all grotesque; and his hair was cut in the fashionable Corinthian mode. All these, plus the brilliant, not to say splendid, lustre of his boots, added up to a gentleman of fashion. But the severity of his hawkish face put it all to rout. She felt, for all his proper dress and deportment, that there was something alien about this man, something more than a little out of the ordinary. Then he saw her through the open door; he bowed slightly and smiled.

The smile changed everything. It was so personal, and yet so without any trace of forwardness or impertinence, that Mariana was taken quite off her guard. She flushed, and before she could recover her composure, Papa was answering Lady Battledore.

"What a bother you are, Emilia. Don't you understand that I am an artist? Our time is not our own to be bullied here and there at every person's beck and whim."

"And am I every person, then, sir?" She glowered at him and Papa visibly retreated. Mariana could not help but wonder what hold this woman had over him.

"Stand down, man, or I'll pull you down." He came closer to her, then remembered his companion and threw up his hands.

"You see, sir, what a house I have come home to."

The stranger turned that dazzling smile on Lady Battledore. "Forgive me, madam. I perceive that this is an inopportune visit." Then to Papa, "Mr. Porter, sir, our business can wait until another time. I apprehend that your lady requires your attention."

"Not long, Mr. Dobyn, I promise," Papa replied.

His companion repeated his previous sketch of a bow. "At your convenience, sir, I do assure you." Another quick look toward Mariana, and he was out the door.

Lady Battledore crowed loudly. "He thought I was your wife, by my life! As if he had not seen me in London a score of times, and even talked to me on more than one occasion. How very curious the world is!" But she returned quickly to her previous, scolding tone. "Now then, you impossible man, have you told this child our dark secret or no?"

Lynval Porter's chagrin was evident. "I tried, Emilia, truly I did, but the words would not come. It needs a woman's touch."

Lady Battledore pursed her lips. "No wonder the poor girl looks at me as if I were escaped from Bedlam. Forgive me, child. Perhaps you had better sit down."

Why was this terrible knot at the bottom of Mariana's stomach? Sitting as she had been bidden, she remained still poised, ready to leap, if necessary, to Papa's assistance. Lady Battledore's first words left her breathless.

"Do you fancy me at all, my girl? I sincerely hope you do, for I am your near relative."

"My . . . relative, ma'am?" Mariana faltered. For one brief, mad moment she thought Lady Emilia was saying that she was her mother, that the stranger before her was the girl who had posed for the delicate ivory miniature in Papa's bedroom. But then she knew it could not be true, though there *was* a likeness.

Her ladyship cast a wary eye at Papa. It half seemed to glitter with her restrained temper. "Why could you not have done this, sir? We agreed it was your place to do so, not mine!"

"You've crossed the Rubicon," said Mr. Porter, who had been trying, ever so discreetly, to slip out of the room. Family scenes after a night of gaming were not his style in the least. Nor, for that matter, were family scenes of any kind. "You may as well go on, Emilia, even in the forthright way you have begun. I daresay neither of us is exactly overloaded with tact."

Lady Emilia heaved a great sigh. "I never dreamt it would be so difficult." She fanned herself furiously, then returned her attention to the girl, who was completely baffled by this entire turn of events. "Oh, pshaw, perhaps there is a certain virtue in being forthright." She paused, steeled herself, then said all in a rush, "Are you aware, child, that your mother is still alive?"

Mariana nodded. "I have always believed so, madam, since my papa has never told me otherwise." The fears returned, and to rid herself of them once for all she asked, "Are you trying to tell me, Lady Battledore, that *you* are my mother?"

To her everlasting credit, Emilia, Lady Battledore, reined in her natural instincts and for once trod gently.

"I would be eternally grateful to the Almighty if I could say 'yes,' my dear, but that is not possible. When I told you I was a near relative, I never thought you would leap to such a conclusion." She sat down beside Mariana at the table and took the girl's hand between her own.

"Your mother is my baby sister, Mariana. She lived for a long while on the continent, but now she has come back to England. Do you think you would like to meet her?"

Relief swept over the girl like a sweet rain. "I beg your pardon, madam. I did not mean . . ."

"No, Mariana. It is all right. I understand. I know how difficult it is for the young to believe their elders were ever youthful. My looks are sadly faded, now, but even I was once called Lady Perilous, because, they said, I was a danger to every male heart in London. It was not true, of course, but it was mightily pleasant to hear." Her protestations were tosh, for she was handsome still.

"And my mother?"

"Oh, she was far lovelier than I. Everyone said she was the loveliest girl that season. I remember how the young beaux used to crowd around her. Why, people would stand on chairs for a better look when she came into a room. If it turned her head, who is to say that was not as it should be? Perhaps her only flaw was that her heart was *too* tender, too easily engaged."

"Not at all," asserted Lynval. "She was left alone too much. Young women can't abide that, though I daresay older ones are often glad for it. You know how I am about cards and dice, Mariana. The table is a terrible mistress."

He was so visibly moved that Lady Battledore took charge once again and rang for fresh tea. Bridie received the instructions with little grace and stomped out.

"There are a few things here," her ladyship commented acidly, "that could do with a little improvement." But she did not go on in that vein, returning instead to the point of her visit.

"The question now seems to be, Mariana, whether you wish to renew your acquaintance with your mother, or be left to sort this all out in your own way. Shall we forget that I ever came to Dublin in search of you?"

Lynval looked almost hopeful, but Mariana cried, "Oh, no, please, Aunt."

"Good, then that part is settled; the next question seems to be a question of *when*. I say get on with it, but you may wish to discuss it with your father and come to a joint decision."

"Nothing to discuss," Lynval growled. "If she needs to go off with you to London, then she must." He awkwardly patted Mariana's arm. "Though I shall miss her like the very deuce."

"Oh, I say, Porter, not the thing at all! She's been with you for years. You can't blame her for wanting to meet her mother. It is only natural."

"Never said it wasn't; I only said I'd miss her, and I shall."

"But who shall look after you, Papa?" asked Mariana a little guiltily, forgetting that only a day ago she had been quite willing to leave him to his own devices. "I won't go off to London without you, and that's certain."

"Not at all, puss. You know I dare not show my face in London the way my finances are presently arranged. If you will be so good, you shall do me a commission."

"Shall I? What is that?"

"Someone must visit the executor of Uncle Forrester's estate. It may not amount to much, but I hesitate to entrust such important matters to the post. It is best that someone go, and since I cannot, you must."

"But what of the expense?"

"Hang the expense; you need a holiday."

"I beg you not to have the slightest worry on that account," Lady Battledore said. "It has all along been my intention to bear what costs there may be."

"But is that quite right?" asked Mariana.

"Will you begrudge me the pleasure, to say nothing of your mother?"

Mariana considered. "Will you give me a day or two, Aunt? I am all in a whirl. First Lucy, and now this." She clapped her fingers to her mouth. "Oh, lauk, I forgot . . . I *must* go to London for the wedding. Lucy could not do without me."

"What, your school chum?" asked Mr. Porter. "How is it you have said nothing of this? Now there is no excuse; you must accept your aunt's very kind offer."

"You would be doing me a great favour, as well," said her ladyship. "There has been little enough of youth in my house for a deal of years. Both it and I need something of a change."

"Then I will come," said Mariana, "and I thank you heartily. I only hope I shall not prove a trouble."

It was arranged then that Mariana should travel with her aunt in two days' time. "But I shall be here again tomorrow! Porter, you shan't escape so easily. We have a great many things to discuss." She looked significantly at her niece. "Not all of them fit for young ears."

"Oh, shall I leave you now?" Mariana inquired. "I shall have a number of things to see to before I can even begin my preparations to travel."

Her aunt shook her head. "If you think your father could stand up to me in the condition he is in, I do not. Look at him, he is nearly asleep on his feet. That is what comes of gaming all night long. And at his age, too." The faintest ghost of a smile indicated that her words were to be taken lightly. "Lynval, my friend, go to bed."

Mr. Porter's answering grin was too brief; it was evident that he *was* very tired. Lady Battledore bade them goodbye and left them alone together, knowing that there was a great deal to be said.

But a silence had fallen between father and child, an awkwardness unlike anything they had known in the past. It lasted for all of five minutes; Lynval sipping his tea, Mariana busying herself with the clearing away.

But it could last no more than those moments; they loved each other too much for that.

"Have you been so unhappy with me, child?" asked Lynval.

She flung her arms about his neck. "Oh, Papa, no! How can you ask such a thing?" She hesitated. "But there are so many things I need to ask you, and I do not quite know how. When you have rested, perhaps we shall have a long conversation."

"Would you not like to ask a little now?"

"Are you not too tired? You look very drawn, and a touch pale."

"That is what comes of keeping gambler's hours," he answered ruefully. "Mr. Dobyn was much too good company."

"Dare I ask?" Mariana only needed to hint; her father understood. "How much I lost? No more than I could afford. Most of the night was spent in talk. Good conversation, too. That man is an unconventional sort, but he has been through it all, and kept his eyes open wide."

"But is he quite a gentleman? It seems to me that I have heard stories . . ."

"Tut, where have you been listening? His antecedents are impeccable, but it is the usual thing, you know: ancient name, no money. Needs an admixture of merchant blood from time to time to keep the coffers full. Seemingly none of the Dobyns were clever enough,

26

or perhaps personable enough, to do that. So he went off to the wars. Splendid chap. Don't know if I'd ever grow tired of him."

He roused himself. "But why are we talking of Tyger Dobyn? We have other, more pressing matters, surely?"

"Would you tell me about my mother?" Then, suddenly shy, "or should that wait?"

"Not entirely. What do you already know of her? You were very young when she went away. I should have talked to you of her long since, I know, but I did not know how. I thought I would wait until you asked, but you never did."

Mariana looked down at her hands, surprised to find them nervously twisting her handkerchief. She had not thought she was so distrait. It was difficult, but she was finally able to say, "I thought she might be dead."

"Oh, my God! Who told you such a thing? Was it something I implied? How wrong I have been. I can see a great harm here, and I ask your forgiveness, child. Men are weak creatures, I fear."

"No, it was not you. You never said anything at all. It was someone else; a nurse, I think, or a governess. I remember asking and being told that my mama was in heaven and I would cause you great sorrow if I even mentioned her name. So of course I did not."

"How abominable! I wish I had the creature at hand this moment!"

"I'm sure it was done for the best." Suddenly something seemed to strike a chord in her mind. "There was a woman . . ." She struggled to remember. "It was at school . . . sometimes when we would play in the garden there was a woman who would come and look at us over the wall. Several days in a row, usually. Then she would go away for a long while, perhaps a year or two, but she always came back."

"What did she look like, this woman?" asked her father guardedly.

She struggled to remember. "Small, rather delicate, I always thought. Dark hair, I believe, though I am not sure, for she always wore a bonnet or a hat."

He pressed her further. "Was she anything like the miniature in my bedroom?"

Mariana considered. "No, not at all. I suppose I merely wanted her to be my mother, though she wasn't."

"Not necessarily true," said her father. "That daub is a shocking likeness, but it was all I had to remember her. I tried to paint her myself, you know, from memory, but it wouldn't come right. I suppose I knew her in too many ways that could not be captured on canvas."

The girl touched his arm. "Did you love her so very much, then, even though she left you?"

"Very much. And the leaving was my fault, not hers. The cause of it, anyway. She was a light, mercurial creature. She was always laughing, or dancing or singing. She needed something better than a man who threw his life away at one gambling hell after another."

She sat very still. "What are you thinking?" he asked her.

"A hard question. I do not want to hurt you."

"I will hurt less when this is all behind us," he said.

"But why . . . why did she not take me with her? Would not most mothers have done that?"

"Oh, God forgive me!" He hid his face from her, then turned it back to face her again. "I cannot allow you to think that," he said slowly. "She did not *leave* you; I kept you from going. I would not let you go. You were the only card I had."

"Why not?" Mariana asked softly. Somehow she already knew why.

"Because I thought I could force her to come home to me. Bad as I was, I could not let her go entirely. I had to have some shred of hope, some link. Do not hate me too much, I pray."

Her briskness was like a breath of fresh air. "Rubbish, Papa. I could never hate you. I know you far too well." She smiled a little to herself, as if she were turning a thought over in her head. "You know, you and I are very much alike, and about two-thirds of the time we think in an identical fashion, but then there is that other third of difference. I always wondered whence came that other percentage, and what my mother was like. Now, it seems, I shall know for myself."

She looked at him lovingly. "And you, sir, are off to your bed. You

28

look as if you would drop from weariness. I hope I have not regained one parent only to lose the first!"

But it was clear that Lynval Porter was already asleep. Even as she watched, his shoulders tipped forward and he cradled his head on the arm lying across the table. He did not answer.

"I SUPPOSE YOU are hinting that she is socially questionable, eh, Porter? Say it straight out, man. The fact is that divorce is a tricky business. One never knows how it is going to go down. It is all very well to rake up old gossip, to point out all those who have been divorced and lived to lead society, but even in our time, among decent people propriety rules."

Lady Battledore looked distinctly uncomfortable as she was saying all this, as any woman should who had married so many husbands, but Mr. Porter knew what she was saying was true. A woman like Lady Webster might desert her husband for a lover three years her junior, marry him, and, as Lady Holland, become one of the fashionable women of the Regent's unorthodox "court," but such were the exception, not the rule.

"Was she happy?" he asked.

Lady Emilia considered. "I think she was at last. She lived with me at Tournai, you know, until the divorce was final and then, after she and Spurrell were wed, they lived in Hanover." She held up a hand to deflect his line of questioning. "He has been dead for some years now, Porter, pray let him rest quietly. I think you should understand that he took very good care of her. Their marriage was successful because he was very kind. He understood her in a deep and basic way that both you and I missed, let alone that devil Cumberland."

Mr. Porter shrugged and looked hang-dog, but Lady Battledore would allow him none of that. "No, no, do not hide your face, I meant no recrimination. In any case, what was between you and my sister was, save for the fact that I cared for you both, none of my affair. I vow I did my best to mend things, but since neither tact nor subtlety are my long suit, I am glad I did no more harm."

Bridie chose that ill-timed moment to sidle into the room and make a great show, now that she knew whom Lady Battledore was, of curtseying to her.

"If it please you, mum," she began, "might I have the pleasure of . . ."

But her ladyship was having none of such toadying behavior.

"Stuff and nonsense! Pleasure, indeed! You should be happy, woman, that I have not boxed your long Irish ears. I know perfectly well that you have been listening outside the door all this time to find what fresh news you may publish, so do not attempt to flim-flam me! My ears, incidentally, are quite as sharp as your own."

Bridie turned quite pale at what she surmised must be coming next, dismissal of a certainty. She saw herself tramping the streets of Dublin looking for work, and the almshouse at the end of it all.

But it was not to come yet, though her ladyship's tongue was not through lashing. "For it was wafted into them, from quite reputable sources, that you have no great opinion of me! That being the case, I will be grateful if you will state your business in brief, and smartly, too!"

Bridie's head popped up stiffly at this barrage, and her curtsey faltered in mid-kneebend. "Oh, indaid? Nothin' I said was at all untrue, yer ladyship, that much I'll insist. Forthright and plain I may be, but Bridie Monaghan has nivver told an untruth in her life, I'll thank ye to know!"

Lady Battledore merely sniffed disbelievingly. She and Bridie indulged themselves in a long moment of glaring at each other before the thaw set in. Her ladyship's mouth began to twitch and the housemaid's poker-stiff back began to relax, and when the Battledore laughter began to pour out, Bridie's snort and snicker joined in, albeit half a beat behind, just in case.

Her ladyship wiped her eyes. "It's been a long time since anyone had the courage to face me down," she chuckled. "You're a rare specimen, Bridie Monaghan." Then, "But don't you be after taking advantage of it!"

Bridie was still uncowed. "Beggin' yer pardon, mum," she began to say while she still carried some advantage, "but I been thinkin'. You know, Miss Mariana has nivver been off on her own, so to speak. There's been school and a bit of travellin', but not out in the world like. Who is to look after her, I'd like to know?"

"Goodness knows, I have servants enough to fulfill the task," Lady Battledore answered. "Am I to assume that you are volunteering for the post?" She raised her eyebrows to her former brother-in-law. "What say you, Lynval?"

But Mariana, entering, intervened before the plot could thicken. "Quite out of the question, Aunt Emilia. Bridie, how could you think of such a thing? Who would look after my father if both of us were gone, not to mention the household?"

Playing upon the old rivalry, she added, "Why, think what Cook might be doing the while you were gone."

"Mother o' God," Bridie breathed. "I daresay yer right, miss, but I do get me the shivers when I think of yerself alone in that wicked city."

Perhaps surprisingly, Lynval took up on the other side from his daughter. "I should certainly be all right, my girl. You know how little attention I need." (Mariana knew this protest to be sincere, for he truly never noticed how much was accorded him.) "I think Bridie *should* accompany you, right enough. A girl your age needs someone from her family to keep her from flying a bit too high, if you know what I mean. Bridie shall stand in as my deputy in the matter."

"Bless you, sir," breathed the housemaid. "I'll be lightin' a candle for you every single day."

Lady Battledore was amazed. "And all this time I believed you to be a God-fearing Protestant."

Slyly Bridie timed her curtsey so that her head was demurely bent as she loosed her final impudence, "Yes, mum, just as I nivver thought you was a real lady." Back up she came. "But I see, mum, as how I have been wrong."

She made her exit wreathed in Lady Battledore's genial laughter.

"She has you there, Emilia! Sees straight through to the bone, does our Bridie. She might have known you for years, what? Think on what an addition she will make to your household."

For a moment her ladyship was faintly alarmed. "Such liberties rush like wildfire through the staff, you know," she said worriedly. "Was I too free with her?"

But Mariana soothed her ruffled feathers. "I will answer for her, Aunt. Truth to tell, I am happy she is coming with me. I shall feel less alone. You will have so many affairs of your own and Lucy will be so wrapped up in the wedding, I shall be glad of Bridie's good sense."

But Lady Battledore had heard only a fragment of the speech.

"*Affairs*, eh? Did you say affairs? You must learn, my girl, not to place stock in malignant gossip!"

And so saying, she swept grandly from the room.

Everything from then went in a great rush. Plans must be laid, both for the journey and for the care of the household; clothes must be sorted, pressed, packed, and a new travelling costume made up; messages sent to Lucy and to Battledore House and all manner of small, last-minute adjustments, errands, calls, and good-byes must be made. It was done with surprising expedition.

And thus it was that Mariana and Lady Battledore found themselves to be resting, nay recuperating, in the snug arms of the Royal George. The crossing had been quite dreadful; even Lady Battledore, who prided herself on an iron constitution, said so. She rested, half-dazed, while Mariana waited on her hand and foot, for Bridie, too, had been laid low by the mal-de-mer.

The furnishings of their rooms were plain. Mariana had discovered early on that it did no good to grimace, far less complain, of Spartan travelling conditions, for Lady Battledore had no idea what she was talking about. But now the great traveller was herself inconvenienced, though there was perhaps no one in the world less sybaritic, no one more able to adapt herself to conditions of travel. She had always considered such to be the hallmark of the true explorer.

The invalid roused herself, looking at Mariana sharply. "Come along, girl, not yet dressed for dinner? Whatever is keeping you?"

Mariana might have been able to smile at this if her ladyship had not been in a trice so absolutely the acme of perfection. Travelling with no maid, under circumstances of great adversity, she still managed, within moments, to look like a fashion plate of the well-to-do matron. Her hair was swept back severely, but with style; her posture, considering the rigours of the trip, superb; the skirt of her up-to-the-moment *robe en caleçons* so narrow that it seemed she might have difficulty walking, but miraculously, she managed very well. Mariana was suitably impressed—by her aunt's energy, if nothing else.

Lady Battledore, on the other hand, viewed Mariana's ensemble with a critical eye and swept it aside with one compliment.

"Very nice, my dear. Just the thing for the George. Sensible and just a little dowdy. Quite perfect."

Since this was Mariana's best frock, the girl was about to protest when something cautioned that it would be in vain. Better by far to bend with the wind, especially when it seemed incontrovertible that her ladyship knew what she was talking about.

This was borne out when Lady Battledore promised for the future, "We shall find you something extravagant and original in London. Not *too* original, you know, but with looks like yours the ordinary will never do!" She beamed on her niece. "How wonderful it will be to have a . . . a . . . what *will* you be, pet? You are my niece, of course, but perhaps not quite yet. Certainly not a mere companion. Let me see . . ." She tapped her fan thoughtfully as if to aid her cogitation. "My *ward*, perhaps. Yes, I can hear them now: 'Who *is* that elegant and ethereal creature?' and some clever-box answering, 'Why, that is Miss Mariana Porter, don't y'know, the ward of Lady Battledore.' . . . It has a ring to it, don't you agree?"

Mariana could only content herself with a nod of acquiescence. After all, what better way to come out than in the reflected glory of a recognised leader of society? But what was this talk of being Lady Battledore's ward? And was she not to be seen with her mother? She surmized that there must be a story behind all this, but now was not the moment to prevail upon her aunt to disclose it.

A discreet tap sounded at the door. "The gentleman presents his compliments, mum, and says as how he'll be waitin' in the supper room."

"Very well," her ladyship replied. "You may say that we shall be joining him directly."

She blandly smoothed over Mariana's surprise. "I had not meant to alarm you, dear. Captain Seymour, with whom we are to sup, is a gentleman I have known since he was a little boy. I believe you'll enjoy Brion's company."

Matchmaking already, Aunt? thought Mariana, raising a mental eyebrow. We shall see about that.

The Royal George, though a first-class establishment, was not grand by any means, but quiet and convenient. It was dedicated to soothing the jangled nerves of travellers, priding itself on a high degree of service. This was evident in the solicitous way the ladies were greeted and ushered toward the supper room. They were crossing the common room when Mariana heard a familiar voice behind her. "Upon my word, what are you doing here, child?"

She turned to see the Marquis of Downsbury quizzing her through his glass. The sight of her old acquaintance made her feel absurdly reassured, as if some important piece of her home life had come along on her great journey.

She presented the Marquis to Lady Battledore, who said, "Join us at supper, Downsbury, won't you?"

"Delighted, madam," the cavalier replied with a deep bow, "but I fear I am no longer on the approved list."

"Ha! You're the one, are you? Thought I recognised the name. Lynval spoke of you." She examined him with a practised eye. "You don't look such a monster to me. Lynval never did know his head from his heel. The girl's in my charge for the nonce and all objections are overruled, at least until I see fit to do otherwise."

The Marquis took Mariana's hand. "What do *you* say, my dear? I would not wish to compromise you with your father."

"I say, sir, that I shall be flattered and honoured to see you whenever you like; here or in any other place. I had intended writing you from London, since our departure from Dublin was swift. I consider myself lucky to have you as a friend, and I will say that before my father, if necessary."

And with the slight emphasis on the word "friend" the Marquis was informed that his suit had been set aside, though in the nicest possible way. In a sense, Mariana knew, it was a great relief.

35

He offered each of the ladies an arm as they proceeded to the supper room.

"Downsbury?" her ladyship murmured thoughtfully. "Would that be Devon?"

"Rutland, actually. I believe we have met before."

"Have we?" The doyenne's tone was a shade frosty. So many people claimed acquaintance, but then, one did know so many people, it was hard to be sure. "Where? Where was it? In London? Recently?" This was something of a snare, for she had not been in London, except briefly, since the past year.

"No, not recently at all, I fear. Quite some time past, in fact. Does your ladyship remember attending a picnic at Rutheven?"

"I never attend picnics. But wait . . . Rutheven? I was only there once, a million years ago. Dullest houseparty I was ever at." She peered at him. "Good grief! Were you called Binky, by any chance?"

"I still sometimes am, madam, to my eternal shame."

She tapped him with her fan. "Not at all. I remember you well. A charming boy who has matured into a charming man."

Mariana was impressed by her aunt's evident sincerity. She began to think of the Marquis in a new light. The rapid transformation from avuncular suitor to man of distinction made her head swim. Her aunt might be interested in him as a conquest, but the simple fact remained that, for whatever reasons, he had already proposed to *her*. It was quite a feather in her cap, if looked at from the right angle.

The man who rose to greet them in the supper room wore a uniform coat of celeste blue with buff facings that admirably set off his lean figure. His hair was bleached by the sun to a tow colour, and he squinted slightly as if staring toward an unseen horizon. Everything about him, in fact, proclaimed the military man, from his large, capable hands to the look of natural authority in his pleasantly weathered countenance. The look he gave Mariana was not *bold*, exactly, but certainly full of masculine inquisitiveness. There was a distinct air of challenge in his demeanour and Mariana, though she could not have said why, found herself faintly uneasy. Though the

Captain was courteous when presented to the Marquis, he appeared somewhat more than attentive when he heard Mariana's name.

Something flickered in his eyes. "I believe Miss Porter and I to be distantly related," he said coolly.

Lady Battledore did not betray surprise by so much as the wink of an eyelash. One might almost have suspected that this information was not entirely unknown to her, and the news seemed to be familiar to the Marquis as well, from his response.

"Related by marriage only, I believe," he said to Mariana. "Captain Seymour is, if I am not mistaken, the nephew of the late Mr. Josiah Forrester of London and Manchester."

"What, *Uncle* Forrester?" said the girl in surprise. The portrait of Papa's uncle swam forward in her mind's eye, and she fancied she saw more than a mere resemblance; Captain Seymour's undoubtedly good-looking face might easily have been a copy of Uncle Forrester's in some far-distant youth. So this was the "rag-tag scamp" (as Papa had characterised him). How curious it felt to discover a cousin one never really believed existed, except as an unpleasant mirage.

And butter wouldn't melt in his mouth, would it? How sly to tell her straight to her face that he was the source of her own father's ruin.

Mariana's fingertips went to her temple, where she fancied she felt a sudden pounding throb. The room and all the people in it had developed an odd tendency to grow smaller and more distant with every second, just as if she were looking into the wrong end of a receding telescope.

"Are you quite well, my dear?" she heard someone ask (it may have been the Marquis), and then she began to feel quite giddy. Strong arms went around her and another voice (Lady Battledore's, this time) began to issue brisk commands. "Put her in the chair, Brion . . . careful, you clod, she is not a sack of flour! You, Downsbury, look in my reticule and fetch my salts!"

Mariana rested on the strong arm, and presently the world came back into focus. Aware after a moment of who it was that supported her, she struggled to be free.

"Really, Captain Seymour, I am quite recovered."

"Are you certain, Miss Porter? Do not move too quickly."

She disregarded his advice with great flair, and in consequence nearly fell to the floor.

"My fault," said her ladyship. "I should have guessed that a delayed attack might come upon her. Latent mal-de-mer. Her maid is laid low already."

"Really?" Captain Seymour seemed doubtful. "You are hardly at sea now."

"Fatigue, then!" snapped Lady Battledore. "In any case, it is quiet that she needs, quiet and rest."

"But what about her supper?" asked the Marquis. "Perhaps a biscuit and a glass of wine for fortitude?"

"Tea and toast. On a tray. In her room, sir," said the commander-general. "That will be all, gentlemen. Good night."

But Captain Seymour was not to be put off so easily. "Lady Emilia, may I not be permitted to assist . . ."

Her ladyship's stare would have frozen grog. "You have done quite enough, sir. Thank you." To the Marquis: "Your servant, your lordship," and she swept Mariana away with every evidence of great solicitude.

Once in their chambers her mood was quite different.

"Vapours, bedad! What were you thinking of, my girl? Leave such posturing for kitchen maids and ninnies, if you please. Find some other mode of expressing your displeasure. Mark you, you may not have such a chance at Seymour again!"

Mariana's head was quite painful now. She wet a cloth with cool water, lay back in a chaise, and applied it to her eyes. "I assure you, Aunt, I am not prone to vapours. It must have been the sea." Then she sat up straight, the cloth falling away.

"*What* did you say? Aunt, what do you mean about having a chance at Captain Seymour? I'd sooner tame a stoat."

"No more of your foolishness, if you don't mind. I've gone without a good supper in service to you tonight. Prating of likes and dislikes does not improve matters."

Mariana, caught midway between indignation and incomprehension, could only murmur, "You do not understand."

"Understand?" said her aunt. "I should think I do, and I must say, I had thought you capable of better behaviour. Captain Seymour is a prize, and don't you forget it. So you believe that young man took away your settlement, eh? No fault of his, I daresay, but I imagine you think that puts no coin in your pocket. The fact is (and you must know it as well as I) that your father might not have left you much in any case, for with seemingly unlimited funds he would have been back at the tables in a sennight." She held up a silencing hand. "No, pray do not dispute with me on a subject I understand as well as any. Sometime before he met my sister I knew your papa. There was nothing in it on his side, but I was quite stricken. I have so little heart now, I trow, because I gave it out complete on the first assay." Her bright gaze softened and she ran a finger along Mariana's cheek. "I might have had a daughter just like you if I had caught him. Perhaps not so pretty, for your mama was a nonpareil, but a toy of my own to fondle and dress in pretty clothes, and to love." She sighed, not deeply, for grand tragedy was not her style, but in a shallow little breath. "I had a rival far too seductive to win against with the weapons at my command. He loved the tables more than any woman."

"But when he met my mama, did not that all change?"

"To some extent, but such men never really alter once they are entrapped. The sad truth of the matter is that if your father once sat down at a table in London he would willingly fling away a fortune in an hour. So you see, perhaps it is just as well that Mr. Forrester chose himself another heir. At least the money will not vanish in a puff of smoke."

"Perhaps you are right," Mariana dubiously agreed, "but I shall never feel comfortable in the presence of Captain Seymour."

"As you wish," her ladyship surprisingly agreed. "There are as good fish in the sea as ever came out of it, and London is the biggest fishpond of all. In all fairness, however, I must allow that I have known Brion Seymour since he was a mere lad and never knew or heard a word of reproach against him. As for the idea of his finagling a decrepit old man into changing his will, that is utter nonsense: first of all because Brion would be incapable of it, and secondly because old Forrester, as I remember him, would never have been bamboozled by anyone."

"As you say," said Mariana meekly.

"Not at all as I say because I say it, only because I believe it is as it is. Yours is a natural prejudice and reflects a commendable love for your father. Nonetheless, for all I care you need never see young Seymour again, except in the way that one sees almost everyone in London."

"How is that?"

"Oh, on the town, in the clubs, at the theatre and the opera. I trust that on those occasions your natural sense of what is proper will allow you to be civil."

"Oh, Aunt, what you must think of me! I would never repay your kindness by being uncivil to any friend of yours. My only wish is that I may not be required to simulate a doting for a person who quite repels me."

"Then I see we shall always dwell in amity, my dear, for I ask no more than that."

Having watched carefully as Mariana consumed every scrap of the substantial repast she had been served on a tray, Lady Battledore prepared to take her leave. "Sleep well, my love, and awaken looking your prettiest. Rest assured that you shall see no more of Captain S. than you desire. Sleep well." She blew a kiss across the room.

"Such a good match it would have been, though," she said wistfully to herself as she closed the door behind her.

Downstairs all was quiet. In a writing room she found the Marquis, who looked up from his letter and laid down his pen. "All well, I trust. Not like Mariana, this behaviour. Would have thought the boy had the looks of the blackest rogue."

"You understood it too, did you?" asked her ladyship.

"My word, how could one miss it? Not the boy's fault at all, you know. Porter himself would have treated him better."

"Still, she is young," said Lady Battledore.

The Marquis looked at her sharply. "Would you go back to that?"

"In an instant, given the opportunity. It is not that I lead such a sad old life, you understand, but only a fool would renounce youth and beauty, no matter on what terms. Wisdom is a comfort, but a demmed poor exchange. Anyway, I am not at all sure I care for the rueful mode. La, yes, I would go back!" Unexpectedly, she grinned. "Not that I expect to be asked, you know."

He nodded. "Sensible. A pity one never appreciates youth until it has quite gone."

"And Mariana?" she asked.

"What about her?"

"Do you appreciate her more now that you feel you have lost her altogether?"

For a moment he said nothing and she thought she might have offended him beyond repair, but he had only been thinking of his reply. "I offered for her, you know."

"Yes."

"Gad, if I had only known what I was doing. Turned old Lynval against me, my oldest friend. Must have looked to the girl as though I cared nothing for her, that it was only a conventional gesture. I never thought I would be capable of such idiocy, but you see" and here he turned his hands out helplessly, "no one is immune."

"You care for her, then?"

"That, madam, is a secret I shall carry to my grave. I am not about to play the fool a second time."

"If it is not you it will be another, who may not care for her as much."

"It will have to be someone who cares for her a very great deal," said the Marquis. "I have never known a fashionable marriage based on penniless participants."

Lady Battledore pulled at her earlobe absently. Presently she bade him good night and went to her chamber.

Mariana had fallen asleep reading *The Golden Wingéd Bird* by candlelight. What a sweet child. A pity she was penniless. Well, if nothing else, it provided a distinct challenge to find her a suitable alliance. And Lady Battledore secretly appreciated nothing so much as a good challenge.

—4—

LADY BATTLEDORE'S COACH, which had been waiting at Swansea, was modern in every way; an ornamental, not to say beautiful, object on the road. Unlike the unwieldy old machines of the past, which merely lumbered along, jolting and shaking every bone in a rider's body, hers went beyond mere comfort and approached luxury. And since her ladyship was herself an amateur whip who often handled the ribbons with all the skill of a member of the Four-Horse Club, the coachman felt confident in travelling at a great clip, and the long miles fairly flew past. But Mariana had been so quiet, so inattentive, that Lady Battledore was a trifle put out. It was not, after all, often that an impecunious young girl could travel in such style, and her ladyship was only human.

Mariana's thoughts were on other things entirely. She could not read her aunt's mind, but compelling questions were going through her own, and this seemed as good a time as any to air them. Bridie, dozing on the other seat, was almost a family member.

"I daresay, Aunt, you wonder that I have not pressed you for intelligence of my mother?"

"Oho!" thought Lady Emilia, "So that is the way the land lies, is it?" Aloud she only said mildly, "I rather imagined you would mention it in your own good time."

Mariana spread her fingers wide, then clapped her hands together in self-exasperation. "I don't know where to begin, you see. I want to know so much . . . and yet . . ."

"And yet you do not want to seem indelicate," said her aunt consolingly. "I know how you must feel. Perhaps you should plunge straight in and ask away."

"If you will excuse my gaucheries?"

"You may be sure that I shall make every allowance," said Lady Emilia gravely. "But there are some things best said in private."

It was obvious to her aunt that Mariana was struggling both to assuage her curiosity and to preserve decorum. The girl hesitated for another long moment, then asked plaintively, "She wasn't a *bad* woman, was she?" There was the faintest flush on her cheek. "I mean, she didn't do anything disgraceful?"

"Should that weigh? She is your mother, for good or ill."

Mariana's blush deepened. "You are right, that was an improper question." She wrinkled her brow, then said forthrightly, "Still, I should like to know."

Lady Battledore put her arm about Mariana's shoulder and hugged. "You would be less than human if you did not." For a few moments the meadows outside the window were allowed to pass in silence. At last she said, "I suppose it depends on what you consider to be disgraceful. I daresay Dublin and London ideas might not be at all the same." Putting a finger under Mariana's chin, she tilted her ward's face until she looked directly into the girl's eyes.

"Your mother is not what the world would label an adventuress, I think. She is a good woman; but she *has* made mistakes."

"What sort of mistakes?" asked Mariana, dreading the answer. She wanted, nay, *needed* to know all these things; still, it was painful.

"She truly loved your father, you know," said Lady Emilia, "but she could not live with him."

Mariana's head went up. "I live with him well enough."

"No, you live with what is left of him. You know only what that treacherous Lady Luck did not suck away. She was his true bride, and I suspect that he is faithful to her still, is he not?"

Mariana said nothing.

"My sister knew another Lynval Porter than you do; charming, profligate, and completely irresponsible."

"That certainly is not my papa."

"*You* were not married to him. You were not brought up in good circumstances, not then forced to watch him gamble away every penny you brought in dowry, not compelled to endure the slights and cuts, and worse, the *pity* of society."

"You are mistaken. He is not like that at all."

"I daresay you are right . . . now. But you must admit that you have only lived with him for a comparatively short time."

"So my mama left him?" asked Mariana with a shade of bitterness. "Was she happy then?"

"Not so very. We all make mistakes. It is hard to give up one's child to strangers."

"Why did she do it, then?"

"Because she was very frightened. She had become embroiled in circumstances beyond her power of imagining. She could see no other way out."

"And you blame my father for that," said Mariana.

"Oh, no, my love. There are no accusations to be made. Each went their own way. Your mother to what she perceived a safe harbour, your father to follow the road every gambler must take. Your mother used a small bequest left her by our mother to assure herself that your schooling would be all that it should be. She and I went to Miss Pecksniff's, too, you know. Miss P. was still alive then, the dear old thing. Her hardest punishment was a tear in the eye, but her girls loved her all the same. They took dreadful advantage, but they loved her."

"I wish it had been as gentle when I was there," commented Mariana, "but I daresay it built my character."

"Were you so very unhappy?"

"Not really. Lucy and I made it a madhouse, I fear, and often suffered the consequences. But pray, go on with your story."

"I wonder if I should," Lady Battledore said. "Perhaps your first recitation of it should come direct from the source, your mother herself." She looked significantly at Bridie, half asleep.

"Goodness, how mysterious. First you leave me with a picture of my father as a heartless brute, then you refuse to continue. Is that quite fair, Aunt?"

Lady Battledore bridled at this. "It would not be fair if it were the truth, but I said nothing about brutishness. You know very well why your father is exiled to Dublin, since he removed himself. He has the fever and must be kept from further contagion."

Mariana knew her aunt was right. In Dublin's limited society the stakes could never rise very high. Papa had done the wisest thing, had chosen the better course.

A sudden shouting up ahead engaged their attention as their coach slowed to a halt.

Lady Battledore put her head out of the window, careful not to dislodge her bonnet. "What is it, Parsons?"

The sturdy man on the box flashed her a wide grin. "'Tis some downy nate 'as got hisself in trouble, mam. Should I help un, mam?"

"Yes, perhaps you had better," agreed Lady Emilia. "I shall have a look for myself, I believe. Mariana, will you please to accompany me?" Mariana and Bridie obediently trailed at her heels as Parsons assisted the ladies from the machine and then approached the other equipage with a tolerant grimace.

"'Ere, mates, could 'ee use another hand?"

The distress of the other coach lay not so much in the ineptitude of the driver as the condition of the road itself. Although in some stretches it was as smooth as a billiard table, in others, poorly maintained, the ruts were prodigious. In this spot more than one coachee had brought his rig to grief, and the one in trouble now was lighter than most and more easily lifted out of the rut. Seven men, including Parsons and Trotter, the groom, took off their coats and helped. It was a matter of brute strength and, with the ladies looking on, the men could not even resort to the oaths customary at such times.

Lady Battledore congratulated them when they were done. "Fetch the medicine, Trotter," she instructed the groom, and he, with a sly look, returned to her ladyship's coach, presently coming back with a silver flask of substantial girth. The men each had a pull and the coachee had two—for the energy, as he said. The passengers, all gentlemen, now donned their coats and prepared to re-enter the coach, save one, who lingered for a moment by the ladies.

"I fancy we have met before, madam," he said respectfully to Lady Battledore, "and I fancy the young lady with you has dazzled me ere now. My name is Dobyn, ma'am, Tyger Dobyn."

"I think we have met," said her ladyship with every air of indifference. "I am Lady Battledore."

Mr. Dobyn bowed, making a leg to Mariana as well.

"And this, sir, is my ward, Miss Porter." She caught Mariana's eye and seemed to flash a warning. "She is not out yet, but shall be presently. Perhaps you would care to be in attendance, sir?"

Was there a hint of a smile in the eyes that rested almost boldly on Mariana's fresh young figure and pretty face? "I should be most gratified, madam."

But a chorus of general hallooing called him back to his seat, and presently the clumsy waggon lumbered off, driver shouting and coachhorn blowing.

It was not until they too were again on their way that Lady Emilia considered their property. She rapped on the roof to get the attention of Parsons on the box. "I say, have you put the medicine away properly?"

"Did you pack the flask back properly, her ladyship wants ter know?" Parsons called to Trotter. But Trotter would have none of it. He had not seen it since passing it to Parsons. The flask of French brandy, the medicine, it seemed, was gone on ahead.

"Humph, I wish them joy of it," said Lady Emilia snappishly. "Though if there is another emergency I do not know just what we shall do."

London, when they reached it, was in a soggy April mood, but nothing could dim Mariana's delight in riding along the familiar thoroughfares. The beloved streets and squares seemed in her eyes to glow with a soft luminescence of their own, even under the leaden sky. The shops, coffee houses, and theatres, the bustle and sheer energy of London raised her spirits in a way that almost made up for being apart from her papa.

The house of Lady Battledore in Portland Square was a revelation to her. Mariana had visited the homes of her friends at school during the holidays and long vacations, but she had seen nothing to compare with what met her eye here. Like that of Lady Emilia's crony, the Countess of Home, Battledore House had been brought into being through the architectural genius of Robert Adam. It seemed to Mariana that it must represent the peak of his undisputed artistry, for the rooms, she could immediately see, were not mere boxes, one opening onto another, but a harmonious sequence of spaces. As her aunt off-handedly took her through them, the girl could see that each hall, even each closet, was a counterpoint enhancing the rooms before and after it. One sensed immediately that the house had been designed for a specific function—to accommodate the flow of the elaborate social parade that was such an integral part of the life of London. Instinctively she gasped when she stood at the base of the great stairs and pictured the grand promenades of lordly men and dazzling women who had traversed them.

Lady Battledore smiled encouragingly. "Yes, you will stand with me at the top. I think we will look well together." It was as if she considered the mansion a mere stage set contrived for an elaborate performance.

"Sometimes I don't know why I live in all this. It is nice enough in its own way, you know, and the servants never intrude, but I could do with a great deal less. My late husband's idea entirely. I'd be as happy in a tent." She reflected on this, considering. "Well, perhaps not quite as happy, since our honoured Prinny has an obsessive fondness for tent-rooms. He likes 'em gaudy, to my mind. But one must remember that he *is* a Hanover."

Mariana's bedchamber was not at all gaudy, but a silken bower of soft greens and pale ivory. She loved it from the moment she and Bridie stepped into the room. A tiny figure scuttled toward the door leading to the backstairs. "Oh, wait," Mariana called, "don't go."

The creature, hardly more than a child, her elfin face peering out from under a huge mobcap, edged carefully back into the chamber. "If yer please, miss, I've done it all, I fink." She seemed poised for flight if Mariana should prove at all formidable.

"It looks very nice," said Mariana gently. "You must have taken a great deal of trouble." The elf smiled swiftly and bobbed a curtsey. "What is your name?"

"Me name's Lily, miss." Another bobbing dip. She was eager to be off. "Will that be all, miss?"

She was so charming in an unconventional way that Mariana longed to keep her there like a toy. "Are you the upstairs maid, then, Lily?"

This extravagant notion brought an involuntary giggle. "Aow, naow, miss. I'm only 'ere to lye out the linens, miss. Missus Marasham is t'one'll be lookin' after yer." Mariana at once pictured a stern and formidable matron, all starch and condescension, but Lily's next words reassured her. "Yer'll like 'er, miss. She's sharp, but she's fair. Be an 'ousekeeper one of these days, or I miss *my* guess."

Bridie was rolling her eyes at such familiarity with a mere tweeny, or in-between maid, but Mariana followed up her questioning. "And you, Lily, what do you want to be?"

Confusion reigned in Lily's face. "Law, miss, I nevver put me 'ead to it. I has ennuf ter do wivvout *thinkin'* as well!"

The door of the dressing room opened and a plump, prematurely grey woman looked out. "Lily, what are you doing? Didn't I send you for lavender?" Then she saw the others. "Oh, Miss Mariana, I never knew you was here. You've caught me quite unawares."

Mariana intervened on the child's behalf. "I'm sorry if I kept Lily from her work. It was only for a moment."

"An' I was jus' goin'!" added Lily, and disappeared as if by magic.

"Bless you, miss, that girl is my mainstay. If they was all as quick and clever as Lily, they'd never be a moment's worry to me or to Housekeeper. She's worth her weight in gold, that one. It wouldn't surprise me to see her go right up the ladder, so to speak."

The very way she used her terms gave Mariana a clear picture of how things were accomplished in a house as large as this. A strict regimen tempered by understanding and mutual respect. It must make for a pleasant household all around.

"You'd be Bridie, I expect," Mrs. Marasham said. "Here, let me help you with those things. Miss Mariana's dressing room is just through here, and your own chamber just beyond, so as to be handy."

When they came back out, Mrs. Marasham went on with the conversation. "Did you have a good trip, miss? They say as how her ladyship's new coach is a marvel of comfort."

But Mariana, grimacing as she remembered the endless bumping over country roads, drew a chuckle from the maid. "Ah, but then, you've come home again to London. That will soon set you up."

"You knew I was from London?"

Now it was Marasham's turn to look surprised. "My stars, I would have thought her ladyship would have told you. Why, I was picked to look after you because I was in service at your father's house in the old days. Lor', miss, I remember you when you wasn't bigger than a clockmaker's mite. Like a tiny little angel you was to look at. I was housemaid then. Name of Cora, d'you remember?"

"No, I fear I do not. I was very young, after all, and not such an angel at all times, I fear."

Mrs. Marasham laid down the apron she had folded and put her fingers to her mouth. "Not half, you wasn't. Like an angel you was to *look* at, as I said, but you was a proper imp for finding mischief. Do you remember your nurse, Nanny Harrow?"

"Oh, yes, she looked after me until I went off to school."

"We come from the same village, Nanny and I, though o' course she was years older. It was a comfort to be with someone from home, being it was my first place an' all." She sighed. "She's gone now, poor thing."

"She died? No one told me."

"Bless you, no, not died. Gone back to Candlebury, where we come from. She was kept in service by her ladyship until she was too old and feeble even to care for herself. No, not dead, but she might as well be, you might say. She loved London, Nanny did, and it must be a terrible thing to be sent away from it, even for her own good."

"But surely it is more peaceful there?"

"Oh, yes, peaceful. I'm sure she hates it. Lives with her niece and a cat and a bird, like a proper old thing. Too old for excitement, she may be, but too young to be put away. Funny she never married. She needed someone like my John, but I suppose he never come her way."

My word, Mariana thought, is the whole world marriage-minded? But aloud she only asked, "Is your husband in service as well?" And having said it, regretted having done so, for Mrs. Marasham certainly was talkative and she was not altogether certain there should be such freedom between mistress and servant. Perhaps it was only that Mrs. Marasham had known her as a child. Unaware of all this, the maidservant answered Mariana's question cheerfully.

"Oh, yes, Lord love you, Marasham is head footman here. Mr. Brill, the butler, says as how he could scarcely do without him. But we'll be off on our own one of these days. In service as a couple, you know, or in a nice little alehouse of our own."

All this time Bridie had not said a word, but had diligently unpacked Mariana's trunks and shaken out her dresses, and was beginning to lay out the toilet articles on the dressing table. She stared into the looking-glass and tried to catch her mistress's eye, but the girl avoided her. Time enough for a scolding later, just now she had things to find out.

"I suppose there must always be a great many guests coming and going in a house the size of this. A great deal to do."

"Oh, ever so, but my John likes it, and, I must say, so do I. Especially as I'll be helping Bridie to look after you."

"And my mother," asked Mariana with as much innocence as she could muster, "is she staying in the house?"

Mrs. Marasham looked quite startled. "Your mother, miss? Why, no, she ain't. So far as I know, she's still in the country. O' course, when she comes up to town she'll be taking a house of her own, won't she?"

This flustered Mariana a trifle, since she knew her mother not at all and had no idea of her plans. "Oh, yes! I daresay she will, I only thought . . . Well, Mrs. Marasham, I don't know that I'll require much looking after. I've managed to do for myself for a long while, and now I have Bridie to take care of me."

Now it was the servant's turn to be discomfited. "Mercy, did I sound as if I was slamming Bridie? I had no meaning to, I assure you both. Oh, no! But you will need more done than Bridie can easily do, what with your come-out, and then Miss Lucy's wedding. I should not be surprised if Lily were called in as well. I expect you will have quite a brilliant season, miss, if you don't mind my saying so. You must take care not to outshine the bride."

"You certainly seem to be quite up on the social season."

"I'll just have Marasham take these trunks to the box room, miss. You won't need them, I should think." She rang and opened the door to push the trunks into the back hall. "I should think I *would* know about the wedding, for isn't my own cousin Miss Lucy's maid? I daresay I knew you'd be coming back to London even before you did; or knew, at least, that Miss Lucy had invited you."

Gone was any thought of sending Marasham away. She was too valuable a source of information. Mariana hoped the channel did not operate in two directions. But since it was available . . . "Have you seen Miss Lucy's betrothed?" she inquired. "I own I am most curious about him. Lucy and I have always been like sisters, but then, suddenly, without a previous mention of him, I find she is to be married."

Marasham's glib and informative chatter seemed to have dried in an instant. Her eyes did not meet Mariana's but concentrated on the tag ends of straightening away the travelling things. Her expression became strangely sedate after her former volubility.

"Lord Robert is very well-known in London, miss. He is very . . . fashionable, as they say. He hobs and nobs with all the bucks and Corinthians, but my cousin says . . . and mind you, I'm not that certain how she knows . . . he is a gentleman for all that."

Then something of her easy conversation returned. "Miss Lucy seems to be near besotted with him, by all accounts. Walks about in a dream, my cousin tells me."

"How lovely for her," Mariana exclaimed sincerely.

Mrs. Marasham barked a short, high laugh. "Don't be too sure o' that, miss. Marriage is not at all a dream, but a serious business. It appears to me that it takes a good deal of sober thought aforehand, so as to avoid tears after."

That gave Mariana something to think about after she had gone.

=5=

WHEN LUCY PAID her first call late the next morning, Mariana understood exactly what Mrs. Marasham's cousin had meant. She could hardly believe that this bright, seductive butterfly was her old friend. In their schooldays Lucy had been a plain, shy, rather "missish" girl on the surface. She seemed a model of propriety, though she was a rebel underneath. Because of her air of innocence, it was always Lucy who led her cronies into troubles while herself sailing safely and serenely upon the thinnest ice. Though others broke through and sank into disgrace, Lucy never lost her footing. Now she seemed quite a different person.

Her hair, for instance, which she had always worn sedately with a centre parting and drawn softly over the ears, was a puff of curls that bobbed and twisted with every movement of her head. She was dressed in a frock of sprigged muslin that, in any other year, might have been out of season, but in a time when young ladies regularly damped their satin, gauze, and muslin to make them cling, seemed refreshingly substantial. In any case, it was quite dry. Her exuberance was infectious.

"*Dearest* Mariana!" she cried, pecking her friend on the cheek, then relenting and giving her a hug. "What a joy to see you at last. Here, let me look at you. You've grown thin as a rail, I believe, although it certainly suits you to perfection! Such lovely, lovely cheekbones, my dear. Is this what comes of languishing in the backwaters of Dublin? Here one must, at the very least, come down with consumption to be so eminently in fashion."

"Have you had consumption, Lucy?" asked Mariana with a twinkle.

Lucy flicked her fan. "La, me? No, my sweeting, I am about to be *married*, and that is the most fashionable thing in London, just at the moment. It is very trying to make oneself over, but I shall show them that I can dazzle the *hoi polloi* as well as anyone going."

She sounded odd and a tiny bit brittle to Mariana's ears, but since sincerity had always been Lucy's keynote in the past, her friend totted it up to the influence of the fashionable world with which Lucy seemed almost overly concerned.

"But you have changed into a swan, Lucy! I hardly recognise you."

Lucy shrugged it off. "You should see me with my Robert. I feel quite dowdy then, he is such a nonpareil. I declare, he takes an hour to tie his cravat and discards half a dozen while he is in the process."

Mariana bit her lips. "You seem frightfully *au courant* with Robert's dressing habits, my love," she observed smoothly, and even this new, fashionable Lucy was drawn up short by that.

"Well . . . that is . . . I . . . the servants say that . . . Oh, Mariana, you are funning me just as you used to do, and I have fallen into the trap as usual. Shall I never become cool and fashionable?"

"Is it, then, unfashionable to giggle with one's old friends? What a dull place this London has become."

Lucy shook her head. "I am not sure it is fashionable even to *have* friends, real and true ones, at any rate. I'm sure you will see that one must learn to keep one's head in London, as well as one's own counsel, for it is a deceiving and shallow place at best."

What on earth had happened to her? Mariana took her hand tenderly, and Lucy said softly, "Dear heart, *you* haven't changed, have you? We shall go on being loving toward one another just as we were in school? I do not think I can bear it if we are not."

"Lucy, you goose, of course we shall be. Nothing shall ever keep us apart," scolded Mariana. "Now let us have an end to such silliness. Tell me all about your beloved Robert. There must be more to him than a perfectly arranged cravat."

The fashionable Lucy disappeared as the Lucy of old plumped herself down on the edge of the bed, legs swinging, and Mariana half-reclined beside her. In just such a way had they always gossiped at school, which made it seem as if they had never been apart at all.

"Let me see," Lucy began, "what shall I tell you and in what order? All the impressive things first, then the ordinary, dullish ones. He is the son of a duke . . . only a younger son, unfortunately, but one older brother is sickly and the other in the army, so hope may spring eternal. He is *quite* fashionable . . . belongs to Davey's, one of the very best sporting clubs, I believe. He drives his own matched bays and dances divinely. What more could one ask?"

"Does he love *you*, Lucy dear?" asked her friend quietly, but Lucy was having none of it. Her whim to play at being a madcap had returned.

"Bless me, I don't know! He declares a passion for me, but that is not quite the same thing, is it? I am not at all sure that love is even permissible in a true marriage-à-la-mode. Do you not think it would tend to make one dull?"

Her chatter suddenly stopped, and she looked straight into Mariana's eyes. "I can see that you think I have altered, love, and I daresay I have. Lord knows, I've tried. Sometimes I get quite giddy from trying. But that is all brummish, you know. Deep underneath I am the same Lucy I have always been. So you see, I must work very hard indeed to be in the fashion, for it is quite against my natural gifts." She sighed comically. "I suppose I should be marrying a country squire and popping a baby every other year. We should come up to town for the season and never notice how old-fashioned we were. We'd look about us at the great world, goggle at all the sights, and then go back to the country quite content with our lot."

"I think that is what I always expected for you, too," agreed Mariana. "What changed you?"

Lucy blushed. "I fell in love."

"With Robert?"

Lucy nodded. "It is quite passé, I know, but it is true. If he had not asked my papa for my hand I think I should have died."

"And he would not like the country?"

Lucy gave a familiar hoot. "I cannot imagine Bob a day away from London Bridge; so I must try very hard to be everything he wants me to be."

"And I take it he wants a marriage-à-la-mode?"

At once Lucy was all brittle and bright again, although a little sad withal. "Doesn't everyone, puss? I daresay I shall get used to it. They say one can adjust to anything."

I don't know, thought Mariana, if I could. Perhaps it had been a mistake to come back to London after all. Everything had so changed.

There was a discreet tap at the door and, summoned, Lily popped her head around the corner of it. "If you please, miss, her ladyship asks will you and Miss Lucy join her in the morning parlour?"

"Of course, Lily. Is something amiss?"

"Oh, no, miss. It's just they's guests come for a cup of chocolate."

"At this hour?"

"Yes, miss, they often do."

When the girl was gone Lucy asked, "Why do you look so surprised? Do they not drink chocolate in Dublin?"

"Not in the morning. What if one were not dressed to receive?"

"Oh, as for that, it is quite the rage to receive in dishabille. It matters not at all. Some great ladies hold forth in great state from their beds. It all depends on what the fashion decree of the week has been. This week . . . all month, in fact . . . it has been chocolate before nuncheon. It breaks up the day by altering the routine, you see."

"Oh, yes, I *see* well enough," moaned Mariana, "but I wonder if I shall ever find a place for myself in all this?"

"Oh, you will," Lucy promised. "It is all in acquiring the knack. After you've had your push, your come-out, you know, you'll find you swim along quite easily."

As the young ladies, arm in arm, entered the morning parlour, an all-too-familiar figure rose to greet them. Lucy ran to him at once and bestowed a kiss upon his cheek.

"Brion, what luck to find you here! I had heard that you were back and I have been wondering how to bring you and Mariana together. See how easily it has all come about."

She whirled to draw Mariana closer. "Dearest, this is Captain Seymour, Robert's groomsman; your opposite number in the wedding party, my sweet. I hope the two of you will find pleasure in each other's company."

"I hope we shall," Captain Seymour said with a low bow. "How do you do, Miss Porter? I trust you have recovered from your indisposition?"

"Quite recovered, Captain." How shameless, she thought, when he must know he was the cause of it. She turned to one of the other guests, a strikingly handsome woman of great elegance. "I am Mariana Porter, how do you do?"

She held out her hand, but the other young woman kept her hands firmly in her lap. She seemed a bit surprised that Mariana should be so forward on no acquaintance at all. "Lady Blanche Westring," said Lady Battledore, as if that explained everything.

"Ah, yes, Miss Porter," said Lady Blanche. Her look made Mariana feel she was a part of some exotic species, and Lady Blanche's further words did nothing to dispel the alienation.

"I understand your home is in Dublin. How odd it is that you have virtually no accent at all. You must have had an excellent teacher."

Mariana looked helplessly at her aunt, but that august creature merely smiled as if she were a cat in cream. "I fear there is some slight misunderstanding," Mariana answered Lady Blanche. "I am London born and bred, except when I was at school. My papa and I have been in Dublin only a year or two."

"Ah," said Lady Blanche, "*that* explains your accent."

Mariana forbore to enquire what she meant, but she surmised that she and her ladyship were not likely to become intimate friends. And no wonder, she thought, considering the people with whom she associates. She glared at Captain Seymour as if *he* had been the one to slight her. Then, recalling what Lucy had said as they came into the room, "Groomsman, Captain?"

"Yes," he replied amiably. "It was a toss between Jeremy and myself." He indicated a slight, gentle-appearing young man near the window. No one seemed to be paying him any mind, but he himself appeared not to notice; he was somehow in the room but not of it. "Jeremy Law," Captain Seymour elaborated. "He, Robert, and I were at school, you know. Cousin Jeremy's a poet. You can spot it by the look in his eye." Surprisingly, he clapped his hands softly together and Mr. Law, as if responding to a prearranged signal, came to himself with a start and focused on the source of the sound. "Come over,"

Seymour commanded. "I daresay Miss Porter reads poetry. Do you not, Miss Porter?"

It issued almost as a challenge, as if she were not clever enough to manage poetry outside the schoolroom. "Yes," she replied, "I do." She smiled shyly at the young man and he responded in kind. It was a fleeting expression, but it lit up his face. "What sort of poetry do you write, Mr. Law?"

"Oh," said Captain Seymour, "Law's not the name on his book."

"Oh? And what is that, pray?" She smiled again at Mr. Law. "You must not let Captain Seymour do all the talking, sir."

The silence that followed was brief but telling. Mariana's voice had carried and heads turned their way. Lucy looked as if she might come to her rescue, but before she could do so Captain Seymour spoke up again.

"You won't get a word out of Jeremy, Miss Porter. My fault, I should have told you. Jeremy cannot speak. Had an accident when he was at Eton. Suits me, though. I hate a man who chatters. Makes him all the better company." He put his arm about Jeremy's shoulder protectively, as if daring her to be unkind, but Mariana recovered quickly.

"Then I must ask *you*, Captain. What is the name of Mr. Law's book and how has he signed it?" Her eyebrows rose into little peaked arcs, for Brion Seymour's face was gradually turning a shade of rosy brown. His jaw tightened and his brows contracted substantially. "Why, Captain," she said in alarm. "Is something the matter?"

With visible effort he reasserted himself. "Why, no, Miss Porter. I am quite well."

But Jeremy, hand to his mouth, was dissolved in silent laughter—so much so that tears sprang from the corners of his eyes. He slapped himself on the thigh, then leaned against Seymour's shoulder, his own shoulders shaking.

"Have I said something amiss?" asked Mariana.

"No, Miss Porter," answered Captain Seymour with an attempt at dignity. "The fault is not yours, but mine." Then he too began to chuckle. "I can't remember the name of his demmed book!" He laughed out loud and disengaged Jeremy from his embrace. "His pseudonym is Quentin Quartermain, so much I recall, but I cannot think of how the book is called."

Mariana had no need of the information. "Why, if he is Quentin Quartermain, his book is called *The Golden Wingéd Bird*, sir. I know it well, for I have in my chamber at this moment a copy on my bedside table." She turned now to the silent poet. "Mr. Law, if I send for the volume, will you inscribe it to me?"

Jeremy could not have been more pleased. He made a gracious bow of assent, and Mariana, seeing Lily, sent her for the book.

"You are my favorite modern poet, sir. I have taken some of the verses by heart." He looked surprised, not to say doubtful. Perhaps many women boasted of such things, but Mariana was sincere.

"'When I leave you, I shall go . . .'" she began to quote softly,

Back to flower of weed or tree;
Plumed as darkly feathered crow,
Tossed as sunlit, sparkling sea.

From you I shall not take flight,
I shall wait until you pass
Walking on a winter night,
Or dancing in a field of grass.

Nets I'll spread I shall devise
Over an indulgent land;
Waiting there to touch your eyes,
Waiting there to brush your hand.

When she had finished there was a brief moment of silence and then a patter of applause. "Oh, Mariana, how lovely!" cried Lucy, and Lady Battledore looked gratified at the success of her protegée. Even Lady Blanche inclined her head graciously.

"Miss Lucy is correct," said Captain Seymour, "you declaimed the lines beautifully. I daresay Jeremy could not have asked for anything better, could you, my friend?"

Lily returned with the slim volume and Jeremy, beaming, took it to a small secretary in the corner and sharpening a quill, began to write upon the flyleaf of the book.

"You have made him very happy, Miss Porter. Not only are you familiar with his work, but you interpret it with all the feeling and sentiment it deserves. You are a remarkable young lady, and I salute you." He lifted his cup of chocolate. He was being so pleasant that it seemed increasingly difficult to resent him.

"When will you be returning to your regiment, Captain Seymour?" asked Lady Battledore from across the room.

"Oh, are you an army man still, sir?" Mariana enquired. "I think I should have guessed you would retire to the country."

He demurred. "I am afraid the Irish gentry can ill afford to be squires, ma'am. I have been off seeking my fortune since I was scarce old enough to hold a drum."

"How very interesting. What regiment, may I ask?" Mariana gave him a small and totally insincere smile. "The Buffs, I'll wager; so easy of entry, and so many of your countrymen seem to favour it. But you were not at La Albuhera, I imagine?" She referred to the near-disastrous battle the previous May in which so many of the regiment lost their lives that it almost seemed dishonour to have survived.

But he took it well. "No, not at Albuhera, Miss Porter, nor, indeed, in the Buffs. I was not in any British regiment, in fact, though I did see action in Spain."

"Action in Spain but not in a British regiment, Captain Seymour?" Mariana's eyebrows lifted high. "You astound me! Were you then enlisted for the French, sir?"

Seymour refused to be rated. "For the Spanish. I had the great honour to be a part of the Ultonia, which is *all* Irish. Perhaps you have heard of the siege of Gerona?" He made it seem doubtful.

"I believe the French pounded it to rubble?"

He nodded gravely and spoke so quietly and solemnly that of a sudden Mariana was quite ashamed. "Out of eight hundred gallant Irishmen only two hundred fifty-three survived. I think you can say we did our part against General St.-Cyr."

She was aware that the attention of the room was on them. Jeremy Law, in particular, seemed to hang on their words. But she was not to give in so easily. "All this for glory, Captain?"

"All this for wages, Miss Porter. I was, at that time, a very poor chap."

All the resentment came flooding back. She inclined her head to him coldly. "I believe we all know the source of your affluence." She paused, then added, "And whose rights went forfeit to give it to you."

"Mariana, how can you?" Lucy breathed.

Lady Blanche curled her lip as if to say, What can you expect? It was Lady Battledore who saved the situation in the most direct way possible, riding roughshod into the conversation as if no tension existed.

"One of my husbands was in Spain. Served in the Irelanda under Cuesta. Dashing fella, looked well in blue." She cackled bawdily. "Looked demmed well out of it, too, if you catch my meaning." Unfurling her fan she tapped a guest on the wrist and said to her, "Pray, do not look so shocked, Lady Blanche. You'll find there is a great deal more to a real man than a fashionable wardrobe."

Lady Blanche allowed a condescending affability. "I protest you are surely correct, Lady Battledore. I fear that I have not had so broad an acquaintance as some, but I willingly bow to your dictum." Then, "By the by, what became of Lord Battledore? Does he live here in London?"

For a moment Lady Battledore only tightened her enigmatic smile, though a knowledgeable observer might have detected a sharp glint in her eyes.

"Blew his head off with a cannonball," she explained. "Ours, not theirs. The damned fool never knew when to bend his neck."

There was a stunned silence after which everyone fell to talking of the wedding preparations. Lady Battledore professed to be much diverted by the description of Lucy's bridal veil of Belgian lace. Even Lady Blanche, the epitome of elegance, was drawn out by the subject.

Mariana, feeling out of sorts as a consequence of having been rude, went to the window and looked out on Portland Square. She was not left alone, however, for a touch on the arm returned her to the morning-room. It was Mr. Law shyly proffering the copy of *The Golden Wingéd Bird*. She took the volume gratefully, but when she would have opened it to read the inscription he stayed her hand. She understood that it was intended to be read at some later time, when she was alone.

"Thank you," she said to him softly. "No matter what you have said, I shall treasure it. You do not need me to tell you how fine your work is, but all my admiration is yours, nonetheless."

With a slight little bow he took up her hand and kissed the fingers lightly. His eyes shone as if she had given him a gift of great price. Then he was gone, bidding goodbye to Lady Battledore and slipping quietly out of the room.

"He is a brave and distinctive talent, my cousin," said Captain Seymour at her side. "I am prouder to know him than almost any other of my acquaintance. I am gratified that you, too, appreciate him."

It rang so patronisingly on her ear that she almost made a retort designed to cut him, then she saw that he was sincere. "So many people treat him as an oddity, a sport," he continued, "because he cannot enter into their vapid conversation. I am glad, for his sake, that he has found a friend who appreciates his true worth."

She did not know how to answer him. On the one hand he was making a bid for friendship, it seemed, but on the other, her resentment had far from dissipated. He seemed to read her thoughts.

"Cannot we be friends, Miss Porter? I protest it was not of my doing that I came into a fortune."

"And will you give it all away, then?" she asked, rather acidly.

He remained genial and not one whit abashed. "By no means. Since I have never been in velvet before, I intend to enjoy it thoroughly while I can. The provisions are so peculiar, I think I may say eccentric, that it remains to be seen whether I shall reap much in the long run, and so I must enjoy while I can.

"What was he like, this uncle of ours?" he asked. "A bit mad, I should think from the conditions he set." At her look he explained his question. "I never met the old gentleman, you know, never in my life."

Mariana was incredulous. "I find that difficult to believe, Captain. Such men as Uncle Forrester are unlikely to leave their fortunes to strangers."

"Nevertheless, it is true. I knew the *name* of our relative, but I never expected to make his acquaintance, much less inherit his goods."

"And so now you need never go back to the rigours of Spain?"

"Only on holiday, once this Corsican bandit is driven to the wall."

"Whom you intend to pursue from a safe distance, I take it."

"My word, Miss Porter, you do have a down on me," he said with some exasperation. "Don't you know that honey is sweeter than brine? I hope you won't treat all the bucks in this unfortunate fashion, else you'll never achieve your aim."

"My aim, sir? And what do you perceive that to be, pray?"

"Why, to get yourself a husband, I should think. Is that not why 'the Battleaxe' brought you to London?"

"'The Battleaxe'? You speak of my aunt. Lady Battledore, if you please. How unkind to ridicule your hostess behind her back."

"I doubt she would be surprised. I've called her that to her face a time or two . . . in private, of course. It is sort of a secret joke between us. I regret that it slipped out in conversation."

"Brion, dear," Lady Blanche was cooing from across the room, "is it not time we made our farewells? We have so many other calls to pay that I shall be quite exhausted by nuncheon." She sounded, in fact, so languid that she might be exhausted already.

Brion smiled good-naturedly, but he pressed Mariana's arm. "Mayn't I return to call on you, Miss Porter? I fancy you might better understand my position if you knew how it all came about."

"No need, Captain. However it happened, the end is the same."

"I think you believe I somehow cheated your father."

"No!" She pulled a face of exaggerated surprise.

"Well, I didn't. Not a speck of it. I daresay he and I should get on together, given the chance. I quite like old rips, and they say your da was quite a flyer in his day."

"Brion!" called Lady Blanche imperatively.

"I believe you are wanted," said Mariana maliciously.

"May I call upon you, at any rate?"

"You are very kind, but I think not. In fact, I may say I *trust* not. I do not understand your motives in wanting to call upon me, but we have, I believe, very little in common."

"Only our mutual uncle?" he asked, undaunted.

"Only a connexion by marriage," retorted Mariana. "One which, if it is regretted by no one else, can certainly find no favour in my eyes. Good day, Captain Seymour."

"Brion, I am waiting!"

Captain Seymour executed a half-bow and said in parting, "Marriage is, after all, an honourable estate, Miss Porter. I leave you to reflect upon that."

And in a moment he was gone, leaving no clue as to the meaning of that cryptic statement. She wondered about it and was to ponder it even further in the days to come. But meanwhile Lucy must have her say.

"Well," she chided when the sound of carriage wheels had faded, "I cannot think what came over you, Mariana. I have never known you to be so rude . . . and to poor Robert's groomsman, too. The poor man was doing his best to win you over, and all you could do was to sulk and simper. What can you have been thinking of? You're not likely to catch a husband that way."

"And is that what *you* did, Lucy . . . *caught* a husband?" asked Mariana sharply. "I hope I shall not have to do such a thing."

Her friend had the grace to flush. "Why, what do you mean? Everyone must get married, sooner or later."

"That may be, or nearly so, but I hope I shall at least have some inclination toward the man I wed, as you do. That certainly is *not* my feeling for Captain Seymour."

To her aunt she said, "I am aware, madam, that the Captain is a favourite of yours, and I suspect there is some little plot in hand, but you cannot hope to pair me off with a man I detest, surely?"

"Oh, indeed not," said Lady Emilia in a stiff parody of the formal tone Mariana had used. "You alone must choose where your heart is to fly. I am sure I am no example."

There was a sharp quiet among them, but it melted and all three of them began to laugh.

When Mariana was alone in her chamber she opened her copy of *The Golden Wingéd Bird*. In it Jeremy Law had written:

I know now, dear Miss Mariana, why this slender book has had no dedication. It was waiting anxiously for you. If it finds favour in your eyes, I am rich beyond dreaming, and blest beyond compare.

How sweet, how gentle he was . . . and how unlike his Irish friend. What strange companions they were. It made her wonder about Lucy's Robert, and about her friend's future happiness.

—6—

IF UNCLE FORRESTER'S lawyer had gone into politics he would of a certainty have been known as "Honest John" Chipworth. He was that sort: plain-speaking, unimaginative, and thoroughly trustworthy. A large man with a bluff manner and the sort of weathered look Mariana associated with country living, he was not at all the kind one thinks of spending his life among writs and documents. Mariana felt at ease with him at once. It was clear that he would not stand on ceremony, and equally clear that this arose not from discourtesy but from a desire to strike straight to the heart of a matter. She suspected that Uncle Forrester might have been very much the same, and that his choice of a lawyer was a case of like calling to like.

"Well, young miss," he said as she was seated in his chambers. "You have taken your time, I must say. I never knew so reluctant an heiress before. I expected you to be pounding down my door long since, but then, I daresay you felt the opportunity would not run away. And you were correct, but you must admit it has been a curious reaction."

Mariana was quite taken aback. "I beg your pardon, sir?"

"I say I expected you sooner and you have surprised me by your laggardness!" He said it a little loudly as if he suspected she were hard of hearing. When she still did not respond but sat there somewhat stunned he asked (a little sharply, she thought), "You *are* Miss Porter, are you not?" She nodded. "Miss *Mariana* Porter?"

"Yes, I am Mariana Porter, but I confess you have me at a disadvantage, Mr. Chipworth, when you say you have been expecting me. I felt certain my father's letter could not yet have reached you. I hardly wanted to present myself before my introduction."

"Letter? What letter? From Lynval, you mean?"

She was a little taken aback at this intimacy. "You know my father?"

"Oh yes, knew him as a boy . . . *and* as a man. Better as a boy, if you take my meaning. No offense meant, of course, but he has proved rather a rum 'un, hasn't he? I suppose he wrote to complain about the terms of the will. A bit ungracious to snap at the hand that is feeding you, no matter how little it offers, what?"

"He did not exactly write to complain," said Mariana sharply, for she did not like to hear Papa so described by a stranger, though admittedly there was just cause in many respects. At least before his reformation. "In point of fact, I have come to complain *for* him, since I do think Uncle Forrester treated him shabbily."

"Had a right, don't you think? His own money, and all that."

"Well, I suppose he did. I don't pretend to know the ins and outs of their quarrel. I only know that Papa's expectations were fearfully brought down."

Mr. Chipworth indulged in a breath of snuff. "And you, miss, how did you feel?" He flourished a large silk handkerchief with surprising delicacy for so hearty a gentleman, sneezed, and looked to Mariana for reply.

"I? My sympathy is entirely with my father. Admittedly it is easier to live well than in cheeseparing fashion, though I daresay we shall get on well enough if we continue to live in Dublin."

"You like it that well, then?"

She considered. "It has many points in its favour, not the least being economy. If one can't live in London, it becomes a matter of weighing disadvantages, doesn't it?"

"You seem to be well practised in such judgements."

"I've had to be. Papa has no head for it. I shouldn't *really* mind Dublin for the foreseeable future. It keeps Papa away from the gaming tables, for one thing."

"You astound me. I should have thought the Irish were great gamblers."

"And so they are," Mariana agreed. "But Papa, you know, has too much pride. When one has been toasted at White's and Almack's, one has a certain reputation to uphold."

Mr. Chipworth nodded understandingly. "So it would seem, but it also appears that your father is not of that noxious breed so given over to the play of the hand that he must wager at any cost."

"I have always thought it was fashion, rather than greed, that drove him on," said the girl, "for he now seems quite content without much of his former pastime."

"And what does he do now instead?" Chipworth enquired.

"He is a painter. Not a great, but rather a good one. His sitters generally profess themselves satisfied, at any rate."

"And he lives well from it?"

"Hardly that, but the legacy will help."

Mr. Chipworth seemed about to choke, for he turned quite red in the face, which alarmed Mariana, but his normal colour soon returned.

"Help? My word, I should say so! I daresay you will not let him worry about a thing. Mustn't be too generous, mind you, or he'll be straight back at the tables."

Generous? What on earth was the man talking about. "You must understand, sir, that my father is quite capable of minding his own money, even though he prefers to leave it in my hands."

Mr. Chipworth, for his part, was beginning to believe the girl a trifle slow, if not outright simple. He leaned across the table and eyed her searchingly. "Miss Porter, Miss Mariana Porter, Miss Porter the daughter of Lynval Porter who was nevvy to Mr. Josiah Forrester? I do have the right Miss Porter, do I?"

"Yes," she replied, beginning to wonder at this odd man who asked the same question over and over. "Whatever else may be in doubt, there is no confusion about that. I *am* Miss Porter and I *have* come to represent my father, with his full permission, in the matter of the legacy to him from his Uncle Josiah Forrester. His letter could have explained all that, and I am sorry that it has not yet arrived, but I have in my reticule the actual document giving me power of attorney in the matter."

Mr. Chipworth looked rather dazed. He wiped his silken square first across his forehead, then over his chops, and lastly over the top of his head in an agitated manner. "My dear Miss Porter, you must forgive me . . . is it possible that . . . ? My *very* dear Miss Porter, this is an unusual situation, quite beyond my expectations. Is it possible that *you* have not yet received a letter from this firm?"

"I, sir? How should *I* have received a letter when the legacy belongs to my father?"

"Quite so, but you see, there is the quizzer. You have not yet received the letter that was sent off the same day as the one to your father?"

"No, but then I left Dublin in rather a hurry. I had an opportunity to travel with my father's . . . with Lady Battledore."

"Lady Battledore? Ah yes, your mother's sister, I believe?" He laughed deprecatingly, but with kindness. "I can never quite keep up with the lady, unlike your beautiful mother, who seems a model of constancy by comparison." He rang a small bell on his desk and a door immediately opened. "Yes, sir?" "Fetch that vinaigrette for Miss Porter, there's a good chap."

"I assure you, Mr. Chipworth, I am quite well. I have no need of smelling salts."

"That may be, Miss Porter, but . . . ah, here we are. Thank you, Rigby. If you need them they will be at hand, Miss Porter."

Quite odd. Odder and odder, thought the girl.

"*So* then," he clasped his hands, "you have *not* had my letter?"

"No."

"And so you did not know that you personally were expected here?"

"No, I did not. For what purpose was I expected, sir?"

He took a long, slightly shuddery breath, relaxed almost as if by personal command, then said, "It is my pleasure, Miss Mariana Porter, to inform you that you too are the recipient of a sum of money from your father's uncle."

"Ah," she said, "that is where the confusion has arisen and the reason for the vinaigrette? I assure you, sir, I am not as flighty as all that. A *sum* of money, you say? But not as much as to my father, of a certainty, that stands to reason."

"A bit more, actually."

"Really? And I hardly so much as laid eyes on the gentleman, nor he on me, to the best of my knowledge."

"Nevertheless . . ." began Mr. Chipworth, but Mariana went on without pause. "Well, that *is* nice. No cheeseparing quite yet, then?"

She waited. He paused. Interminably, it seemed.

Finally, "How much *is* the legacy, Mr. Chipworth?" she was driven to ask. "More than my father's six hundred, you say?"

"Hmm," he said, clearing his throat. "Yes, rather a bit more." He wrote a number ending in a series of noughts upon a scrap of paper and passed it over to her. "What do you say to that, miss?"

She blinked, but nodded. "Aside from the fact that you have omitted the decimal, I think it quite handsome. It will considerably alter our life style. For a little while, at least."

"No decimal omitted, Miss Porter."

Her hand went to her lips. "Really? Upon my word!" Then she rallied. "I daresay I shall adjust to affluence, however." Smiling, he wrote again, adding zeros and thrust the paper back to her. Now she removed a handkerchief from her reticule and pressed it nervously to her lips. "Perhaps the vinaigrette, after all, if you would be so kind." He waved it back and forth and her colour returned.

"You see, Miss Porter, aside from certain small bequests . . . and, of course, your father's legacy . . . a few trifles and loose ends yet to be tied up . . . the fact is that between yourself, my client's other nevvy, and the City Merchant's Benevolent Fund, the late Josiah Forrester has divided his estate equally." Mariana was grateful that the vinaigrette was set firmly on the table beside her without question. She could not have supported questions just then.

When at last the room stopped swimming before her eyes, she took another deep breath and straightened her spine. "And how much does that amount to, sir?"

"Well . . . in round figures, mind you, but after taxes . . . I should hazard in the neighbourhood of twenty thousand pounds a year. You are a wealthy young woman, Miss Porter."

"Yes," replied Miss Porter faintly. "It appears I am."

"There are, however," said Mr. Chipworth, "certain provisions."

Ah, now it came. It would all be taken away again. Still, they might eke out a *living*, after all. How odd to have a fortune within one's very grasp, only to lose it in the next breath. "And what provisions would those be, sir?"

He cleared his throat awkwardly. "Actually, there are only two of any importance. The first one is . . . and you must not take it ill, for I know it was laid on with the best intentions . . ."

Her heart sank. "What is it?" Something impossible to fulfill, no doubt. Was Papa's share of the money so hedged about?

"It is that no portion of this money shall in any way or fashion be made over or fall under the control of your father."

"But how unfair! Do you mean to say that Papa is to be poor the while I am wealthy? What sort of man *was* this uncle of ours? No wonder if Papa and he did not get on. My own father to have no share in my good fortune? Quite out of the question!"

"I applaud your filial piety, miss, but hear me out."

Breathlessly Mariana sank back into her chair.

"The provision is quite specific. If you refuse to abide by it, the entire fortune passes to Captain Seymour and the Benevolent Fund. I beg you to consider carefully."

"Oh, dear," she cried, more to herself than to him, "this is so difficult! On the one hand, I may live with Papa in genteel poverty, always on the edge of things, and on the other, I may live any way I like, but only by denying Papa a share in it."

The lawyer waved a chiding finger. "You do not *listen*, you see. The provision states only that you must not *sign over* or place any *control* of the money in your father's hands. In other words, you may give your father what allowance you like, but the *control* is bound to remain with you."

"Oh," said Mariana, "that puts quite another light on the matter."

"I thought it might," agreed Mr. Chipworth.

"But think of poor Papa! All this money, and he not to play at the tables? How difficult for him!"

He eyed her keenly. "My word, you sound almost pleased. I take it you disapprove of gaming, then?"

"I disapprove of nothing that does not become an obsession, but in London Papa was never able to be moderate. Besides, if he gambles he does not paint. I leave it to you which is best for him?"

"Quite so, but he has a choice all the same, you know," Chipworth reminded her.

"Does he? What choice is that?"

"Your father still has *his* six hundred a year. He may fling that away as soon as he chooses. He might go more carefully, though, I believe, knowing that he must *ask* his daughter for more." He spread out his hands and her lips curved. "What a nice smile, Miss Porter. It makes you quite radiant. What are you thinking, pray?"

"I am thinking, sir, what a wise, kind, and generous man was my papa's uncle in providing both for Papa and for our future as well. He has left my father both security and a full measure of self-esteem. I make that to be wisdom indeed."

Mr. Chipworth agreed completely. And the more he saw of this lass, the more he liked her. "But there is another provision still, you will remember."

She settled comfortably. "I await it with full confidence."

Looking over the top rim of his spectacles and watching her carefully, he continued. "It is not an easy provision, Miss Porter. I fear, indeed, that you will take great exception to it."

"Please go on," she said steadily.

"Not to put too fine a point on it, you must marry within one year or forfeit a substantial portion of the money."

Still holding steady, "How much must I forfeit?"

"One-half, I am afraid."

She let out her breath. "Ah, but that is not so very terrible, is it? Ten thousand a year is still very considerable."

"And if not married within the second year," he went on, "it descends by half again, and so on each year." He shrugged lamely. "I had no part in this, Miss Porter. It was your uncle's plan entirely. The conditions apply to Captain Seymour as well."

She calculated mentally. "So that means that within ten years time I should be beggared unless I marry?"

"I believe that is correct. So you see, it is in your interests to wed quickly."

"So it would appear." She knit her brows. "What becomes of the money if I do not marry?"

"Very gradually, as you paid forfeit, it would transfer to the other legatees." His fingers drummed upon the desk top. "And so, you see, it becomes more complicated. It is the same for Seymour."

A foolish thought occurred to Mariana and she said it aloud before she thought. "I hope you are not suggesting," she laughed, "that Captain Seymour and I develop a *tendre* for each other."

"Not if you do not fancy each other, certainly," he said gravely, "but I hope you will hear me out. The fact is that the provisions for both of you are rather more narrow than I have yet related."

Mariana's eyebrows arched a little at that. "How so?"

"Harumph! Well, the fact is . . . well, you see . . . the fact is . . . the fact is that both you and the Captain must marry within the family. It would, I should think, solve a great deal if you came to some terms and legally bound yourself to each other."

"But Captain Seymour and I are not related by blood."

"Oh, that I know . . . the extended family, I should have said. Your uncle wished to keep his money within the bounds of the family as he knew it, you see."

He delicately took another pinch of snuff from his box and as delicately placed it in one nostril, sneezed, and delicately flicked away the residue. "He was a great one for family connexions, your greatuncle."

"So I see," said Mariana as she arose. "Thank you for your time, Mr. Chipworth." She paused. "One other thing before I go. How would I go about discovering what *other* male relatives I may possess?" She smiled dazzlingly. "It would not pay to limit my options, do you think? I assure you, Captain Seymour is not at all to my taste!"

=7=

MARIANA WAS NOT so stunned by her good fortune that she was unable to take it in. Though Lucy sighed and swooned over her imminent opportunities, sheer commonsense told her that when the news became general, she would quickly become the target of numerous offers upon the mere promise of her expectations, for not all of the will's provisions were likely to seep out just at first. Later, when all the details had made the rounds (she laughed to think), a great many family trees and obscure genealogies would be scoured. There was no doubt that she would soon find herself knee-high in proposals from recently discovered male connexions. She wondered to what extent the law would allow such connexions to be within the family, for to be sure, we are all cousins by way of Adam and Eve.

Lucy took a more pragmatic approach. As soon as she was given leave she went directly to Mariana's armoire and began inspecting the clothing she found there.

"You are so lucky," she said, "to have discovered your great good fortune before your aunt spent more than a few pennies on you."

"Whyever do you say that?" Mariana asked in surprise. "I do not think my aunt would have begrudged me anything."

Lucy agreed. "But *you* would always have held back. Now you will have no excuse. I shall drag you, kicking and screaming if necessary, you know, to every fashionable shop and dressmaker in London. We shall buy dozens and dozens of things, look them over at our leisure, try them on, parade in them, pick them through, and throw back what does not suit. I shall send for my own dressmaker at once and you shall begin to be fitted for all manner of things. Ball gowns first, because they *are* such a delight and you will need so many, then morning frocks and a great variety of costumes for the afternoon. A riding habit in black ribbed silk, I think, or perhaps in blue velvet. With your colouring you can wear anything! Oh, Mariana, we shall have such fun. What will you choose to do first?"

"Pay off my father's debts," said her friend decisively, "and then visit a bookseller, for I have almost nothing to read while I wait for my prospective beaux to call."

She almost laughed at the expression on the other's face. "To read!" Lucy exclaimed. "Mariana, you really must understand your new position."

"And then," continued the wealthy Miss Porter with a secret smile, "we shall get into my aunt's coach and take the costumiers of London by storm, just as you wish. I shall have party frocks and morning frocks and ball gowns and walking costumes and a riding habit, not in black but in russet broadcloth. And I shall have a whole roomful of pretty hats, boots, and silly, impractical little slippers!"

In fact, as it came about, Mariana discovered that the whole ritual of shopping took on a decidedly different tone once one *had* money to spend, and it mattered little if one spent it or not. The mere ability to spend was almost enough, after the first glorious excitement. There was so much to see, to do, to hear. So much to occupy one; so much to divert one's attention. Truly, London must be the most delightful city in the world. One could ride or stroll, as one chose, for the smooth flagstones of the elevated pavements kept walkers out of reach of the orderly lines of swift-moving carriages, each of which kept so sensibly to the left, avoiding the danger of collision.

Bond Street, itself the most famous of all the streets of shops, she found rather dingy and inconvenient, but oh! the marvels that were offered there. The girls quickly discovered the joy of lingering over the selection of a single item and coming away with the sense of an afternoon well spent. At five-ish they would at last return to their homes for tea and an hour or two of leisure before dressing for dinner and whatever evening diversion was to follow. It was all quite gay and giddy, and Mariana, eminently sensible Mariana, loved every minute of it.

But even Mariana might have been surprised when a certain visitor came to Battledore House one afternoon, and even more surprised at his errand. It was the Marquis, who was shown into a parlour and offered tea by her ladyship. At length the gentleman came round to the purpose of his visit.

"Since we have something of a shared past, Lady Battledore," he began, "that is, since we know who each other are and where we stand, and since you seem, in a way at any rate, to be Miss Porter's London guardian, I wonder if you will do me the honour of allowing me to call upon her . . . as an old family friend, naturally."

"Naturally?" asked her ladyship. "Naturally is hardly a word to use, sir. I apprehend that her father has forbidden you to address her?"

"Not exactly," said the Marquis, a little flustered. "That is, it was not couched in exactly those terms. The fact is that when I offered for her, he somehow took it as a personal remonstrance. I fear I did not present my suit in the best light."

"Ah," said Lady Battledore amiably, "but were you serious?"

"Serious?"

"Yes. Did you actually mean to marry the gel?"

The Marquis flushed an apoplectic scarlet. "Damme, madam, what d'ye take me for? If you were a man I'd consider calling you out for such a question!"

She smiled in a self-satisfied way. "I take it that the answer is in the affirmative. Pray, sir, do not let your feathers become unduly ruffled, for it was a natural question, and one that you should not find surprising.

"You are a man of 'a certain age,' as they say," she went on, parenthetically adding, "such a kindly phrase, I think, since I fall into the same square. And you are still unmarried. One in such circumstances should not take a little probing amiss." She continued to regard him quizzically, a flicker in her eyes. "You are still . . . ah . . . thirsty at the fountain, I take it?"

If the Marquis had been less of a gentleman in the true sense of the word, he might have been very rude indeed, but he contented himself with a terse, "Quite *capable*, madam, if that is what you mean."

"No encumbrances of a familial or . . . um . . . emotional nature?"

"None."

"No embarrassing offspring or anything of that sort?"

"What sort of question is that?"

"Take no offence, I pray. It happens to the best of us. The King himself had to scotch such a family affair recently, you know."

"No, I do *not* know, and I prefer not to be told things of that sort. What the King does is his own affair, not mine."

"Capital," she said lightly. "Am I to take it that you are in good physical condition?"

"Both my teeth and my heart are sound." The Marquis regarded her ladyship with what might, in another instance, have passed for controlled disdain. "I am surprised you do not enquire after my holdings," he commented frostily.

But Lady Battledore was now all wreathed in smiles. She felt he had passed her rigorous testing. "No need for that, since my man reported on it yesterday afternoon. I do not mind saying that if the gel accepts *you* she'll have made quite a catch."

"Well, I'll be blowed," the Marquis exploded inelegantly. "Then why all this catechism?"

In answer the lady opened her eyes very wide, expressing candid innocence, and said, "Why, sir, if I am to override a father's express wishes in such a matter, I must be sure of a suitor's true eligibility. The gel's reputation might be ruined by the wrong associations, is that not so?"

He hardly knew how to take her, and so made do with a deep sigh of resignation and a disbelieving shake of the head. "Is Miss Porter at home today, madam?"

Lady Battledore really looked regretful. "Alas, no. She has had to visit a lawyer on some business of her father's a good deal lately. But I shall certainly acquaint her with your visit."

"And I may return soon?"

"By all means."

The Marquis rose to make his adieu, but as the servant was showing him out he turned to her ladyship once again.

"Pray, madam, what chances fall to me in this, do you think?" He could not comprehend all the many levels of her reply.

"Some chances, sir, some, if you but press your luck. Faint heart, they truly say, ne'er won fair lady. Who is to plumb the mind of a young gel?"

By which, I think, we may rightly assume that Mariana had not entirely acquainted her aunt with the provisions of Josiah Forrester's will. She had, after all, a great deal to consider, and, being resolutely sensible, she wanted to have it all straight in her head before trusting herself upon the seas of fashion, where not a few novice mariners have sunk without a trace.

Even though she had not yet come out, Mariana was permitted certain chaperoned appearances. She went one evening with her aunt to a rout in the company of Lucy, her dear Bob, and the Marquis. This assemblage was to take place in the house of a great merchant whose wife desired to move up in society and had been widely advised to make this a first step, and perhaps society chose to come for the pleasure and diversion of inspecting a house they had never seen, but if Mariana had expected opulence she was much mistaken; if brilliance, she had been misinformed.

The invitations to assemblies such as this merely advised that so-and-so would be *at home* on such-and-such an evening, though if "home" implies warmth, kindness, or ease, the wording was misleading. The house was usually stripped from bottom to top of all but the most ornamental furnishings and the rest hidden away somewhere to make room for the great crowd expected. Our party knew they were in the right street long before the house was reached by the number of carriages that blocked the way, and they might, as Lady Battledore pointed out, easily recognise the house by its state of illumination. Every shutter was thrown back, every curtain flung aside. One could look through the windows and see, in the intense blaze of light, the constant motion within. To Mariana it seemed a roiling, boiling mass of flesh. It was daunting, but she steeled herself. It was, she knew, as important a first evening for her as for the merchant and his wife.

The movement inside appeared even more exaggerated when their party came to the entrance of the principal apartment, for there a distinct bottleneck had formed as the host and hostess, in an advanced state of shock occasioned by the presence of the *ton* and their own unaccustomed position, greeted each visitor with the same blank smile, for all the world as if they knew everyone or, conversely, knew no one at all. The crush was everything. There was no entertainment, no music, no cards, no place even to sit down. All one was expected to do, or *could* do, was twist and turn, be elbowed and buffeted from room to room.

Communication of any normal kind was impossible. When Mariana and Lucy recognised a long-forgotten school friend, they could not even talk to her. It was impossible to converse except by a series of winks, grimaces, and face-pullings that would have put the simian kingdom to shame. The friend was swept away and lost in the flood and Lucy and Mariana could only ask each other, mouthing in broad fashion, "What was her name?"

The torture was short-lived, however, for in a quarter of an hour the Battledore party was once again standing in the street awaiting their carriage.

"Now then, niece, what did you think?" asked her ladyship. "Do you understand why I choose to spend so much of my time in travel?"

Mariana was too stunned to give more than speechless assent. The experience had seemed so dreadful, so exhausting, and pointless withal, that she really could not conceive why people of intelligence would do such things, or, having done them, would submit to them a second time. Yet here was Lucy clamouring to continue on to another such affair in another street, and Bob lazily agreeing, for his own reasons, that it might be a tolerable thing to do. Mariana begged to be excused, whereupon Lucy labelled her a spoil-fun and the Marquis looked vastly relieved. Lord Robert merely looked down his nose.

Try as she would, Mariana found she could not summon any warm feelings for Lucy's darling Bob. She sought but found no common ground with him, not even a metaphorical pebble upon which to build a closer connexion. And built it must be, she felt, if she and Lucy were to remain close friends. She was never sure whether Lord Robert's languid posture was real or affectation. She only hoped that what Lucy fancied *she* saw in him was bedrock real.

Though she in future avoided routs, there were many other fêtes, smaller parties and outings, which Mariana did enjoy. Mrs. Siddons took the town by storm in *The Gamester*, with George Cook, looking distinguished still, for all his fifty years or more. There was an exciting new panorama on the subject of the bombardment of Flushing, with bombs bursting in air and rockets piercing the roofs of houses shown as being afire, the streets full of fleeing inhabitants half-mad with terror. A disquieting picture in all respects, and very lifelike, she thought, though without such a good command of *personality* as seen in Papa's best work, a critique with which the Marquis ardently agreed.

There were as well musical evenings and concerts, less well attended, where persons of quality sometimes seemed even to listen to the artistry of the musicians. From time to time Mariana saw Jeremy Law at such restrained evenings. He would bow and kiss her hand, but otherwise pressed no further. Often she would turn the pages of his book, *The Golden Wingéd Bird*, and wonder at the inscription he had placed in it. Was it merely social puffery, or had she for a brief moment made a friend whom she now seemed in some way to have lost?

=8=

THE GOWN FOR Mariana's first ball was nearly finished, the final fitting in progress. Mr. Tiburn, the great dressmaker, professionally known as Madame Trinita, dabbled about the hem, lifting, draping, and reshaping the fall of the fragile fabric to suit his exacting taste. Margate muslin was all the rage this season, and this creation was, as befitted the presentation costume of a young girl, embroidered in a soft white scarcely different from the muslin itself. The great departure, and Madame Trinita swore it would create fashion history, was the use of the tiny white silk flowers to trim the shoulder and adorn the sheer overskirt. The mameluke sleeves themselves needed no embellishment.

"You are blest, niece," pronounced Lady Battledore, "in being young enough to forego the plaguey stays. I wish I were still supple enough to do without 'em. It would make my life a great deal sweeter."

"Oo, but your ladyship," declared the dressmaker after carefully removing the pins from his mouth, "stays are all the fashion again! Everyone will be wearing them, and you are, as always, in the first rank. I daresay that presently even the very young such as Miss Mariana will be forced into them. And it's not all bad, you know. When I think what some ladies look like without their stays, I must just laugh to myself, really I must!"

The coming-out ball was a very few days away, and only the fact that her mother had not made an appearance at all clouded Mariana's gaiety. But each time she tried to broach the matter to her aunt she found herself put off with the discussion of a new cap, or a tidbit of gossip that simply could not wait, or, *in extremis*, a plea for patience and understanding.

Lucy, as always, had an answer for this state of affairs, though she blushed and stammered before saying it in the brittle accents of Mayfair, "Puss, I cannot *believe* you are such a dolly! The whole town is talking about it."

"About my being a dolly, Lucy?"

"No, you noodle," said her schoolmate in exasperation, "about the fact that your mother is finally coming out of retirement. Why, my mama says that society is all agog! It is not every day that the heroine of a great romantic misadventure returns to face the world that cast her out."

"Oh, Lucy, they didn't, did they? I mean, were doors actually shut against her?"

"Well," Lucy temporized, "not exactly, but very nearly. She couldn't go to court, you know. I mean, it isn't as if it were the *modern* day, is it? People simply didn't divorce then, even for the very best of reasons."

"What did they do when they were unhappy in their marriage?"

Lucy shrugged. "Put up with it, I suppose. Or took lovers, as all those wicked Whig ladies seem to have done."

"Then I think my mother must have been very courageous," Mariana said gravely. "And just think what it must mean to her to come back now, if they were so very dreadful."

"Ye-e-s," Lucy seemed to agree reluctantly.

"Why do you say it like that?"

Lucy's eyes rolled dramatically. "Think how frightened she must be, but what strength of character it shows! Unless she is perfectly horrid and hard, waiting only to make her entrance. And since you, dear, are her daughter, I cannot bring myself to think that of her."

Mariana was almost drawn in, but pulled back just in time. "Lucy, what are you talking about? You seem to be of the opinion that I know all about my mother and her scandalous past . . . but I assure you, I know nothing at all. I've asked Aunt, but she says I must wait, and so wait I do."

"There, you see?" said her friend. "That is what comes of being discreet. It really is most vexing. I am sure you *are* fuddled, sweet, but I thought you were only being reluctant out of diffidence, not innocence. Do you mean to say you really do not know?"

"Not a thing. I was not even sure she was alive until Aunt turned up in Dublin."

Lucy was awestruck. Or seemed to be. "Fancy! You *are* a sheltered creature. We might still be at Miss Pecksniff's for all you've learned of the world. Did your papa never say? How did he explain it?"

"By saying nothing at all. I am certain he meant it for the best," said Mariana with that flash of ire she always felt when anyone implied the least criticism of her father.

Surprisingly, Lucy agreed. "I know. I daren't ask my father very much, either. He is a puss, you know, but a father is a father."

It was evident that she wanted to ask more, but taking heed, she drew away from the shoals of conversational disaster and moved briskly to another topic, one of never-ending fascination.

"What are you wearing to the opera tonight? You remember that your aunt is attending with my mama and papa, and that you are coming along to keep me company?"

"What about your dear Lord Robert?"

"La, Bob and I cannot be tied together *all* the time. He will see enough of me when we are married. I daresay he will attend, but not in our party. What shall you wear?"

"Oh," Mariana said vaguely, "I hadn't thought."

"I knew you would say that!" It was a crow of triumph. "I have made up my mind that this time I shall have *my* say. Here you are, probably one of the richest girls in London, and you care nothing for your appearance. That is quite shameful, Mariana! Have you no pride?"

"I have not much vanity, I think. I've never learned it."

"Then I shall decide everything. It will be such fun. Like dressing a doll of life-size."

"I think I shall manage," said Mariana firmly. "I have been dressing myself for some time now. I don't understand it. Why does everyone think I must become a bird of paradise? You and my aunt . . . the very people in the shops. One would have thought Madame Trinita had found his ultimate place in life when he began fitting me."

"Oh, dear," Lucy sighed, "when will you learn? It is expected of you now. You have been a drab little hen for far too long. Lord, if I had your looks and your chances, not to mention your income!"

"You would have done the exact same," smiled Mariana. "I daresay you would have settled on Lord Robert no matter what chances you had." And with a scarcely suppressed giggle of accord Lucy flushed prettily.

Lucy's grandpapa had almost been in trade. Not too close, for he had a country spread and his factories were in the north, but close enough so that when his daughter married Lucy's father, she kept very great state at even the slightest of functions. Dinner was no exception, although there were only an intimate ten about the table. Mariana was placed between an elderly major general and a rising politician who wished to curry his favour. Contrary to accepted form, they all but talked over her head. The only respite was an occasional mischievous glance from Lucy and understanding looks from the Marquis, who was seated near his hostess. The situation was rescued by Lady Battledore, who spoke with bright amusement about her travels. If this was great society, Mariana thought, God save me from it.

The announcement that they would be hearing Signior Paisello's *Barbiere di Siviglia* cheered her somewhat, for it was one of her favourite opera buffas, but she wondered whether her fashionable companions would hear more than a few notes. The theatre was brilliant, the candlelight directed and reflected back and forth to every part of the auditorium, but it seemed to her that the audience was more brilliant still. The boxes, the circle, and the pit seemed filled to a crush with those come to see and be seen rather than to hear.

The Marquis agreed with her. Gazing critically through his quizzing glass, he opined dourly, "A bunch of demmed snobs, what? Not a music lover among 'em."

And Lord Robert, who had after all joined them, absently agreed. Then he leaned forward. "Stap me, if it ain't Seymour! And who is it with 'im? Blanche Westring'll have her nose out of joint, or I'm blowed."

Despite herself, Mariana's eyes followed his pointing finger. Truly the girl with Brion Seymour was enchanting, even from this distance. Her Titus-cropped copper hair had been lightly dusted with silver powder to contrive a delicate effect that resembled nothing so much as a light morning frost. It admirably suited the girl's *gamine* little face and lively expression, but another aspect was revealed as she carelessly threw back her mantle and her elegantly sloping shoulders emerged from a froth of lace. Brion leaned over her solicitously as he took the wrap. He may have murmured something complimentary, for his companion's eyes lighted and she dropped her lashes, coquetry well learnt. Mariana felt a distinct pang, which she thought very odd, since she had no feeling for Captain Seymour except a sort of continuing annoyance. She looked quickly, guiltily away just as a sibilantly continuous whisper spread through the assemblage. All eyes turned toward the Royal Box.

"Damme," said the Marquis, who had more or less attached himself to their party. "It's Cumberland."

Lucy's father looked apologetically at the ladies, saying to his wife, "I offer my pardons, m'dear. I had no idea he was in town. If I had known . . ."

Lucy's mama stared straight ahead. It was a signal, all knew, that she had banished the Duke of Cumberland, along with his scandalous aura, from her mind, nay, from her very. existence. For women like Lucy's mother, such dangerous men were not allowed to exist. Lucy's father turned explicitly to Mariana and her aunt. "I beg your pardon, no slight was intended."

"None taken, sir," said Lady Battledore coolly.

The Duke and the woman with him were seated now, their flock of satellites ranged behind them. The face of the woman was in shadow, but the clear light of the candles illuminated that of the King's son. Whatever he might be morally, Mariana thought she had never seen such a handsome profile. It was nearly classical in its symmetry. The head was gracefully set on a strong neck, the jaw firm without appearing stubborn, the ear well shaped, and though the general expression seemed one of austerity, there was a kind of grandeur there as well. So this, then, was the monarch's fourth son? He looked every inch the royal scion.

"That woman is Mrs. Page," Lucy whispered from behind her fan.

"They say she is *his* mistress as well as the mistress of his *valet*! Isn't it shocking?"

"Enough, Lucy," said her father. "Remember who you are."

Lucy dropped her eyes, but at that moment the Duke turned toward his companion and the pitiless wash of light illuminated his countenance completely, cruelly exaggerating every portion of the ruined visage, which had been concealed by the angle of his head. Instinctively Mariana gasped, and as if in response, the severe eagle-gaze turned in their direction. The Duke's eyes and Mariana's locked across the curve of the circle, held for the briefest moment, then broke.

"Well, he'll know you again," said Lucy, who had looked up just in time to observe the exchange. "Don't let him upset you. Everyone will know it was not of your doing."

Lady Battledore looked distinctly annoyed, and Lucy's mother closed her fan with a sharp snap.

"If you cannot be discreet, Lucy," she hissed, "at least be silent."

Mariana was baffled. She felt as if a cold wind had swept over her, quite destroying the safe, warm refuge she thought she had found. What had a royal duke to do with her? She noticed that her hands were trembling and she clenched them tightly together until she could feel her rings cutting into her fingers.

"Steady, girl," she heard her aunt murmur. "You mustn't give them more to talk about." Mariana tried to comply, and her aunt imperceptibly conveyed her approval. "That's right. Lift your chin. Look at me and smile."

Mariana's face felt as if it were frozen in place but she forced her lips to curve upward. What on earth was happening? It was a bad dream, was it not, and she would soon awaken safe in her own bed.

"Now smile at Lord Robert," Aunt Emilia whispered. "Robert, say something bright to make us laugh."

But for once the imperturbable Lord Robert was confounded. "Stap me, can't think of a blasted thing! 'S gone straight out of my head." He was so bewildered, so unlike the Mayfair dandy she thought she knew, that even Mariana could laugh without pretense, and as if by magic, the tension eased at once. The curious eyes of the crowd sought other cynosures. The dreadful moment was past.

"Should we take our leave, d'ye think?" asked the Marquis.

"That is up to Mariana," said Lucy's mother stiffly. "Personally, I think it would be a mistake," and Mariana quickly agreed.

"No. I do not know what is happening, but I won't turn tail in the face of it."

"Gad, what bottom!" exclaimed Robert admiringly. The Marquis squeezed her arm and shot her a look of congratulation. "Good gel. If you survive this, you're made, I don't doubt."

But Lucy, on her other side, was trembling. "I had no idea, my sweet. Can you forgive me?"

And from across the way Mariana perceived that Brion was staring straight at her with a curious look in his eye.

Mercifully the music had begun, the overture to Signior Paisello's *Barbiere di Siviglia*. Presently the Count and then Figaro were anxiously awaiting Rosina's appearance at the window and the audience was hushed, all fashion deferring to the outpouring of melody. Leaning back into the shadows Mariana looked again at the Royal Box, but its inhabitants too had withdrawn into a curtained obscurity.

At the interval they left their seats quickly. Mariana, able to contain herself no longer, pressed Lucy for details, but her friend only stammered and blushed mightily. "Please, dearest, not here." Behind her fan she said in an aside, "It is Robert, you know; he is so proper."

"Am I, by Jove?" asked her intended, peering round the little screen. "Dashed if this ain't the first time I've heard of it. I daresay you won't believe it, but I'm not at all shocked by fifteen-year-old news. Tell away if you like or not, but don't run me in on it. Am I right, Marquis?"

The Marquis was left with the uncomfortable choice of do or don't. "Harrumph!" he said, then launched into a furious spate of social pinpointing. "Look, over there is that amusing scoundrel Lord Barrymore, the Duke and Duchess of Rutland just behind him, and Mrs. Damer in that party of five or six just under the chandelier."

At the name of the famous sculptress Mariana's attention was caught. Following his direction she saw a striking woman of late middle age, but one to whom the years had added distinction rather than decay. The pleasing face was an almost perfect oval, the brow wide but not enough to depart from the rule of Greek proportion. Her figure, draped in a simple gown of classical design, seemed slight, but her movements were graceful in the extreme, and, Mariana was pleased to see, her neck was quite as long as Mariana's own, a fact Lucy was quick to note. "Oh, Lud," she said, "another swan."

It was the animation of Mrs. Damer's features that drew a feeling of sympathy. Here, Mariana thought, was a woman whom one might be proud to call friend, not because of her accomplishments or lineage but because of what her expression bespoke of interior beauty. The artist smiled and Mariana found herself smiling in return. A woman beside the artist whispered into her ear and Mrs. Damer seemed to look at Mariana even more thoughtfully. She moved forward through the throng and the girl found herself moving to meet her.

"I am Mrs. Damer," she said kindly.

"Yes, madam, they have told me so," Mariana replied. "It is a great honor to know you." She hardly knew what to say next. "My name is Mariana Porter."

"Yes," said Mrs. Damer, "they have told *me* so. Your mother and I were great friends many years ago. I hope that you and I will be the same."

"Thank you," said Mariana faintly. "They say my mother is coming back into society."

The finely shaped eyebrows shot upward. "*Is* she? How very brave of her. Please express to your mother that both you and she are welcome to my house at any time." She pressed Mariana's hand. "I mean that, you know. I hope you will visit me soon."

The opera's second act was even more enchanting than the first, the delightful "good night" quintet being particularly felicitous. Mariana enjoyed it the more when she perceived that the Royal Box was vacant. Perhaps the duke did not enjoy opera buffa. At the scene change she looked about her curiously. Mrs. Damer nodded and smiled, and her acceptance seemed to trigger other acknowledgements.

"Oh," whispered Lucy, "you've done it, you beauty. They all will come to call at Battledore House, now, you'll see."

Mr. Seymour and his little copper-haired friend were not in their places, however. And it did not matter to Mariana in the least— did it?

—9—

"But please, Aunt. You *must* tell me!"

Lady Battledore was not at all happy at the turn matters had taken. Mariana had certainly acquitted herself well enough this evening, but she should not have had to do so. Mere chance had brought about the brief confrontation, but it had been enough to electrify the spectators. And just before the gel's coming out, too. Well, there would be no regretted invitations now. Everyone would come, if only out of curiosity.

"I was afraid of this," she said, as if in expiation. "I had thought I could safely wait and let your mother deal with it; indeed I had counted on it. Now I can see that will not be possible."

"Why were they all staring at me? And what have I to do with the King's son?"

"Nothing, actually."

"But they all *think* I do?"

"Perhaps. I should not worry about it. It is all such foolishness."

But her niece was not to be shunted aside. "What is it they think, Aunt, true or not?"

Lady Battledore's expression became less gentle. She was an experienced old warrior in the social battles of her kind, and she knew well enough when blunt fact is kinder than gentle evasions.

"In point of fact, they wonder if he is your father."

Mariana had been completely unprepared for such a thing as this.

"I . . . my father?" Then, carefully watching her aunt's face, "Is he?"

"Certainly not, but they will think what they choose."

"And Lucy's mama and father, do they believe such a thing?"

Lady Emilia's familiar bark of a laugh returned. "Stuff and non-sense! Do you think they would allow you to associate with their precious daughter if they believed it for an instant? No one who can count would give it room!"

Mariana sat up very straight and tried to look as grown-up as possible. "Perhaps you had better tell me about it now, rather than waiting for my mother?"

"I hardly know where to begin. It is always all very well to say begin at the beginning, but I scarcely know where that is. Tell me, my dear, how is your history? Have you learned of the great cam-paign in Flanders?"

Mariana felt absurdly like a schoolgirl again. "Not very much. I think I must have been very young."

Aunt Emilia chuckled dryly. "Yes, very young. I doubt if you could talk yet." She paused as if recollecting. "I hadn't expected to give a history lesson, but it was in 1793 that Lord Northrup and I went to Flanders."

"I was two!" Mariana interjected. "I could certainly talk by that time."

"You are doing very well in the matter now. Let me get on with it. Lord Northrup, at the time my husband, dear man, was on the Duke of York's staff. Very proud of himself, as he should have been. Winter quarters were in Tournai. The fighting had all but stopped and the King's Hanoverian troops were in cantonments around the city, so it was quiet most of the time, you see. Usually the men were employed merely in readying for fighting again in the spring."

She paused, remembering. "It was so cold that winter! It makes me shiver to think of it. I seem to recall that there was a bit of discontent when the King sent his Hanoverians new and warmer coats than the English soldiers had. I have always believed that he loved his German subjects better than the Britons. Blood tells, you know."

As if she had said something unfortunate, she skidded on along into her narrative. "You must not believe that Tournai was the end of the world. It was no ordinary encampment, but quite civilized. It was, I believe, the seat of the Merovingian kings . . . or was it the Carolingians? . . . At any rate, it was decidedly lively that year. You would have thought we were in London . . . balls and dinners and theatre parties. There was hardly any danger, you see, and I entertained a great deal. It was expected of me. But every now and again I would have a letter from London, sometimes from your mama, sometimes from a 'well-meaning' friend, but the general undercurrent was always the same. Your papa was making a name for himself at the tables."

"I daresay I know this part," said Mariana, "he cannot resist."

"Then I need not discomfit you with a recitation of what was going on, except to say that he was a fool with the cards and dice. It was a disease with him."

"How did it take my mother?"

"Not at all well. Since it was evident that they were not getting on all that famously, I thought a change of scene might do both of them good and I invited her to visit me. I had no idea what it would precipitate. I only meant it to give her a change of perspective . . . a rest from the strain of London. The encampment was prodigiously gay, what with all the young officers and the emigrés. I expected Lynval to come after her in quick time, to be honest, and that it would all patch up well enough."

"But he didn't?"

"No; he hardly seemed to miss her, from all reports, and she, I believe, was resigned to the idea that she had lost him to the tables forever. It was natural to cast about for solace; unfortunately, she found it all too quickly."

When Mariana would have spoken her aunt held up a finger. "You must not blame her too much, you know. Your mother had always been pretty . . . prettier by far than I . . . and used to a good deal of attention. I am sure the lack was felt, but in Tournai she was back in the thick of it.

"At first I was delighted to see her laughing again. It does so much for the complexion to be happy, you know. But among the Light Dragoons was a particularly good-looking man whom she had known when she was among the Queen's ladies at Kew."

"The Queen's ladies? I didn't know she had been."

Aunt Emilia nodded. "Oh, yes; the Princess Augusta is your godmother, I believe. She and your mother were thick as cream at one time."

She was now sweeping along in her narrative at such a rate that Mariana's head felt a little swimmy. "In any case," her aunt went on, or rather back to her original subject, "the young officer was excessively liked at Tournai . . . by everyone. Oh, I don't suppose he would have been at all the thing in London. Too bluff, too manly. He couldn't have stood the life at Kew for three days running, but in army society he was a different thing. A true Hussar; lively and open, completely good-natured."

Knowing the answer already, Mariana was impelled to ask the question. "Who was he?"

"His name is Prince Ernest, the man in the Royal Box tonight."

Sadly Mariana thought of that ruined face.

"He was a prince of the blood, after all, and your mama was *very* lonely. It was a dangerous combination for any woman, especially one who feels she has been jilted for a gaming table.

"Quite honestly, even if she had been free nothing could have come of it. The Royal Marriage Act was already in force and the King would never have approved of a non-dynastic marriage, nor even would Parliament. Look at the scandal about poor Maria Fitzherbert."

"So the Prince was merely dallying with her, do you mean?"

Lady Emilia shook her head violently. "Oh, quite the contrary, my dear. Within a very short while he was completely mad about her."

"And she about him? Were they lovers, Aunt?"

Emilia shook her head. "That I cannot say for sure. Nothing could have come of it, probably. It is all very well for someone like myself to marry at leisure, repent at will, but the Royal Marriage Act forbade it for the king's offspring. Mrs. Fitzherbert discovered that, didn't she?"

"And so, I gather, you are saying that because of this little flirtation my mama was ruined?" asked Mariana. "What a dreadful thing society can be! I shall never give in to it. I shall make it my business to do always just what I like! They'll not pillory me as they did my mother."

"You've not heard all."

"I've heard enough. They say the Duke of Cumberland is the wickedest man in England. If he ruined my mother, I believe it!"

Lady Emilia sighed. "How quick you young things are to condemn. You never knew him then. All you have heard came later. He would have married her, I think, if he could. Another officer might have been able to simply resign his commission, but the royal rules were well laid out; the King was adamant."

"I daresay kings don't chastise their sons too severely," said Mariana scornfully.

"Enough so that he was removed from his regiment, the regiment he loved, and transferred to the Command of the Second Cavalry, a totally different arm of the service."

"Was that when Mama came back to obtain the divorce?"

"Yes, but your father dragged his feet. I suppose he thought he could hold her despite everything."

Yes, Mariana reflected, that was congruent with her knowledge of her father.

"Your mother was to join Ernest in May. I have no idea what plans they had made. A small house in Hanover, perhaps, and a morganatic marriage, but . . ."

Something in Lady Emilia's tone. "But . . . Aunt?"

"It was war, my dear. One fine morning Ernest rode out into the field as a handsome and dashing young Prince-hussar. By evening he was doomed to be a cripple for life, and his face had become the ruin you saw tonight."

Mariana gasped a little, thinking of that visage. "And Mama?"

"He wouldn't have her. My dear sweet sister, who was quite convinced that she loved him, was turned back at the door time after time. Such a fool! He was too damnably proud, like all the Hanovers, and the Stuarts before 'em."

"But did she . . . ?"

"When she finally returned to London the news had preceded her. Oh, everyone was sorry, she was well liked, after all, but socially she was a ruined woman."

"And that is why she has stayed away at present?"

Her aunt nodded understandingly. "Oh, yes, your mother understands all too well that she must not be present at your coming out. It would ruin everything. And she knows, too well, my dear, what social ruination means."

Mariana sat quite silently, examining her hands, stretching out her fingers aimlessly. Her aunt looked at her keenly.

"What are you thinking, Mariana? I can hear something buzzing in that head of yours."

"It is nothing," protested the girl. "Nothing."

But next morning Mariana was bright and early at the office of the solicitor, Mr. Chipworth. Weem, the clerk to whom she first spoke, at first protested, but she gave him little quarter. She had need to see his master, and see him she would. Did he not know who she was?

He did not, and she informed him, and saw, for the first time, what a power the scent of money can be. He, who had only been confronted with biddable, quiet women in these chambers, was swept aside as the heiress thrust herself past the little gate and into the sanctum sanctorum. There she found Mr. Chipworth ruminating over a pipe. Presently, her business concluded, she thrust herself out again. Mariana had decided how the first installment of her inheritance should be employed.

—10—

MARIANA, ALREADY DRESSED, lingered in the Long Gallery of her aunt's house, peering up at the dim portraits by Van Dyck and Lely, by Gainsborough and Stuart, without knowing exactly what she sought. Perhaps it was wisdom she hoped to glean from her predecessors, or even some look of kindness from the pale, proud faces.

Wandering the house she had already peered into the ballroom, so soon to be the centre of the house, but now still and empty like a great gold and white shell in which one might almost hear an echo of the sea, or at the very least the music and faint laughter from a hundred past entertainments. She tried to be excited, to anticipate, but the evening ahead was too unreal to imagine.

In the rooms below the dinner party was about to begin. She should, she knew, already be there with Aunt Emilia. She must again, and this time with her new awareness, endure the curious scrutiny of those social arbiters whom her aunt believed might best serve or be enlisted in her cause. And, Mariana had come to believe, it *was* Lady Battledore's own ends that were served by all this.

For herself she gave not a snap of her fingers for all the social fol-de-lal. Once dear Lucy was married and off on her wedding trip, Mariana knew that she herself would be as happy . . . nay, a great deal happier . . . in Dublin with her father than in this unfriendly city. Eager as she had been to return, London was no longer her home. Perhaps Dublin was not either, but she missed it. Even cantankerous Bridie pined for Ireland. It was evident not so much in her usual litany of complaint as in the peaky way she went about, and from one poignant question, asked off-handedly and in an unlikely soft voice: "Will we be goin' back to home at all, miss, before the summer is gone?"

And yet Mariana had taken a decisive step to remain in London, of which even her aunt was as yet unaware. Was she putting her foot right, she wondered, or should she have consulted wiser heads than her own?

Mrs. Marasham found her, seemingly in colloquy with her ancestors. "If you please, Miss Mariana, your aunt is all of a pother. The dinner guests will be here presently and she requires you." The kindly under-housekeeper looked sharply at the girl. "Is all aright, miss?"

Mariana caught her breath in a tiny, convulsive movement. "I suppose I am a little nervous at facing strangers," she confessed. She fancied Mrs. Marasham might think she was daft, what with the many times larger number of people coming later, to the ball. But they were different, somehow; infinitely less daunting.

"Quickest done, miss, soonest mended, they say. I dare predict it will all come right once you've made a beginning." Mariana was grateful for the plain comfort of common sense.

They descended the great stair together, Mrs. Marasham keeping a practised eye out for last-minute requirements, Lily hovering nearby to carry out her commands. Lady Emilia waited at the foot.

"You look lovely, my dear, quite the picture of the sacrificial victim approaching the altar. Can you not manage at least a small smile?" She pinched her niece's cheeks to bring a little colour to them. "Pity you are too young for paint . . . No, what am I saying? It is your youth that will win them all. You must not be afraid, my child. They are only people."

And three hours later Mariana knew that her aunt had been right. The dinner guests admittedly had been only people. Proud people. Certainly very distinguished people. Very, very rich people, for the most part, but kind within their limits. She had already been acquainted with some of them—Lucy's mother and father—Lord Beresford—the Marquis, of course—Lady Stoneham, doyenne of the circle that still moved about the King's family.

It had somewhat puzzled Mariana at first to learn that there were, in effect, two courts, and had been for a number of years: the more staid group who played whist on innumerable sedate evenings with King, Queen and daughters, and the racier, glittering butterflies who followed the fortunes of Prinny. Both groups were represented here tonight, however. Since the Prince was now Regent and the poor old King confined for his own good, the fashionable lot were more in evidence. Undoubtedly, as an old campaigner, Lady Battledore knew what she was about.

Mariana knew almost none of the men who were brought in constant succession to be introduced, to write their names on her dance card, to bow and be replaced by others. None of them, certainly, had any notion of the turmoil within her. If she seemed a little austere, a little stern and remote, it merely added to the mystery of this newly eligible young heiress.

Jeremy Law climbed the stairs and bent low over her hand. For the first time her smile was one of genuine pleasure. She pressed his hand in return and thanked him for his inscription in her copy of *The Golden Wingéd Bird*.

"I feel quite as if we have already become old friends."

His own answering smile was enough to make up for his inability to speak. She allowed him to sign for two dances. They were spaced widely enough apart to seem oases in the broad expanse of the evening.

On the other hand, when Captain Seymour arrived in the company of Lady Blanche she felt an unaccountable increase in her disdain of him. Look at him, the great gowk; broad-shouldered, narrow in the hip, and that smug look of *Le Chevalier parfait*, a picture-book knight. Looking down the stair at him their eyes caught, and horror of horrors, he had the gall actually to wink at her! It was enough to make her jaw slacken. Thank goodness no one had seen. She shuddered to think what Lady Blanche's caustic tongue would have made of it.

She was dimly aware that her aunt was making introductions and she did her part by rote, determined to banish Brion Seymour to his proper place. He was just the sort of man she instinctively disliked. So superior, so sure of himself, so extravagantly unconscious of his manhood.

97

Not but what he *should* be masculine, naturally; but need he make one so aware of it?

The great ballroom seemed already filled with people, and still they continued to arrive. Was all of London to be in attendance? Lady Blanche was cool as a snow queen when she at last reached the top of the stair. Ice blue satin and diamonds contributed to the effect. Captain Seymour, thankfully, declared to play the gentleman and signed her card with decorum. One might almost think the unfortunate wink had been a mere facial tic. Something in his manner assured her that it was not.

Hardly had Captain Seymour and Lady Blanche moved on toward the ballroom when a sibilant murmur sped through the crowd. "He is coming . . . he has come . . . he is here!" And as the Red Sea must have parted, so did the throng yet making its way up the stair. The Great Prince had arrived.

The Regent was no longer the plump Adonis he had been in his youth. Disappointment, and especially dissipation, had taken their toll. The balladeers had taken to substituting "Georgie Porgie" for "Rowley Powley" in the old rhyme, and indeed, the Prince had "kissed the girls and made them cry" many a time. He was still only in his late forties, but he tried too hard to conceal it. The puffy, overblown features, waxy and almost copper-colored from the oils and unguents used on them, would have indicated a much older man to the uninitiated. His chin sagged, his eyes watered, and even his absurdly tight corseting could not conceal the fact that he had become a gross parody of the young prince who had enchanted the nation only a few years before.

Still, he had learnt his lessons well. He remained gracious and affable, moving among the guests with that sure, light-footed step that many overweighted persons possess, and even now there remained about him an aura that belied his excesses. It occurred to Mariana that the Prince Regent was all that the Hanovers might ever have aspired to be: German opulence married to the effeteness of the English upper class. George was, in his own way, both enviable and pitiful. Not that he would have subscribed to either view.

He was hardly out of breath when he reached the top of the stair, though a gracious pause to greet one or two of his friends might have been a ruse to disguise his effort. In any case, he greeted Lady Battledore as an old friend.

"How well you look, Lady Emilia. It takes me quite back to my youth, when you were the lure for every eye."

Her ladyship made a stately curtsey. "Your Royal Highness, may I have the honour to present to you my niece, Miss Mariana Porter."

Mariana, too, dipped low before the Prince, but he drew her up at once. "My dear Miss Porter, you are quite ravishing. How is it that we have not met before this?"

Mariana blushed. "I have but lately come from Dublin, sir, where I lived with my father."

"Dublin, eh? Dull hole for a young gel like you. I daresay these young bloods will see to it that you never have to return to it." The Prince Regent bowed low over the girl's hand and as he did so, a peculiar creaking noise seemed to emanate from somewhere near them. It was evident that Lady Battledore recognised the sound and a warning glance from her eyes told Mariana to say nothing. The Prince paid no attention at all, but taking Mariana's card in his pudgy hand, quickly set his name, or rather the initials G. R., beside the first two dances, a minuet and a *contra-danse*. Mariana recognised that she had been done a great honour. The first minuet might be expected, since she was the guest of honour, but the first "country-dance" in addition—well, that was something!

Now, surrounded by admirers, the Regent continued upon his way into the ballroom. Before the line of arriving guests could begin again, the mystery of the creaking was explained when Lady Battledore raised her fan before her lips and said succinctly, "Corset stays, my dear. He's laced too tightly! Let him set the pace on the floor, or he may faint from the effort."

When at last the musicians in their gallery struck up the stately measures of the opening dance, Mariana succumbed to a brief moment of freezing panic, but the Prince Regent gave her such an encouraging smile and led her out with such elegance and grace that her confidence swelled and the feel of the music communicated itself to her. In only a few turns she imagined that her body was giving itself over to the compelling intoxication of rhythm and balance, of step and counterstep. In the Prince's capable hands the country-dance went on to raise her spirits. This stout Florizel was no longer faintly amusing, but a kind of psychopomp leading her into another world. By the time he surrendered her to her next companion, she was already transformed.

Soon, when the cotillion was finished and her partner, briefly a young god, was once more a callow, overheated young beau, she began to believe the dance itself was speaking to her. "Live!" it was commanding. "Take me into your spirit and soul. Let me live through you." After that, for a long while, her companions did not concern her; she inspired them and they were present to lift with her against the rhythm, to partner her in a pursuit of ecstasy. Even when, in the ordinary way, they were poor sticks upon the floor, she made them into something far more than they were. Some of the guests began to notice this, how she could seem almost transfigured, and they inwardly applauded it, but others took her glorification to use toward their own ends.

Lady Blanche was one of these. Mariana was not sure why the lady so disliked her, but she was sure that it was not an accident that she was allowed to overhear an unpleasant scrap of conversation.

"Quite like her famous mother must have been," Lady Blanche said acidly to Lord Brompton, and he, who had known Mariana's mother and admired her, agreed with alacrity. Others who had overheard the exchange, as Lady Blanche had perhaps intended, understood that something quite different had been meant. It lay a film across the brightness to reflect how many others here might be thinking of her in that fashion. Oh, it was cruel, but she knew how much it was the way of the world.

She longed to communicate something of this to her aunt, but it was impossible. There were other ways of justification, however, and because she knew that Lady Blanche would like to lay claim to Captain Seymour, and despite the notion she held that she did not, herself, much like him, when it came time to step out with him she did it with great flair. Oddly enough, she found that she enjoyed it. Unlike her previous dances she was quite aware, in a heightened sort of way, of each step he was about to take, even before he took it, and she matched hers to it. The spirit of the dance had not deserted her;

it had enfolded her into itself, and seemed to be moving through her and through Captain Seymour as well.

Both of them knew it, and perhaps he was as baffled as she was. Before this he had thought her more than a little spoiled, not to say prim in an irritating way that led him to bait her just a trifle, but now something had changed, and the dance expressed itself through them. The music played expressly for the two of them; their partners in quadrille were mere geometric supports, mere balances and checks to their own movements.

Mariana saw that Lucy was aglow with the same invigoration as she danced with her lover, and even he, his posing thrown away, became acceptable as Lucy's bridegroom. It made Mariana question her own relation to Brion Seymour. Who was he, really, and what was he?

When the time came round (for he was only once on her card) they separated reluctantly, and each knew it as clearly as the other. Although she danced with others all the evening, with Jeremy Law, with the Marquis, with Lord Brompton, and even with the formerly despised Lord Robert, her eyes and Seymour's sought each other out almost unconsciously, and she found, though she could not have admitted it, that she was most comfortable when he was somewhere in her immediate vicinity. She could then give herself over once more to the exhilaration of the dance, and become itself.

She must, by the rules of society, go down to supper with the Regent, and she awaited that experience with some curiosity now that she had lost her incapacitating awe of him. He seemed to her rather more a jolly uncle than a sovereign. That there was a great fallacy in this sort of thinking, she knew, but her knowledge did not persuade her, and for his part, the Prince did nothing to convince her of it. Rather, he showed her every mark of favour; hung upon her words and presented her to one and all as if she were truly *his* niece, and not merely that of his hostess, Lady Emilia. It could not help but create a triumph, and she could see from the way Lady Emilia glowed that her aunt felt she had done her proudly.

When Mariana found herself alone for a few welcome moments with Lucy, her school friend was jubilant. "Oh, I knew you should win over all, my pet!" she enthused. "Just look at us! Who at poor Miss Pecksniff's would recognise us for the ink-grubby minxes who terrorized the mistresses? They would never guess who we are!"

"I am not sure that I know myself who we are," confessed Mariana. "It all seems such a dream that I wonder who I shall be when I wake up."

"I know who I shall be," declared Lucy, her grip firm on the future. "I shall be Lord Robert Jessup's lady, and that is exactly who I wish to be!" They giggled and threw their arms about each other in mutual satisfaction.

"But what of you and Captain S.?" Lucy asked archly. "I seemed to see that Lady Blanche was quite overwhelmed at the vision of the two of you together."

And Mariana did not know what to answer.

The Marquis had been waiting patiently for his second dance with her and had watched her carefully throughout the evening. He was proud as only a close friend can be, and he wished fervently that Lynval Porter were still his friend as well, and were present to see her in her hour of glory. He knew also that any thought he had entertained of wedding her had been a fancy. She belonged to all this glow of youth about him. There were others here his own age and older, but he saw them and himself as only a dull backcloth against which the bright gaiety of youth could show itself. He had been so afraid that Mariana would be unhappy on this night, but she was not, and he was strangely content to know it.

Now he saw that she was dancing a variation on the German Landler which they called a *valse*, and that she was dancing it with young Seymour. He remained content at the sight of them, reflecting only how well they looked together.

At the evening's end Mariana was exhausted, aching in every bone, and happy beyond compare. The Prince continued gracious as he made his adieu. More than one older gentleman regretted aloud that he had not been able to take a turn with her, while others made a point of remarking how like her mother she was, and asking after her mother's return.

Only a few remained reserved in manner. Lady Blanche, on the arm of Captain Seymour, was artificially bright while remaining cold. The Captain himself was an enigma. Despite the evidence of the dance, he said only a "very good night," and intimated nothing more. Even Lucy took note of his curious behaviour.

"I would have thought for all the world that he was a virtual stranger by the way he conducted himself," she said. "I vow I am curious to know what is behind all that, aren't you?"

Mariana did not know what to think of it. Her own feelings about the Captain were in such a state of revisement that she did not feel capable of guessing what his might be. It was all a great puzzle, but there were many other things to dream of this evening. She wondered if it would be like this always, that she would float upon the music like a blossom on a stream? How marvelous, how very beautiful life could be if it could always remain as it was on the night of one's first ball.

—11—

THE NEXT AFTERNOON she was again in Mr. Chipworth's offices, this time welcomed rather than discouraged by the clerk. Rigby, it appeared to Mariana, had been apprised of her status, for he ushered her into the inner chamber with great and solicitous ceremony. Mr. Chipworth was in a benign frame of mind, actually smiling as she came in.

"Ah, Miss Porter, so good to see you again." She took the chair opposite him and unbuttoned her gloves at the wrist for comfort. "I believe," he said with an understated joyousness, "that I have found the house you require."

"*The* house? Do you mean it? How could you *know* what I require, since we have hardly discussed it? I have not even thoroughly considered it myself."

"Weem, fetch me the papers," called Chipworth out the door. "Miss Porter doubts my attentiveness on her behalf." He smiled again to show that he was joking, but he was evidently quite serious. "Ah, yes, here we are. Now then, you see . . ."

Mariana was not so much bewildered (for she *had* instructed him to begin a search for a residence in London) as opposed to being taken for granted. How could this kind but condescendingly avuncular gentleman have any idea what she required?

"Small, but very select," he pointed out. "Drawing room, three parlours, the usual chambers for sleeping and for dressing, for dining, and for merely taking tea. Kitchens, of course, and . . . why, the lot. And at a good price, too. Good location in Baillie Street by Rottingdean Square. Not too small for your needs, not too large for a sensible staff. What do you say, shall we have a look?"

"I should appreciate a little less haste, sir, if you please," Mariana replied in that severe tone her friends recognised as a warning. "First of all, what do you consider a good price? For I must warn you that though I have come into substantial money, I have no intention of being parted from it unnecessarily."

He beamed even more broadly. "Just so, just so. The price, Miss Porter, can never be bettered, for it is no price at all! The house is already yours."

"What on earth do you mean?"

Mr. Chipworth played a little tattoo with his fingers on the edge of his desk in evidence of enormous self-satisfaction. "Part of the estate, miss, part of your own inheritance!" He leaned forward confidentially. "The fact is, you may even faintly remember it, though I doubt it."

"Remember it, sir?"

But rather than make tedious explanations Mr. Chipworth bustled her out of his chambers and into his waiting phaeton. Rigby stood by to hand her into the equipage and Mr. Chipworth gave him one last instruction. "Mind the office, and if Captain Seymour should communicate, say to him that I believe an advertisement . . . discreet, of course, and carefully worded . . . emphasise that, *very* discreet . . . that such an advertisement would best suit the purpose. After I shall have consulted with Miss Porter I shall discuss it with him in greater detail. Shall we go, my dear?" The horse boy relinquishing their heads, the chestnut pair trotted smartly up the street.

Mariana delayed until they were under way before enquiring casually, "Pray, *what* advertisement will you discuss with me?"

Mr. Chipworth opened his eyes quite wide. "Why, bless me, Miss Porter, the very one we spoke of a few days past."

"We spoke of an advertisement? And what one is that, sir? I am all at sea. I do not in the least remember a discussion on that subject."

He snapped the reins to quicken the pace and nodded assent. "I daresay, yes, I daresay. But you will find, my very dear young miss, that Chipworth is a man who can follow a hint. Find you other candidates besides Captain Seymour, you said, and presto! it is done."

"Oh, but I did not mean . . ." The enormity of the act assailed her and she felt her voice rise to a squeak. "Do you mean to say that you have *advertised* for a husband as if I were a situation to be filled?" Her indignation was so great that she felt herself beginning to tremble.

"Mind this corner," the solicitor advised, "it is a bit sharp." She held on for dear life. She had no idea that people drove so madly in town. She would swear that at least one and probably two of the phaeton's wheels had left the ground as they cut the turn. When they had returned to a moderate pace Mr. Chipworth continued his explanation.

"Only a small advertisement, Miss Porter, and it has not yet *been* placed. It should be a wide-ranging one, I believe. Descendants of Jefferson and Adelaide Forrester, you know, grandparents of the deceased. That sort of thing weeds out a portion of the scoundrels and false claims."

But Mariana was still puzzled. "Do you think that Uncle had all that much family? I never heard so. I believe his relations are few."

"On your father's side, yes," Chipworth agreed. "But there are still the Seymour connections. Black sheep, perhaps, but good blood, demmed good blood!" At her sidelong look he chuckled. "Come to that, we are all related, eh? Cousins through Mr. Adam and his missus. I assure you, miss, that it will be a thorough search and that no gentleman will come into your fair presence until he has been closely examined, past and present."

Like a horse, thought Mariana; like a stud-horse.

"And what does Captain Seymour think of all this?"

They turned into Rottingdean Square. "Oh, he agrees with you. No *tendre* between the two of you, I told him. After all, you were quite specific about that, weren't you? He quite understood. He's a gentleman, that Captain Seymour. He'd never press a lady unwanted."

"And when was this conversation?" Mariana asked quietly.

They turned now into Baillie Street. "Why, this very morning, Miss Porter. But he was in a great hurry, you see, and I neglected to mention the advertisement." They drew up. "Ah, here we are."

The house was quite simply a jewel box. Nearly perfect in every way. As the solicitor had said, it was the very size she required, with room for expansion in the rear. Baillie Street being closed at the far end, it was at once *privé* and easily accessible. The façade was as elegant as any by Mr. Stuart or the popular brothers Adam, and once inside, the columned hall, classical but restrained, and the drawing room opening into a commodious library made Mariana's fingers itch for drawing paper and pens. The garden was exquisite.

But it was the upper chambers that made her decision inevitable; Mr. Chipworth had been right. She found herself allocating the rooms in her head: a small bedroom for Papa, with a large, north-lit studio adjacent; a small suite for herself; even a chamber and dressing room for . . . for whom? Some unknown occupant who would have as much right there as herself.

As she stood in the doorway of that chamber, Mr. Chipworth looked beyond her shoulder. "For the chaperone, eh? Just right."

Mariana's head all but spun to regard him. "Chaperone?"

He had the grace to look embarrassed. "Well, I assumed . . . well, hang it, no young lady can . . . No young lady can live *alone*, Miss Porter!"

She smiled at him sweetly enough to remove the barb from her words, pointed though they were. "I have no intention of doing so, sir, but if I should . . ." She left the implication that it would be her own affair. Mr. Chipworth was beginning to realise that this was no missish schoolgirl.

It was on the more sedate return journey that she found herself returning to the question of Captain Seymour and the advertisement.

"I believe the male cousins . . . that is, you see, I believe that *you* will have a wider choice than Captain Seymour, Miss Porter. I believe you have more . . . well, the fact is, there is a paucity of female relations in your family, I believe. The Captain will have a deal of trouble. And then, too . . ." He shifted uncomfortably in his seat. "There is the question of Lady Blanche Westring."

"What on earth has Lady Blanche to do with it?"

"You are acquainted with her, then?"

"Yes," Mariana replied, picturing the tall, cool beauty.

Mr. Chipworth applied just the tiniest bit of the whip, then said confidentially, "Lady Blanche has, I believe, serious intentions in regard to the Captain, but the Captain is bound by the terms of the will. He is caught, you see, between his attachment to Lady Blanche and his need to marry within the family."

The solicitor pursed his lips judiciously, looked about as if in fear to be overheard, even there in the middle of the street, and spoke carefully. "There seems to be . . . ah . . . little affection between you and Captain Seymour, Miss Porter, thus another . . . ah . . . candidate must be located if ever he is to come into his inheritance."

Was that why? Had she only imagined that current between them as they danced? Had things seemed different only because it was imperative that Brion Seymour find an acceptable cousin to marry to avoid losing his deviously gained inheritance? What was this hard hurting lump within her chest? Why did it seem so difficult to breathe?

"And if no one is found?" How hard it was for her to shape the words.

"Why, then as you know, the money comes to you and the Benevolent Fund. Eventually, that is."

"And the Captain is penniless?"

Mr. Chipworth all but laughed. "Hardly penniless, should he marry Lady Blanche Westring, Miss Porter. Her fortune is greater than your own, I believe. Certainly enough to support two in style."

The chaise that paused beside them at this moment was near enough so that Mariana could hear a strain of bright, giddy laughter, infectious and young. Smiling, she leaned forward to catch a glimpse of the happy pair. The young woman's hair was clipped into a mass of curls above a pretty, heart-shaped face. She returned Mariana's smile confidently, but her escort's laughter was somewhat stilled as his eyes met those of Mariana. Captain Seymour had not even the grace to flush or look discomfited.

Mr. Chipworth too saw them, and his eyes filled with admiration. "Demmed if he ain't doing his best, the enterprising lad. I wonder which branch of the family that lass is from?"

Mariana made no reply, but taking up the whip she touched the chestnut trotters smartly.

A night or two later she saw the Captain again. She, with her aunt, Jeremy Law, the Marquis, and the engaged couple, had once again gone to the theatre, but had not cared for the play.

"I fear *The Duenna* is a bit fusty for this generation," said Lady Emilia, "yet I can remember when it was racy and all the rage. How sad it is that nothing stays."

"I say," Lord Robert suggested, as if he had not heard her, "shall we go on to Lady Bassingbrook's house? She has an E.O. table, you know. Damn fine fun."

But the Marquis was scornful. "What, roly-poly? You do favour a quick slide, m'boy!"

"With all respect, sir, but you cannot believe that Georgie Bassingbrook would fleece her friends?"

"Why not?" laughed Lady Emilia, quite regaining her spirit. "What else are friends for?"

"Well," Lord Robert continued, "she has whatever your pleasure: French hazard, faro, macao, *chemin-de-fer*."

Jeremy Law made a quick flutter of his fingers, then pantomimed throwing something into the air. The Marquis smiled and translated, "In short, anything to relieve you of your money."

"Is it true," asked Lucy breathlessly, "that Lady Bassingbrook has a service of plate made from silver coin?"

"Not mine, at any rate," Robert protested. "I've only been there the one time with Seymour. Jeremy might know." He addressed Mr. Law in a loud tone of voice, "Jer-e-my, is there such a service at Lady Bass-ing-brook's?"

Jeremy made a mock shudder and put his hands over his ears.

"Oh, Robert," chided Lucy crossly, "Mr. Law is mute, not deaf!"

Lord Robert had the grace to look abashed. He clapped Jeremy on the shoulder. "Sorry, old chap, I keep forgettin'. I ain't used to dummies, y'know."

Everyone else in the party looked appalled, except Jeremy, who laughed soundlessly but heartily, almost staggering in his hilarity.

"Lud, Lord Robert, I wonder what you will be when you mature?" said Lady Battledore. "I hope that will not be afar off."

From the puzzled look she got in return, it was evident that Lord Robert had no idea what she was talking about. With a great show of uninterest Mariana turned the subject back to its previous course. "So the Captain is a gambler as well as a soldier, is he?"

Lord Robert professed amazement. "Upon my buttons, miss, you sound as if the two were incompatible. Why, I am told that on St. James's Street there is a house devoted exclusively to Guardsmen with back pay.

"Brion's lucky, though," he added, "and smart. Always has been. Only a pigeon plunges when he's slid. Brion always comes out ahead."

Mariana could not but smile a little wryly to herself. Poor Uncle Forrester had carefully kept his money away from one gamester, only to leave it, all unknowingly, to another. She had a sudden, irrational desire to see for herself how quickly her adversary might be expected to "slide."

"What do you think, Lucy, are we chaperones enough for each at such a place as Lady Bassingbrook's? Or will you join us, Aunt?"

Lucy was aghast. "Mariana, you cannot mean it? Lady Battledore, set her to rights, I pray."

"Oh, lauk, no! I have always wondered what that woman hid behind her lace curtains. I have no intention of passing up the opportunity to find out."

The Marquis was less sanguine, and counselled against it. "M'dear," he murmured to Mariana, "think of what your father would say."

Mariana barely contained her laugh. "If my Papa were here, sir, he would have skipped the theatre and gone straight to the play!"

There was no doubt that Lucy was outnumbered; there was also little evidence that she protested overmuch.

Lady Bassingbrook's house was in Jermyn Square, an ideal situation for her occupation. The lady herself was a tall, rather horsy blonde woman, well into her second youth. Only a liberal application of "lead and red" alleviated the inroads that time had made upon her countenance. Somewhat to Lucy's surprise, she greeted Lord Robert as an old friend.

"Why, your Lordship, I believe your friend Captain Seymour is raising a great stir at the whist table. He is a very demon at cards. If he were not such a gentleman, I would question his motives."

Mariana smiled winningly. "How fortunate for your peace of mind, madame, that he is heir to great wealth."

Lady Bassingbrook raised a quizzing-glass to her eye and examined this unknown carefully. "Have we had the pleasure?" she asked in a tone to freeze monkey-brass.

Mariana had learnt her lessons well in a short time. Taking a deep breath, she *condescended*. "I believe you kept a place especially for my father," she said carelessly. "He told me of it often."

Her ladyship shook her head. "No, you are mistaken, I fear. I never kept a permanent place for any but two dear friends: Lord Kenyon, who married a very young girl and has gone all moral, and . . ." She broke off, leaned forward slightly, and peered at Mariana again.

"Good God! You're not Lynnie Porter's gel? Dear heaven! You are, you minx!"

She was quickly introduced to the rest of the party, looked sharply at Lady Battledore as if she knew her, but said nothing, then began to draw first one and then another person into her orbit. Taking Mariana by the arm and worrying their way down the long salon, she introduced her over and over as "Lynnie's daughter, Lynnie Porter's daughter," leaving Lucy, open-mouthed and chagrined, trailing in their wake with Lady Battledore. The Marquis stayed close to them, but Lord Robert had drifted off to look for Captain Seymour. By the time the procession had reached the entrance to the whist room, Brion and a lady friend were already coming toward them. It was not Lady Blanche, but the pretty child who had been with him in the chaise.

They made an annoyingly handsome couple, her coppery head reaching just past his shoulder, his campaign-brown complexion setting off the Devonshire cream of her skin. Well, let them be happy, Mariana thought; the money will go where it is destined. Even in the short while she had been here she could see how seductive the play must be to some people. She felt a quickening at the click of the dice, the riffle of the cards. She was obviously Papa's daughter in ways she had not considered.

Captain Seymour bowed low over Lady Battledore's hand, "Good evening, Miss Lucy, Marquis. Miss Porter, I see that you and my friend Jeremy have much in common. I trust you enjoyed the theatre—or, since you left so early, perhaps you did not?"

She strove mightily to be civil to him, trying not to match the dancing partner of a few evenings past with this urbane gamester. "I find I prefer the opera," she replied. "Music often carries where mere words fail."

With only the ghost of a smile he explained, "My cousin is not a great admirer of the Italians, I fear, so I have missed much this season." He hesitated. "I do beg your pardon, may I present my cousin, Miss Rosalba? We have become acquainted by reason of our family connexion, but we discover we have much else in common."

Miss Rosalba's bell-like little laugh chimed out as if he had made a great joke, perhaps one understood only by themselves. The group stood there a little awkwardly, no one having anything to add, but not knowing how to break away. Just as Lady Battledore was coming to the rescue by drawing Mariana with her toward some other acquaintances, there was a great commotion at the whist table behind them.

The handsomely tailored man with the hawkish features who had been sitting there so quietly had half risen from his chair. The man next to him, an emigré by the look of him, shifted in his seat uneasily. He held his cards close against his chest, while the other hand rested flat against the table top. Oddly, although he shifted, his hands did not.

"Zounds! What's Tyger about?" asked Lord Robert, joining them.

"There will be trouble, I fear," agreed the Marquis. "Perhaps the ladies . . ." But Lady Battledore scotched this notion with a hard stare.

"Don't be a lily, man," she snapped.

Mariana and Lucy both took in the scene with wide eyes and fluttering pulses. Lucy's mouth trembled just a little as she clutched the arm of her fiancé. "Who is that man, Robert? He seems quite dangerous, doesn't he?"

"You are quite right, Miss Lucy," Brion Seymour said. "I have a notion that his neighbour was playing in error."

Tyger Dobyn took up the pointed candlesnuffers from the playing table and with one swift, plunging motion pinned the foreigner's hand to the baize. "I ask your pardon," he said in a cool voice, "if the ace of spades is not under your hand."

In the moment of shocked silence that followed, the other player with a whimper threw down his cards and wrenched the snuffers from his injured hand. He stumbled backward and fled the room, and the ace of spades, all bloodied, lay face up on the table.

The Tyger resumed his seat. "Shall we continue, gentlemen?" And the play resumed.

Mariana was not certain which of two emotions outweighed the other in her mind: horror at the brutality she had witnessed, or admiration for the bottom with which it was displayed.

The men of the party, even Jeremy, showed no such squeamishness. Lord Robert, in particular, seemed almost jubilant. "Top hole, Tyger!" he exclaimed. "That'll teach the demmed Froggies not to be muck-snipes in respectable English games, what?" The other men in the establishment appeared to agree, but only Brion's lady cousin, of the women, said anything aloud. With a little catch of her breath she only murmured, "You are a fantastik, sir."

All the company understood her to mean, in that moment, that she was giving notice that her sights were switched from Captain Seymour to the gentleman pugilist, but Tyger's amber eyes met Brion's over the lady's copper hair, his eyes raised in question, and Brion grinned engagingly.

Lady Bassingbrook approached with great presence, followed by a waiter with a tray on which sat a bottle and a single crystal tumbler. "Your brandywine, sir," she said, and as the waiter presented the filled glass, "To your health!"

Tyger's full lips curved into a smile. Really, Mariana concluded, despite his air of rascality there was a sort of coarse attractiveness about him. He seemed to radiate a kind of leonine power that she assumed most women would find attractive. She felt she understood Miss Rosalba's response to him.

She remembered him now, of course, from that brief moment in Dublin when he had escorted her father home from the club. Probably after winning all his money, she reflected. That seemed to be his profession.

As if he read her thoughts, Dobyn raised his glass. "To all the fair ladies," he toasted, "the known and the unknown." Mariana found herself blushing furiously for no reason at all.

"You remember Lynnie Porter, Tyger, do you not?" Lady Bassingbrook was asking. "This is his daughter, Miss Mariana Porter."

He made a slight half-bow. "Your servant, Miss Porter. So pleasant to make your acquaintance again. I regret we were not introduced when I had the honour of visiting with your father in Dublin. It would have made Dublin all the more pleasant." He bowed, too, to Lady Battledore. "Your servant, madam. I trust your journey was not too arduous?"

She acknowledged him with a smile. It was evident that for some reason Captain Seymour was not at all pleased with this turn of events. Nor was Miss Rosalba. The Marquis merely looked pained but resigned, rather like an experienced schoolmaster forced to monitor an unruly band of rapscallions. Even so, he seemed somewhat less pleased when the Tyger continued his attention to Lady Emilia.

"As something of an habitué here, madam, may I have the honour of escorting you about?" Why did his eyes twinkle? "And Miss Porter too, of course."

"Yes, why not do that, Tyger?" neighed Lady Bassingbrook horsily. "I doubt not that the gel will find her father's blood runs quick."

Jeremy looked rather alarmed at the suggestion. He hovered nearby as if he believed harm might be inflicted by Tyger's very presence. The Tyger brushed back a lock of coarse, amber-colored hair and lifted an eyebrow in Captain Seymour's direction. "If you will excuse us, cousin?"

"Cousin?" squealed Lucy in a transport of discovery. "Are you and Brion truly related?"

"Yes, Miss Lucy," answered the Tyger with the faintest hint of a smile. "Our mothers were sisters, and, they say, no more alike than the Captain and I. My aunt, I believe, was a pillar of the community, whilst my dear mother had a taste . . . how shall I say? . . . a taste for adventure."

"I cannot think why you have never told me this, Brion!" said Lucy. "How very exciting it is."

Lord Robert leapt to his friend's rescue. "Oh, come now, my love.

114

You know what a dashed modest fellow Brion is. I daresay he didn't care to boast."

One would not have thought that a face could be so utterly devoid of expression as Captain Seymour's became.

Suddenly a faint nausea overtook Mariana, a kind of revulsion with this world that had darkened her father's life and bid fair, if she succumbed to the lure of it, to darken her own. She tugged at the lace on Lady Battledore's sleeve. "Aunt, you remember that we are being waited upon by the Archbishop at mid-morning. Perhaps we should not linger?"

"Afraid the smell of the company might rub off, luv?" asked the copper-haired Miss Rosalba. "I daresay the old geezer 'imself'as been 'ere a time or two. Wotcher say, Brion?"

Tyger Dobyn seemed completely unruffled. He bowed over Lady Battledore's hand again. "Another time, perhaps?" Her ladyship condescended graciously with an inclination of her head. Miss Rosalba sniffed haughtily and Lucy giggled to see how the older woman had thawed. Brion was very still, very watchful.

"Goodnight, sir," said Mariana. "Goodnight, Captain Seymour, Miss Rosalba." She noted with satisfaction how much less spectacular that copper-penny hair seemed when the owner's nose was so conspicuously out of joint.

When they were in the carriage Lucy gave full vent to her astonishment. "Imagine Captain Seymour being cousin to that rake! Whatever do you think of that?"

"And what was that puffery about expecting the Archbishop for breakfast, Mariana?" asked her aunt. "You know that isn't true!"

Jeremy Law perforce kept his tongue, but Lord Robert, half asleep, was understood to murmur, "Capital chap, Tyger. Fancy him and Brion havin' a cousin like that little red-headed girl."

"Well, as to that," said Lucy, "I don't believe she was their cousin at all!"

—12—

MARASHAM MADE IT his business to seek Mariana out in the morning room. "If you please, miss, there is a personage asking to speak to you."

"A gentleman, do you mean, Marasham?"

"He *is* of the male sex, miss," said the manservant grudgingly.

"Did he give his name?" What on earth was this charade?

"His name appears to be Dobyn, if you please, Miss Mariana."

The girl hardly knew what to think. Obviously Marasham was expressing his disapproval. In a way, this might be a test of their future relationship. How she began here might very well determine the course they would follow.

"Dobyn?" She pretended to cogitate. "Ah, the Tyger. Don't you know who he is, Marasham? He is quite famous, I believe."

Marasham seemed frozen. "Yes, miss, I know who he is."

"Then perhaps you will show him in?"

"In here?" There, she had won the round by shock.

"Perhaps the library would be better, don't you think?"

"Much better, miss. I shall be close by in the event that . . ."

"Thank you, I don't believe that will be necessary. Mr. Dobyn and I are acquainted."

The final stroke. He would never recover. She must alert Mrs. Marasham that emotional first aid was in order. She had hoped he would enter her employ, and she hardly wanted to lose her new butler before he had even taken up his duties.

Tyger Dobyn was resplendent in carnation velvet, the cut admirably displaying the extreme breadth of his shoulders. The wild lock of glossy hair fell across his forehead, but otherwise he was immaculately in fashion. Why, then, she wondered, did he so incline one's thoughts to tinker camps and caravans? The tawny eyes gave off a lustrous glow as he bent above her hand.

"Your servant, Miss Porter. I trust it is not untoward of me to call so soon upon our meeting?"

The young woman looked at him warily. "I wonder if such a brief and mischanceful encounter could properly qualify as an introduction, sir, if you take my meaning? I daresay you mean to pay your respects to my aunt."

He was not at all chagrined. "I shall be happy to see the Lady Emilia, but are you really going to force me through the social maze before I am allowed to tender you my respects? I allow I had thought better of you than that. I had believed, in fact, that I detected a certain rapport between us. Was I, then, so mistaken?"

Mariana could not, with any honesty, deny the truth of that response. Yet she had a great many reservations about such an acquaintance. Despite that aura of maddeningly masculine presence about him, Dobyn was certainly only a borderline gentleman. And yet, questionable or no, he seemed to have all the strings of social connexion at his fingertips. He was even an intimate of the Regent, her aunt had told her. And since she *did* know all of this, how was it that he had been able, from his first words, to put himself so unreservedly in charge of this situation? How was it that she found herself so completely at her ease in his presence? And, good heavens, what did that say about herself?

She rang for Marasham. Would he advise her ladyship that Mr. Dobyn had come to pay a morning call?

"I was about to order up a pot of chocolate, Mr. Dobyn. Will you join me?"

"The Archbishop is not to be with us, then?" he asked solemnly.

Mariana's composure remained unruffled. "I believe he is detained. Sad how these churchmen have no life of their own, is it not? Chocolate?"

"Chocolate is a bit sweet for my palate, and I find it has a bitter undertaste. I would prefer coffee, if it is no great trouble."

While they waited the pugilist drew from his pocket a paper that seemed to be torn from a gazette. "Did you place this notice, Miss Porter?"

Mariana scanned the paragraph he indicated.

All persons holding notes against the name of Mr. Lynval Porter should communicate with Mr. John Chipworth, solicitor, at his chambers in Pennyroyal Street, where upon presentation of proven notes, such notes as found valid will be paid in full.

"Why, yes, I did. Or, rather, Mr. Chipworth placed it at my behest. Do you hold such notes, Mr. Dobyn?"

"As you know, I spent some time in Dublin recently." He looked a little uncomfortable, as if he were not used to being in such an anomalous situation. "Your father is never a man to refuse good play."

He made a gesture of spreading his hands, as if to show his essential innocence. "The notes are not for large sums, but they offered me a convenient opportunity as well."

"An opportunity, sir?"

"I mean an opportunity of seeing you again, Miss Porter. I would forgive the notes as quick as nothing if you bade me."

Mariana's laugh rang freely. "Oh, this is like a play, then? You will forgive my father's debts if I will surrender my virtue?"

He had the audacity to grin at her. "Not so baldly as all that, I beg of you. Credit me with a bit of subtlety. I must watch my steps, you know, since I am, after all, only an interloper in society."

Mariana found she quite liked him, even if he were indisputably a "personage," as Marasham put it. By the time the refreshment arrived they were chattering away like magpies.

"Just leave it there, Lily. I'll pour."

"As you say, miss." Then, conspiratorially, "'Er Ladyship will be 'ere presently, miss. I've brought another cup." And she slipped out discreetly.

"Shall I pour you a cup, Mr. Dobyn?"

"Gladly, if it will lengthen the time before you have me thrown out of the door."

She found she was laughing again. "What a droll idea. Whyever should I do that?"

"It wouldn't be the first time," he answered with no embarrassment. "The Lady Emilia once had it done when my entreaties became too importunate. That jockum at the door remembers it well enough."

So that explained Marasham's reluctance to admit the caller. "How very curious, Mr. Dobyn. If you chose to pique my interest, sir, you have certainly done so. In what way were you importunate with Aunt Emilia?"

"I had the temerity to propose marriage to her, but I fear she laughed me out of countenance."

Mariana sat quite still, not sure she had really heard what she seemed to have done. Aunt Emilia? "You proposed to my aunt, Mr. Dobyn?"

"I did."

"But . . . but she is . . . ah . . . my aunt is . . ."

"She is not so *very* much my senior, if that is what you are thinking. And you must admit, she is very rich." He shrugged in a quite light-hearted way. "But I must confess, she was more sensible than I. The offer gave her a great deal of amusement."

"I should have thought so." Her brow wrinkled a little. "And now you pay your addresses to me? Why do you think I will not be as amused?"

He pulled a long face at this. "I trow, Miss Porter, I am quite addled about you. Dash my wigs, do you think I should so expose myself to ridicule if I did not find you ravishing? I thought about you all night long; tossed and turned until dawn. I only put off coming here so late in the morning because I feared to inconvenience you."

"Do not pay attention to all that, Mariana," said her aunt, coming into the morning room, enveloped in a voluminous robe and with ribbons on her cap. "Do you like this, my dear? What do you think?" She turned for inspection. "It just arrived from my dote in Turkey. It is called a caftan or coftan, or some such. They all wear them there, you know." She admired herself in the looking-glass. "But I do think a turban, rather than a cap."

"You look wonderful, Aunt." And indeed, so she did. Now that Mariana looked at her in a different light, there was no question as to how she had been married so many times, for she was a handsome woman, at any age she chose to admit.

"My very humble respects, Lady Battledore," said Tyger. "Miss Porter is quite right. Gold brocade suits you to a fare-thee-well." Then reverting to her earlier remark, "But why, if you please, should she pay no attention to what I was saying?"

Aunt Emilia beamed kindly upon him. "If I am not greatly mistaken, sir, far from tossing and turning all night, you have not yet been to bed at all. The only tossing you may have been doing was with a dice cup." Then to Mariana, "Has he proposed to you yet, my dear?"

"Not yet, Aunt," said Mariana, eyes demurely down, "although he may have been on the verge."

"Now dash it all," Tyger cried with a beaming smile, "this is quite unfair! A fellah has no chance at all these days."

"Do you propose to all fashionable beauties, Mr. Dobyn," asked Mariana, "or only to heiresses?"

"Heiresses and widows," he replied with extreme candour. "Bedad, I'm in no position to marry poor!"

"You might do worse, Mariana," said Lady Emilia, as if the subject were seriously under discussion. "Consider: strong, healthy, no more filled with masculine conceit than most of his race, and honest enough for all that, even if his candour is a part of the scheme."

"With such a testimonial, Miss Porter, how can you refuse me?" asked Dobyn. "I can furnish additional, if required." Then a sort of cloud passed over his face. "I say, you aren't in love with old Seymour, are you? I never encroach upon another man's territory."

"My heart is entirely free, Mr. Dobyn," laughed the girl. "You may storm it if you can."

"Splendid! We'll all start off neck and neck, as the saying is."

"All whom, sir?"

"What, haven't I been clear? So far no other applicants have turned up, have they? Just the three of us, I mean?"

"Mr. Dobyn, I am all at sea. What three, pray?"

"Why, I thought you knew it all along and I see you don't." He

120

struck the heel of his palm to his temple. "To the best of my information, Miss Porter, you have only three male cousins . . . eligible male cousins, I should say . . . from whom to choose. Brion . . . Captain Seymour, that is . . . Jeremy, and myself."

"Jeremy Law?"

"Why, of course. Dashed if I didn't think you already knew, the way you've been seen all over with him, to the opera and the theatre, not to say Lady Bassingbrook's."

Her head was awhirl. Mr. Chipworth's advertisement had not even appeared, and she had three eligible cousins already. Mr. Dobyn was not about to end his proposals at this early point.

"Naturally, I believe you will find my suit the most advantageous."

Lady Battledore sipped her chocolate meditatively. Mariana asked, with more curiosity than surprise, "Why on earth should I do that?"

He was not taken aback in the least. "Well, think of the advantages. Item: not too terribly bad looking. Item: already known quantity . . . rake, gambler, Corinthian, and all that. Item: I should require an allowance, but not control of your fortune . . . and that is an important point, you must admit."

"All good reasons, Mariana," said Lady Emilia wisely.

"But there is one more, Miss Porter, and a very compelling one from my standpoint."

"Pray, what is that, sir?"

"Just this: I fancy we should get on together. Deuce take it, Miss Porter, but I quite like your style!"

Marasham slipped in and announced decisively, "The Marquis of Downsbury, madam."

"Oh, good! Show him in," replied her ladyship. "Downsbury, dear man, what do you think of my caftan?"

"Suits you to the ground, my lady. Makes you a queen and something of a dasher at the same time." He studied her, then added, "Though if you don't jump into my jaws for saying it . . ."

"It is the cap, isn't it? A turban, do you think?"

"Capital!" he agreed. "A turban. Just the thing." Then to Mariana, "I stopped only to remind you, miss, that you asked me to escort you to Strawberry Hill today. I think it is wise to go quite early, since it is a goodish drive to Twickenham."

"La, off to Strawberry Hill, are you? How grand. Shall I accompany you? I haven't been in a dog's age and Mrs. Damer is one of my dear dotes."

Since her aunt seemed quite anxious not to be left behind, Mariana agreed at once. "In caftan and turban, Aunt? I think it would be admirable. You have brought the calash, Marquis? Then there is room for you as well, Mr. Dobyn. We shall make an excursion of it!"

Perhaps the Marquis had expected to be alone with the fetching Miss Porter, you say? Well, perhaps he had, but he was not. He took it well and entertained the Lady Emilia the whole journey.

═13═

STRAWBERRY HILL, AN unassuming country house transformed into a pseudo-Gothick castle by its owner, had been left to Mrs. Damer as a life residence. This owner was the famous Horace Walpole, the Fourth Earl of Oxford, author of the romantic *The Castle of Otranto* and other, less extravagant works, some of which were printed at the private press of Strawberry Hill itself. The property was entailed upon Lord Waldgrave, but Mrs. Damer lived as though it were her own. The comments of Lord Waldgrave have not been recorded.

In the coach the excursioners discussed their hostess freely. Or rather, Lady Battledore rattled on and the others perforce must listen.

"Oh, lauk, she knows everyone there is to know, from the old King to Garrick's German widow. She's famous for her busts, you know."

"Is she, by Jove?" said Tyger, perking up, but subsiding again as Lady Emilia continued.

"Oh, yes, She's done a ton of the great ones, I believe. Did Nelson after the Nile. Did Handel. But I've heard the one she most regrets is Napoleon. Oh, she's quite the thing! Though, mind you, they *do* say . . ."

The Marquis interposed quickly. "I will hear nothing ill of her, I warn you, madam. She is to me a great and clever lady."

"Oh, clever, I daresay. And a Whig to the death, if that pleases you. Personally, I never trust a woman who meddles in politics or other male affairs."

The others all laughed at this, knowing how active a meddler

Lady Battledore herself was, but she merely smiled complacently as if she had led the joking herself.

"Have *you* met her, Mr. Dobyn?" Mariana asked him, sure that he was the only relative stranger among them.

"Alas, I have only admired her from afar," Tyger admitted. "Her usual circle is, I fear, far above my ambition." This from a confidant of the Regent!

"I wonder, then," retorted Lady Battledore, "what that says of us."

The journey passed very quickly amid much merriment. Everyone seemed to like everyone else, and at a pleasant spot along the river they stopped to picnic from a hamper Cook had quickly prepared. Since she had packed for an expected pair enough to feed a half-dozen, the extra mouths were well enough filled; the coachman and groom had a hamper of their own. Indeed, when they were done there were crumbs enough to feed the swans, who came to them greedily, like hungry princes. At the end of another short ride they found themselves at Strawberry Hill. As they arrived, so did Jeremy, to everyone's pleasure.

Privately, Mariana was more than a little taken aback when faced with the famous showplace. What had originally been a small cottage had been enlarged to a mockery of towers, crenellated battlements, and pointed-arch windows. It was difficult to escape the sense that it was rather ridiculous, but the warmth of Mrs. Damer outshone all else.

She greeted them all by name, even Tyger Dobyn, whom she had never met but knew by report. But it was Mr. Law for whom her greatest enthusiasm was revealed.

"Jeremy! My dearest boy! I had no idea you were coming. *What* a delightful surprise."

And Jeremy, to the wonder of his companions, began moving his fingers in rapid and ingenious combinations that formed a language Mrs. Damer obviously understood. They chattered away for several moments, she speaking and he signing, for all the world as if it were the most natural thing ever.

At last Mrs. Damer turned back to the others. "I hope you had not thought of returning to London today, you know. No one ever does that. What with the others, I daresay we shall have a pleasant evening party."

"Others?" asked Lady Emilia. "I hope we are not inconvenient."

But the elderly sculptress would have none of such thinking. "We shall enjoy ourselves, as you shall see. In fact, you have saved my own evening, I believe. My late husband's niece, you know, is expected. Blanche is a proper girl, I daresay, but excessively formal, with a cutting tongue. I find I need a leavening agent, if you follow."

"That would be the Lady Blanche Westring?" enquired the Marquis.

Mariana's heart sank, for she remembered all too well her previous encounters with that lady. Mrs. Damer was correct in saying that her tongue was a cutter. It was sword-sharp.

"And the boy who is with her," continued their hostess, "is a brave lad who was at Gerona . . ." She paused, perplexed. "Or was he at Albuhera?"

"If you speak of Captain Seymour," Mariana interjected, "I believe he was at Gerona, for he was a part of the Irish Ultonia."

Both the Marquis and Lady Emilia looked sharply at her and Jeremy seemed to smile a bit to himself. Only Tyger Dobyn looked a little ruffled. But even he said, "Well met," as if spending the day with his cousin was exactly the tonic he needed.

They had a goodly hour before the others were due, and Mrs. Damer proudly led a tour of the house through chambers and galleries, libraries and sitting rooms, all seemingly added as the occasion required with rarely a nod to unity. The Tribune, as one cabinet was called, was choked with a bizarre, disunited collection of memorabilia that included miniatures, bronzes, and enamels, as well as The Great Seal of King Theodore of Corsica and an ancient bronze phallus that amused Lady Emilia no end. Not having the collector's mania herself, Mariana thought it a pity that the scramble of oddities somewhat obscured the individual beauties of the pieces themselves. She much preferred a painting by Conway in which Mrs. Damer, as a girl of nineteen, leaned against a statuary pedestal, chisel in one hand, mallet in the other, a study of the artist as beauty.

Certainly there was no question that Lady Blanche was also a great beauty. When she arrived, it took no discerning eye to see that both the Marquis and Tyger Dobyn breathed a little more deeply as she came into the sitting room where they were all enjoying a cup of superior bohea. She was dressed in a high-waisted classical gown of sapphire that brought out the rather chilly blue of her altogether admirable eyes. Mariana felt quite in the shade, but Brion Seymour seemed disposed to pay her his previous warm attention. Remembering how quickly he had seemed to turn from ardent dancing partner on the evening of her ball to a more distant position as a mere acquaintance a short time later, she was not at all sure what she thought of him now, but he seemed disposed to be friendly.

"Lovely frock, Miss Porter. Pale yellow suits you dashedly well."

Coolly she answered, "Thank you."

"Coming out into the great world seems to have had an admirable effect. Did you enjoy your ball?"

"Very much, thank you," said more coolly still.

"I was deucedly sorry not to have afforded a greater conversation with you last evening, but my cousin Tyger seemed to have taken the situation in hand."

Her eyes changed from blue to steely gray. She said, more sharply than she had intended, "I daresay *your* companion occupied you suitably."

His eyebrow raised lazily. "Now what in the world can you mean by that?"

Mariana flushed furiously. It had been a gauche thing to say. What a fool she felt! But headlong she rushed on. "She is another of your cousins, I believe you said? Could she not secure you the inheritance? She seems suitable."

His eyes probed her expression. "A nice girl, Rosalba, but not, I fear, for me." He came nearer. "Miss Porter, cannot we be friends?"

A dozen flustering images flooded Mariana's mind: his attendance upon Lady Blanche, his hot and cold behaviour at the ball, the all-too-pretty copper-haired cousin who looked up at him so adoringly, and, not least, his obvious personal delight in the play of the cards. The fact was that he needed a wife, and what could not be hidden was that in marrying her his wealth would be doubled. It was dreadful to find herself thinking in such terms, but there it was.

It also hurt, she found.

She set her jaw a little more firmly and looked him straight in the eye so that there should be no mistaking *her* attitude in the matter. "I have no feeling of a kind that would gratify you, I believe, Captain Seymour. In all honesty, I think I should warn you that any overture you should feel inclined to make at this time could only be viewed by me . . . and perhaps by others . . . with a certain amount of suspicion."

Brion Seymour's face went quite pale beneath the brown. It was as if she had dealt him a mortal blow. But he spoke quite calmly and showed no ill feeling on his part.

"I appreciate your position, Miss Porter. I shall not again trouble you with my addresses."

As he turned away from her Mariana was pricked by something undeniably like remorse. She knew how much she had scored on him, humbled him, and it gave her no pleasure at all.

"Please, Captain Seymour . . . I shouldn't have said such a thing to you."

Seymour turned back to her, his face still pale, but too composed to show his angry hurt, though she felt it. "Our uncle, Miss Porter, was well known to be an eccentric. Sometimes I wonder at the humanity of a man who would place his kin in such a position as you and I find ourselves."

"As to that, I cannot say," she answered him, "since I never really knew Uncle Forrester, but I do know that you are not a wealthy man—as poor as my papa, I imagine—and I cannot chide you for wanting to alter your station."

Brion Seymour shook his head slowly and sadly. "That bit of well-intentioned pomposity, Miss Porter, is the sharpest slice of all. I swear, you find my armour's chink at every point. But I am not such a fortune hunter as you suspect me to be. I do not deny the very great value of the inheritance, but I still hold my commission, you know, and I would stand no poor chance of rising, I believe. I would return to my regiment at once but for one odd notion." He took her hand again. "I have said I would not bother you again with my addresses, but I feel it right to tell you this. I think that Uncle Josiah *meant* the two of us for each other. I think he intended some sort of alliance between the two sides of his family. And without really

127

knowing either one of us, his manipulations have brought us to this equally untenable position." He stopped for a moment, and Mariana fancied she could hear her pulse pounding in her ears so loudly that she nearly missed his next words.

"I believe I could care for you very much, very deeply, Miss Mariana."

She held her breath, afraid of what he might say next.

"And that makes it all the more difficult, does it not? Even my protestations must seem suspect in your eyes," he said regretfully.

Mariana became aware of Lady Blanche's glacial smile directed at them from across the room. She had an impression of ice and fire mixed together in one personality. An impossible combination, but she guessed that even without the Forrester inheritance, Captain Seymour would not have far to go if he wished to avoid rejoining the Ultonians. Why should it concern her, after all?

She excused herself and moved across the room.

It pleased Mariana that the more she talked to Mrs. Damer, the more she liked the older woman. She found in her the self-sufficiency of the artist, an unforced independence very rare among the society women she had met since she had returned to London. Perhaps it was merely the natural culmination of her years of worldly experience, but whatever caused it, Mariana was charmed by the sheen of gentility it lent to every utterance.

She saw from the corner of her eye that Lady Blanche and Captain Seymour seemed to have naturally gravitated toward each other, and, given a few moments with her hostess, she inquired about the nimble finger movements which she and Jeremy had used. "It seemed almost like a natural conversation, you were so quick with it," she said admiringly. "Will you tell me where it comes from? Or is it a private language between yourself and Mr. Law?"

Mrs. Damer's eyes crinkled amiably. "I wish I could lay claim to having invented it. It would be quite a feather. But the honour goes to an old friend." She looked carefully at Mariana. "You really *are* interested, aren't you? How unusual a girl you are." Then she continued seriously. "There are many forms of sign language, you know. I understand that the people of the Sudan use it, Lord Howe tells me that the Indians of America have developed it quite extensively, and if you were ever to visit Naples, my dear, you would soon see how the language of gesture supplements speech. I hardly think the Neapolitans could get along without it!"

"But a friend developed this one that Jeremy . . . that is, Mr. Law . . . was using?" She had not meant to betray how easily she and the young poet had fallen into an informal, almost familial relationship, but there it was.

"I gather that you and Jeremy have become friends," observed Mrs. Damer approvingly. "I am so happy about that. He has few real ones, I fear. His life is not easy." She hesitated, then went on with what she had been about to say. "A young woman could do worse, you know, than form an alliance with such a fine man."

Mariana sidestepped the issue carefully. "I can guess how frustrating it must be to have no ready expression of one's thoughts. Even writing must seem a clumsy substitution."

Mrs. Damer agreed. "The language is not difficult to master. The Abbé de l'Epée, who taught it to me, was a distant connexion of my mother. He did not invent it, of course, but certainly he is entitled to the credit for systematising it. When I learnt it as a sort of girlish game I never guessed how grateful I would be to teach it to someone else. As you say, it opened up a whole new mode of expression for Jeremy." She spoke lightly. "I could quickly teach you the fundamentals."

"Oh, that would be wonderful! But I am a very slow learner."

"All the better, if you are serious. The secret of doing anything well is doing it with care," Mrs. Damer answered. "Perhaps after we have eaten we might make a start, if you like. Soon you will be able to take Jeremy by surprise." The two exchanged a smile of complicity at the notion of affording this pleasure to their friend.

The collation was simple, but superb in quality. A game pie, veal arabesque, and jugged hare were the main courses, and a hedgehog dessert delighted Mariana, who had never seen slivered almonds put to such use on a pudding. Wines she could not judge, but Tyger seemed to find them very much to his taste.

When the ladies left the table to afford the gentlemen some time with their brandy and cigars, Mrs. Damer taught Mariana a few signing gestures, as she had promised, but soon Lady Blanche intimated a need to be entertained. The hostess suggested instead that her ladyship entertain the idea of giving pleasure to the rest of the company.

"Have you never heard Blanche sing, Lady Emilia? Ah, then you have a great treat in store." To Lady Blanche she said, "Will you not do us this honour, my pet? You know how much it will please me."

"Oh, very well," Lady Blanche agreed negligently, but the little toss of her head betrayed her true feelings. Lady Blanche, Mariana felt, was one of those people who must always be coaxed to give of their best, seemingly preferring to clutch their talents close to their hearts rather than share them. And later, with Brion at the clavier, she came into her own. Her voice was small but naturally pure, a cool, clear tone that interpreted the Italian songs, and later an aria of Mr. Handel, with all the eloquence they deserved.

When Mariana said as much to her aunt, Lady Battledore expressed amazement. "I declare, I am much surprised. One would have thought the art demanded passion, but a voice like this illustrates quite the reverse." She gave her niece a wry smile. "My tongue wants to find something cruel to say, but I cannot; how it frustrates me to hear her sing so divinely!"

But Tyger seemed to have no ear for music. All through the songs he seemed ill at ease, and, when Lady Blanche turned to the arias, he fidgeted quite openly, too ill at ease to go unnoticed. After several baleful looks from Lady Battledore, he murmured into Mariana's ear, "I say, Miss Porter, are you game for a turn in the garden? For I swear, I can take no more of this."

As unobtrusively as possible they slipped into the hall and then into the conservatory from which a window gave access to the gardens.

"Who would have thought she was such a nightingale?" asked the Tyger. "Could a man be married to that and stay sane, d'ye think?"

"I suppose an unmusical man might not," conceded Mariana, "but you know, there are others who would appreciate it. I imagine Captain Seymour must, since he is accompanying her."

"Do I hear a bit of an edge in your voice?" asked Tyger. "I suppose old Brion might be attractive to women, eh? Sensitive, upstanding, and all that? Are you one of 'em, Miss Porter?"

Mariana sidestepped the question as though it had never been asked. "Do you not care for music then, Mr. Dobyn?"

"Oh, music, yes. A tavern glee, a ballad of the right sort, and especially a good and lively fiddle tune, but this . . . no, it is not for me. I feel as if I have just escaped from church, God save me."

Appraisingly, she looked at him through the dusk. "I wonder what sort of man you really are."

He pulled a comic face. "What d'ye mean? I am a man like most men, I suppose."

"No," she contradicted, "you are not. You play at being the buffoon as if you carried the lightest of hearts, and yet last night I saw you at your most brutal."

He pretended to be amazed. "D'you mean with the Frenchie? That sort has no claim to gentleness, if that is what you mean. He is a cheat, and there is no place for that among gentlemen. He needed a lesson and I taught him one, that's all." His expression became a sombre one. "I grew up in a rough world, Miss Mariana, not all good breeding and gentility like Cousin Brion. Whatever I know I taught myself. I'll say nothing about my mam, but I'll tell you this much, I battled my way up out of the stews by my own wits. I found there were so-called gentlemen who would pay to see me brawl, and that was my introduction to 'the fancy,' as the fighting world is called by some."

He drew a deep breath as if it hurt to remember. "I've come to a place where the highest in this country calls himself my friend, and I've never looked back, not once."

"Why did you do all that?"

"Why, you ask? You've not heard a word I said, or else not taken it in. I came up out of places like Vinegar Yard, miss. I seen horrors when I was but a wee lad that I'd not repeat to you now. And what I did to the Frenchie was a tickle compared to what'd happen to him in some places. I am not joking when I tell you that there is more than one den where they'd cut his bloody hand off at the wrist for doing what he did."

Whether it was the notion of the horrors he communicated, or the coolness of the evening Mariana never knew, but of a sudden she began to shiver uncontrollably. She had to grit her teeth to keep them from chattering. Tyger was all concern.

"Dash me, if you haven't caught a chill, my girl. My fault for dragging you out here. Let me put my arm about you and we'll hurry back in. I daresay you must have a wrap, eh?"

Mariana allowed no such thing, but drew back just as a drawling voice behind them said, "Charming. Isn't it delightful the wiles these country girls learn among the upper classes? And Mr. Dobyn has *learned* all about the upper classes, has he not?"

"I don't know what you think you saw, Lady Blanche," said the Tyger in confusion, "but this lady has done nothing to deserve such a reproach."

"Of course not, old chap," said Brion. "What d'you take us for? Come, Miss Mariana, shall I escort you back into the drawing room?"

But Mariana's chin lifted defiantly, although she kept her tone as light as possible. "We found it rather stuffy inside and were just about to take a turn about the garden. Won't you join us?"

"How right you are for seeking a breath of air," agreed Mrs. Damer, coming out through the tall drawing-room windows. "But Miss Porter, I have brought your wrap. The air is deceptive." She turned to her companions, the Marquis and Lady Emilia. "The garden is just right for a walk at this hour, don't you agree?"

"So lovely," said Lady Battledore. "Shall I still be able to see your famous lilies?"

Mrs. Damer linked her arm in Mariana's. "This way, my sweet. What a pity that the lilies have closed for the night. But the scent of the roses lingers."

Suddenly Mariana realised that one member of the party was missing. "Where has Mr. Law got to, ma'am?" she asked her hostess.

"Jeremy? Oh, he is preparing a surprise, I believe, but you must not say that I told you so. Jeremy is so good and clever, I always marvel that a clever woman has not snapped him up ere now."

They promenaded about the famous gardens; Mrs. Damer with Mariana, Lady Blanche between a chastened Tyger and a bemused Brion, with the Marquis and Lady Battledore bringing up the train.

When they had advanced some distance ahead of the others, Mrs. Damer spoke to Mariana in an undertone. "Do you think it quite wise to make Lady Blanche your enemy, my dear?"

Mariana sighed. "I seem to do it without effort."

"I should be careful with her. She is an able antagonist, I believe, and you have given her cause for considerable pique."

"Do you mean Captain Seymour?"

"I know nothing of that. I had reference to her music, you know."

"Oh, but I enjoyed her music. It was Mr. Dobyn who . . ." She stopped in mid-protest. "She would never understand that, would she?"

"I fear not," said Mrs. Damer. "Tell me, does Mr. Dobyn mean all that much to you?"

Mariana could not help giggling. "The Tyger? How could one take seriously a suitor who has already proposed to one's aunt? I know that Aunt Emilia is still very much in her prime, but truly . . ."

Mrs. Damer stopped in mid-step. "Oh, my sweet child, have I found the canker in the bud? Can it be that you are the tiniest bit a prig?"

Abashed, Mariana hung her head. "Perhaps I am, but whoever did hear of a pugilist marrying a lady?"

"My friend Lord Barrymore for one," chuckled her hostess. "His great crony, Hooper, married Martha de Barri, Barrymore's beautiful cousin. And they have been tolerably happy, I believe." This was said very dryly, and Mariana took it as a faint reproof.

"But my aunt . . ."

"Is, as you say, still a handsome woman, and not too much older than Mr. Dobyn. Maturity has its compensations too, you know."

Mariana felt that she could hardly dispute that with a lady of sixty-five.

By the time the others had caught up, Lady Blanche was in a finer mood. Playing two men off against each other had made her far more amiable, and when Mariana made it a point to compliment her on her rendition of the aria from *Serse*, she took it with surprising graciousness.

"Music, you know, is really the only passion that moves me. I daresay if I were not who I am I might have been a singer myself. Does that shock you, Miss Porter? There are skeletons in everyone's closet."

Seeing this amiable exchange Mrs. Damer nodded encouragingly at Mariana and roguishly tipped her a wink that luckily was undetected by Lady Blanche.

But the great surprise of the evening was Jeremy's. After having been absent from their company since dinner he appeared with several sheets of heavy paper lashed together to form a book. And what a fascinating book it was! For in it Jeremy proved himself not only a poet, but an artist of rare distinction as well. Carefully arranged, picture by picture, were the basic gestures of the Abbé de l'Epée's manual language, so clearly and cleverly illustrated that anyone who chose to do so could master the rudiments in a comparatively short time. With a grand gesture of homage Jeremy Law laid the book on Mariana's lap.

She was quite overwhelmed. "For me, do you mean? But Jeremy . . . that is, Mr. Law . . . this is far too valuable for any one person. You must keep it and publish it. Why, think what this could mean to all those who, like yourself, cannot speak . . . and, unlike you, are not poets enough to find a way around it."

Everyone agreed. "She is right, my friend," said Mrs. Damer. "What you have begun here is greater than any mere convenience. You must go on with this, you know, for it is a fine beginning."

Jeremy began to gesture animatedly, and Mrs. Damer translated.

"He says, my dear, that he *will* go on with it, that he has every intention of doing so, but that this first effort is for you and you alone, for you are the only one of his adult friends who ever expressed a desire to hear him in the only way that he can speak."

There were tears in Mariana's eyes as she accepted the gift.

"You make me very proud, Mr. Law, but your poetry speaks to all who read it."

Jeremy gazed at her gently and made a sign that only later she understood to mean "beautiful." But somehow she comprehended it.

Later in the evening Mariana was visiting alone with Mrs. Damer before retiring. She explained how much she had enjoyed Jeremy's poetry long before she knew him. "Of course, in those days I used to imagine Quentin Quartermain reading his words aloud to me, but now . . ."

"Does it weigh nothing that the poet is real, and your friend?" asked her hostess.

"Oh, yes. Certainly it does! I hope I am not so shallow as that. Besides, in a short while, if I apply myself, I shall be able to 'see' him read his own poems, or at least sign them. Isn't the little book he made for me a wonder?" She looked around. "Now where did I put it? I know I had it only a few moments ago."

"In the drawing room, perhaps, when you were showing it to your aunt?"

"Yes, of course. I must have left it on the table. No, do not trouble to ring. I believe I know just where it is. No need to bother the servants."

Candlestick in hand, Mariana descended the shadowy stairway. What a queer day this had been. No one seemed to be all of a piece. Lady Blanche with her beautiful voice and sharp tongue, the Tyger combining gentleness with such ferocity, the ambiguous Captain Seymour, and Jeremy. Dear Jeremy and his touching gesture. What a dear boy he was. She corrected herself. No, not a boy. Jeremy Law was a gentle and sensitive man.

Carefully she picked her way through the darkened drawing room. Ah, she was right. Unerringly she put her fingers exactly on the booklet and sighed with relief. What a pity if it had been lost. She knew that Jeremy would gladly have made another, but that would not have been the same. She was very thankful to have found it so easily.

From somewhere nearby acrimonious voices, though pitched low, carried through the empty rooms. Two people, a man and a woman, were quarrelling unhappily in the library. Though Mariana had no desire to eavesdrop, she could not but hear one phrase delivered in Captain Seymour's battle-trained voice.

"There can be no question of broken vows, Lady Blanche, where none were made!"

Mariana had no desire to be involved or caught up in the dispute, whatever it might concern. She quickened her step, to scurry up the staircase to the safety of her own chamber. But fate was against her. The pages of Jeremy's little booklet, only lightly lashed together, came undone, began to slip from her grasp. In her efforts to retain them she found herself juggling, trying to balance both the pages and the candlestick. The candle, guttering, escaped the holder and fell to the floor. The pages of the manuscript scattered.

"Oh . . . oh, zounds!" she moaned in exasperation. Just when she needed her calm and confidence, this must happen! Mariana fell to her knees, gathering the papers, unsure where the candle had rolled, and at that moment the door of the library was flung open. Framed in the doorway, backlit by the illumination within, Lady Blanche was quite magnificent in her anger. Visions of beautiful, scorned Medea flashed into Mariana's mind. The light of battle was clearly in her ladyship's eyes.

"There are, sir," she all but hissed, "other men in Christendom!"

Mariana, in the shadows, she passed by undetected, but Captain Seymour had the advantage of the candelabrum in his hand. It was obvious when he emerged that he had not tried to detain Lady Blanche, but he appeared to be as startled to find Mariana on her knees in the hall as she to be found there.

"You seem to be in some difficulty, Miss Porter. May I relight your candle for you? Shall I escort you to your chamber door?"

His tone of amusement so annoyed Mariana that her own tone was icy. "Thank you, Captain. I am sure I can find my own way."

The door of the smoking room opened. Tyger Dobyn, glass in hand, watched them with considerable concentration before he raised his eyebrows and beckoned to Brion. "Since the lady requires no assistance, Cousin, perhaps I might share a word with you?"

"By all means, Cousin," Brion answered pleasantly. "Good night, Miss Porter. Sleep well."

Tyger said nothing to her at all.

—14—

TYGER DOBYN WAS unaccountably missing from the breakfast table and Lady Blanche was frostier than ever. One could imagine that icy glints struck from her eyes each time she raised her head and the repast, as a result, was endured in almost complete silence. Though Mariana was all but devoured with curiosity, she felt it wisest not to enquire. True to her position as hostess, Mrs. Damer valiantly endeavoured to keep the conversation moving, but responses were few and desultory. It was as if everyone were taking their cue from Lady Blanche, and her jaw was so rigidly clenched that it was a wonder even food could pass her lips. Something was certainly in the air, for the wind was up and, from the look of things, definitely out of someone's sails. From time to time Lady Battledore would begin one of her sprightly monologues, but she too soon ran out of energy in the face of the other breakfasters' apathy. Jeremy's fingers twitched nervously and Brion sought Mariana's eyes as frequently as she avoided his. It was only when Mrs. Damer submitted an interesting proposal to Mariana that Lady Blanche seemed at all distracted from her own self-contemplation.

"I should be happy, Miss Porter," said the sculptress, "if one day soon you could be persuaded to visit my studio in London with an eye toward sitting for me. I have a fancy to do a head of you. The planes of your face are quite striking enough to lend themselves to it, I think."

Mariana was pleased but could not help flushing, especially as her aunt nodded immediate agreement. "Capital idea, gel! You won't be young forever; on the other hand, with those bones it may not signify."

137

Lady Blanche's chilly tone cut across the exchange like a silver knife. "I wonder, Mrs. Damer, that you have not proposed that *I* sit for you, as more than one artist has done." She moved her shoulders and slightly stretched her neck to a more becoming angle.

"Indeed, Lady Blanche, I can well believe it, though yours is the sort of beauty to which mere sculpture could never do justice. For that, one must have paint. No marble could define, for example, the texture of your skin or the quality of your eyes, which are remarkably fine. What a pity it is, I always think, that we no longer favour polychrome."

Mrs. Damer's own eyes, in which there lurked the slightest hint of amusement, sought Mariana's. "One day next week, then, Miss Porter?"

Brion Seymour, of course, rode off as he had come, as escort to Lady Blanche, and Jeremy Law elected to spend another day with his friend Mrs. Damer. As Mariana was departing with her aunt and the Marquis, Jeremy took her hand and drew her away from the others for a little while, choosing the conservatory for a most disjointed and, on Mariana's part, awkward exchange. The upshot flattered as much as troubled her, for at the end he held her left hand tenderly in his and mimed the slipping of a ring upon the third finger.

She did not answer. She did not know how to make an appropriate reply. But Jeremy seemed to understand. With his cigar cutters he clipped a blossom from a flowering bush and offered it to her with an impish grin. She understood what he was saying—that she must not be troubled that she had no answer. Gently he led her back to the others. Mariana was more than a little bemused. Three proposals in a day.

The carriage had hardly left the grounds of Strawberry Hill before Lady Emilia began to interrogate her niece.

"Talk of ninnyhammers, miss! What did you do to encourage that great oaf last evening?"

"Nothing, Aunt."

"Do not 'nothing' me out of my own carriage, pray. We all saw that little exchange in the garden."

"What you saw," said Mariana with dignity, "was much misunderstood by all of you."

"Oh, pish! I know Tyger Dobyn. You never should have been alone with him."

"So I discovered," said her niece with spirit, and in only a moment they were all laughing, as merry as grigs as the carriage jerked and jolted on its way to London.

"To be honest," the Marquis confided, "I was much surprised when your aunt told me he had made a proposal. I had it in my head that his cap was set for Lady Blanche, you see."

"I feel that Lady Blanche may share your opinion," Mariana agreed. "I hope she is not soon disabused of the thought."

Lady Emilia hooted at this. "His cap is set for Lady Blanche, for Lady Anne, for Miss Cecily, for Miss Beverly, for any widow with a mite! Tyger Dobyn leans toward marrying wealthily, and he ain't too particular. Though I am not sure how far he will get with the snow maiden. She needs a firm hand and he too much plays the fool."

"By that, I imagine," said the Marquis, "you mean he does not scruple to hide his motives. Perhaps he and young Seymour should settle the matter with fisticuffs."

"What matter is that?" Mariana asked innocently.

"Why, which of them will have *you*, miss, and which Lady Blanche."

This was all said with such a straight face that for a moment the girl did not understand that her leg was being pulled energetically.

"Fie, Marquis. Captain Seymour is a gentleman," said her ladyship, carrying the jest. "He is no match for such as the Tyger."

"Then you have seen the Tyger in the ring, have you, Aunt?" asked Mariana, falling in with their humour, since she perceived that only by joining could she hope to divert their conversation away from herself.

"Ladies do not attend such exhibitions, I am sure," the Marquis remonstrated, but Lady Emilia surprised them both.

"Then I am no lady," she said spiritedly. "Do you think I would let such an opportunity escape me? Demme, of course I have seen him. And I was on the arm of the Prince too, sir, if that saves my reputation!"

"I am sure, madam," he answered with great reserve, "that it is not my place to criticise your conduct." Then he could not help asking curiously, "Whom was he pitted against?"

"Aha! Thought that would catch you! Against Mendoza, man, and came out the winner. A fine match, and ever so exciting! My husband had reason to be grateful. He won much at your hands." And with that indecorous thought she let the subject drop, or at least kept her musings to herself.

The drive homeward seemed longer by far than the excursion out toward Strawberry Hill, but for Mariana there was a welcome treat in store. The Marquis, who had grown oddly silent, had been let off at his rooms and Lady Emilia repaired immediately to her chamber, leaving Mariana to wonder if something had escaped her. It seemed that both had acted very oddly. And all of a sudden, too. But Marasham diverted her thoughts before she could follow her aunt up the stair.

"A gentleman to see you, miss." She noted that this time, at least, it was a gentleman, not merely "a personage." "I left him waiting in the drawing room, but he may have changed. Very restless he seems."

She finally located her visitor in the library where he was poring over a heavy tome.

"Papa!"

Energetically he snapped the book shut. "Daughter," he answered so severely that Mariana thought, What, has he heard already?

Lynval Porter shook his head sadly, then unexpectedly sneezed. It took a bit off the edge of his old Roman pose. "Demmed dust! Does no one clean in here?" But he reverted to his serious mien.

"Daughter, I am displeased. And I came to London to tell you so."

Well, it couldn't be about last evening's misunderstanding, then. Her face fell. "I suppose you've heard about the money. Are you very angry with me for it?"

"Not for your getting it, if that is what you mean." He stood up with feet wide apart in a belligerent stance. "I don't mind you *having* the demmed money, but what you propose to do with it!"

"What?" Mariana was baffled. What dreadful thing had she done to so annoy him? "Do you mean the house?"

"Be demmed the house!" he roared. "How dare you shame me in the face of the world?"

Mariana was by now almost in tears. "My dear, how could you say such a thing as that? What on earth have I done that you should use me so?"

Lynval waved the gazette in front of her. "This, missy! This outrage!" With a visibly trembling hand he pointed to the notice placed by Chipworth. "I can pay me own debts! I do not hide behind the skirts of any woman, let alone my daughter!" He fumed wordlessly for a moment. Then, becoming more rational, having observed that Mariana's agitation was as great as his own, he went on in a quieter tone.

"I *am* happy for you, you know. I daresay I should have fallen back into my own ways before the year was out if that fortune had come to me. But damme, gel, I pay my own notes. I can do it, you know, now that I have no great, hulking female eating me out of house and home." This last was said with such a wry smile that his daughter's heart quite melted. Both understood what the inheritance meant, that things now could never be the same.

Lynval's eyes softened. "Dublin town is almightily empty without you, my dear. Is Bridie watching over you properly?"

"Yes, Papa, she is." Then, "Papa, will you come back to London? I shall take a house with a studio just for you, a fine large one."

Porter shook his head. "Nay, lass. London is not for the likes of me. I am like a drunkard here. I never know when I have reached the limit of anything. Perhaps it is as well that Chipworth handle the payment of the duns as they come in, but the paying will come from my share, not yours. Bedad! A man has his pride!"

She knew him well enough not to press the matter further, and they sat together for a little while in companionable silence. Finished were the tears and reproaches, but Mariana still had something to ask, and she hardly knew how to say it.

"Shall you mind dreadfully if I marry, Papa?"

"Mind? Of course I shall mind, gel! What father would not?" But abandoning his air of mock severity, he drew her toward him and kissed her on the brow. "But if you are happy, when the time comes I shall be happy for you as well, never doubt that."

Suddenly a thought occurred to her. "Oh, Papa, are you very busy today?"

"Not remarkably, why do you ask?"

"I need to ask your advice about the house I am thinking of purchasing. Will you look at it with me?"

"Certainly, my love, if it will please you. But don't be expecting to ask me about the decoration and such. I know nothing of that."

Mariana flew up the stair to change into town clothes, stopping at the door of her aunt's chamber to apprise her of the plan. Lady Battledore was sitting in a slipper chair by the window, a letter in her hand.

"I have something to tell you, Mariana."

"Yes, Aunt? I am listening."

"And," Lady Battledore cautioned, "you must promise to be very calm."

The girl was quite puzzled. "I *am* calm, Aunt," she said with a little laugh. "Are you quite well?"

"I?" Lady Emilia asked. "Oh, *I* am well enough, but you must take a deep breath and let your body go all loose and limp. Perhaps you should sit down for a moment and count to ten."

"Aunt!" Mariana cried in a little exasperation. "I am perfectly well and quite calm, except that you are distressing me. What *is* the matter? You are not at all yourself."

Her aunt beamed. "Oh, yes I am. Quite myself. But I have news, such news!"

Mariana knew it at once. "She is here? In London?"

"No, not in London. As I told you, she fears the effect her presence might have on your season, but she *is* in England."

"Where, Aunt, where?"

"She is living in a house the late Lord Spurrell left her in Lamorna, near Penzance."

"Oh, in Cornwall! I love Cornwall!"

"So does your mother. We spent our childhood there. In fact, if I remember, your parents spent their honeymoon with Squire Lovell at Trove."

142

Which made Mariana remember. "He's here, you know."

"Not Squire Lovell, surely?" asked Lady Emilia playfully. She was in a rare mood, Mariana could see.

"No, my papa. I had thought to take him to see the house I have an interest in." She thought aloud. "I wonder what it will be like when they see each other again?"

Her aunt became a little more serious. "You must not be spinning fantasies, my girl. I daresay he will not be in London when she arrives. In any case, I doubt that he will want to see her anymore than she will want to see him. You must not expect that. A great many years have gone by."

"But wouldn't they be curious?" asked Mariana. "I know *I* would be."

Lady Emilia shook her head. "Curiosity is not *always* the most compelling force in life, dear, as you will find in later years. Comfort and peace of mind often mean a great deal more."

"But . . ." Mariana began, then clapped her hand to her mouth. "Oh, Lud! Papa! Excuse me, Aunt, but I've left Papa dangling his heels in the hall!" She tugged at the bellcord and in a moment Lily appeared in the doorway. "Lily, just pop down to my father and say to him that I regret detaining him and that we shall be off to Baillie Street shortly."

Lily bobbed her way out and Mariana returned to the subject at hand. "But honestly, Aunt, do you think that Papa and my mama cannot even meet in society? What a sad thing that will be."

"Oh, society," said her aunt disparagingly. "Who knows about society? They might be ostracised, or taken up as the hit of the season. One never knows. My only caution, dear, is not to expect too much. Certainly not to indulge yourself in romantic fantasies. These are hard times. A woman must keep her wits about her."

Lily bobbed back into the room. "Beg pardon, miss, but 'ee's garn."

"Who's gone? Papa? How very odd. Did he leave a message?"

Lily curtsied nervously as if the sudden departure might somehow be construed as her fault. "Naow, miss. I guv 'im yer message an' 'ee says 'Baillie Street, is it?' an' then 'ee just up an' went, quick as anything!"

This was recited so brightly and with such an English-sparrow demeanour that both women smiled. "Very well, Lily, you may go." But to her aunt Mariana confided. "How very peculiar. Just when I was depending on him to help me decide about the house."

"Perhaps not so odd," Lady Emilia disagreed. "Where is it, did you say? Not Baillie Street?"

"Yes. Quite delightful, too. Just off Rottingdean Square. I can hardly wait until you see it." Something in her aunt's expression stopped her in mid-speech.

"My dear child, are you joking?"

"Not at all. Number twelve. Such a pretty little house."

Lady Emilia drew her breath and let it out very slowly. "Yes, I daresay it still is."

"Still, Aunt Emilia?"

"I cannot think how this has come about," said her ladyship, "but it is most peculiar. Did you not know that number twelve is the house you lived in as a child? The house where your father and mother were at first so happy and then so sad? No wonder he took flight."

"Oh," said her niece. "So that is why I felt so at home there? It is such a love of a house. I cannot bear to let it go, though I suppose I must, mustn't I?" She tried to mask her disappointment, though it was not easy.

"Not necessarily," replied Lady Emilia pragmatically. "A house is only a dwelling, after all. Your father is not to live in London? Then you should do exactly as you like. You can even refurnish it in the same style, if you like. I daresay the moveables are in the attic here, though they will be vastly out of date." She considered. "I think your mother would be quite pleased to come home again."

Thus it was that Mariana set out for her house not with Lynval but with Lady Emilia. The invitation had been calculated on the knowledge that her aunt would allow no sentiment to overweigh. Her advice would be invaluably cool and sensible—the very qualities Mariana needed at the moment.

Mr. Chipworth passed the whole situation off quite blandly.

"'Pon my honour, Miss Porter, I never thought to look up the antecedents. I would have done eventually, of course, but it hardly seemed needful." He stole a look at her out of the corner of his eye. "That puts you off it, eh? Unhappy memories and all that?"

But truthfully, it did not, despite the notion she had that Mr. Chipworth was not representing things quite as accurately as he pretended. The house *was* a jewel; nothing had changed that. The clean lines of it, the exquisitely laid-out little garden (well tended over the years by someone who took pride in it), and the practical consideration that no matter what, it was exactly what she needed.

Lady Emilia looked it over with a somewhat sterner eye. "Needs airing," was her first, pithy remark, followed by a sharp look at the condition. "Bit of dry rot there, is it, Chipworth? Gutters need replacing. I should revamp the kitchen quarters entirely, Mariana. Time has changed what needs to be accepted. The earth closets are a disaster!"

But all in all, she was inclined to admit that it was not at all a poor choice. "Quickly done, I should think. Especially as you have money to spare. Nothing makes a workman so nimble as the thought of secured money in his pocket!"

It was something of a relief to Mariana that her judgement was borne out by an old, probably wiser head. But something else entirely convinced her that she had made the right choice. It was the warm, cherished, and beloved feeling she felt here, at once protected and completely at ease. She did not think it was a mood she would find elsewhere.

But as they were leaving, just as they swept round the corner into Rottingdean Square, the sense of supreme well-being abated by the merest trifle. Against the ornate railings that sheltered the square's garden lounged a man she was almost sure she had seen before. Seen quite recently, and not in this quarter of the town. How very odd that it should cast even this slight cloud upon the day. Perhaps it was only her imagination.

"Aunt," she asked, "do you see that man?"

Lady Battledore turned her head and peered past her curiously. "What man, dear? I see no one at all."

And when Mariana looked back no man was there, which was curious, because there was hardly any place that could conceal him. Unless he had vaulted over the railing into the garden, which was most unlikely, since it was reserved for the residents of the square only. But he was certainly no longer in view.

And again, another odd thing only a little while later. As they reached Battledore House they could see Marasham on the front steps exchanging courtesies with a liveried footman. As their carriage drew up the footman bowed and walked quickly away.

"Egad!" exclaimed her ladyship. "I know that livery, but whose the devil is it?"

"Why, that was the Duke's man, ma'am," Marasham answered. "He was requesting a bit of information of me."

"Duke? What duke would be making enquiries here?"

"Why, His Grace, the Duke of Cumberland, your ladyship," said Marasham in a surprised tone. "He made out as if it was all quite known to your ladyship. I thought as how it was all right. Not that I had anything to tell him, you know."

"Well, what was he asking, man?" Lady Emilia snapped testily. "Good Lord, have you set up as a news service?"

Marasham withdrew into an immense dignity. "I am sure I had no intention of giving away any private information, ma'am. The man asked me, quite natural-like, if your ladyship had left the message for the Duke. Not *a* message, mind you, ma'am, but *the* message."

"What message? I left no message! What on earth are you gabbling about?"

"He said, your ladyship, that you was to have left a message as to when Lady Spurrell was expected. And he was quite insistent that I must know."

"Good grief, what utter rot! And what in the world did you tell him, Marasham?"

The footman answered very quietly, so quietly as to have the effect of shouting, which demonstrably he could *not* have done. "I told him, your ladyship, that I did not know.

"And that," he added, "is all I told him, ma'am, because in truth I do *not* know."

Mariana thought that it was a fair answer.

=15=

IN THE VERY nature of things, Lucy had to be told of the house and all the great plans immediately. Lucy, of course, *had* a house, since she would be moving into Lord Robert's family home after the wedding in St. James's. Not for her the giddy pleasures of selecting and matching and painting and arranging, so she must do it all at second-hand. Mariana offered the ideal opportunity. It was such fun, rather like playing at dolls with real rooms, real furniture. But it had its drawbacks as well, even if only by contrast.

"And you shall be living, Mariana, in light! All white and pale greens and citron yellows, with that perfectly exquisite blue carpet you have chosen for your sitting room, while I must go off to a gloomy mansion," she mourned.

But Mariana had little sympathy. "Quite grand in its gloominess, I believe, Lucy. You will settle in with a flourish, and then, after a baby or two, when you are having a little respite, I daresay you will start rearranging everything to your taste."

Lucy was aghast. "A baby or two? Why not say three or four? My dear, I hope I am to have a *bit* of a run as a young bride before I am turned into a factory for heirs! Have mercy, puss, I am not ready for such sobriety."

"Oh, lud," Mariana pretended chagrin. "And here I was expecting to be a godmother right off."

"You have not been a bridesmaid yet. Pray be content."

And the house *was* coming along well. The necessary physical alterations had been easily accomplished except for the new kitchen in the rear yard, and that was nearly done. Hired workers, supplemented and directed by servants from Portland Square, laboured long and fruitful hours. Mrs. Marasham, who was to be installed as housekeeper, saw to that for the most part, but Mariana had not shirked her own responsibilities. If the house were to be well done-up, well run, she knew, it must take its energy from the source; and, as it was her house, her taste, her money, and her responsibility, the source was necessarily herself.

Which is to say she enjoyed every moment of it.

It was not easy. Less so, since she had still an unending round of social responsibility. Routs, balls, assemblies, concerts, suppers, dinners, teas, nuncheons, all must perforce be fitted in. It was expected. It was imperative.

Jeremy proved, surprisingly, to be of great help. The question of romance had been tabled for the time, through Mrs. Damer's good offices, and they had become something more useful—friends. Jeremy's eye for the nuance of colour was extraordinary, his grasp of design superb. Often when he and Mariana were chattering away at a great pace in finger movements upon some particular point of artistry, Lucy would cover her eyes mockingly.

"Stop, stop it! You are deafening! And I feel quite left out!"

It was amusing, but then Mariana would always have to think how to explain what had been said, for in a brief time, through application and enthusiasm, she had become quite extravagantly proficient at signing. To the point, indeed, that she no longer needed to think of the symbol or movement, but merely of the thought she wished to convey.

"I swan, I am quite jealous," Lucy professed. But she would never try to master the art herself.

One morning Mr. Chipworth sent Rigby round to Battledore House. "Would it be convenient, Miss Porter, to visit himself . . . that is, to wait upon Mr. Chipworth on a matter of business?"

"I imagine it can be arranged, Mr. Rigby. Will you have some chocolate?"

He blinked. "Yes, please. That'ud be very nice, if it is quite convenient."

"And some buttered toast? You look, if you will pardon me, sir, as if you had not had time for a very good breakfast this morning.

No, not that slice, I believe it is a little burnt. Oh, you like it burnt? . . . When?"

"When, miss?" Mumbling through his repast.

"When to visit Mr. Chipworth, Mr. Rigby?"

Brushing the crumbs away from his whiskers. "Ah . . . this afternoon, miss, if that is quite convenient. I am particularly to say, 'if it is quite convenient,' you see."

Mariana cocked her head to one side in a pretty way. "What is in the air, Mr. Rigby? Something portentous, I imagine."

He looked quite alarmed at the question. "Oh, I'm sure I could never say, Miss Porter." He rose hurriedly, napkin and crumbs scattering. "Only if it is convenient." Sidling toward the door crabwise he recollected, paused quizzically. "Beg pardon, Miss Porter, is it?"

"Quite convenient, Mr. Rigby. Shall we say at two?"

"Thank you, miss. At two."

Things were coming along well at Baillie Street, and she had no reason to put the solicitor off. But she was surprised and a little mortified on arriving to see who else had been summoned.

Captain Seymour seemed as uncomfortable in the situation as she, though he smiled amiably enough and bent over her hand.

"A pleasure to see you again, Miss Porter."

"Thank you." Said coolly but without rancour.

"Your father is well?"

"Yes, thank you."

"And your aunt, she is well too?"

A little more stiffly now. What was he up to? Why were his eyes twinkling when only a moment ago they had been wary? "Lady Battledore *is* well, thank you."

"I believe I have heard that your mother is returning to London soon?"

Mariana smiled rather thinly. "The world at large seems conversant with my affairs, does it not? Yes, my mother is resting in the country, but she will, I believe, be coming to London."

"Resting? Mrs. Porter is ill, then?"

"There *is* no Mrs. Porter, sir. Or, though I daresay there may be one or two in London, even several, there are of no connexion to my mother, whose name is now Lady Spurrell."

"Ah?" The conversation was effectively cut short. From then on it limped and halted, touching general topics only and carefully skirting personal references until Seymour said, "And I believe you have taken a house of your own?"

"How well informed you are, Captain. Yes, I have bought the house I lived in as a child."

"And your mother will live there with you?"

There, it was out. She had not yet said it to herself, but trust the gallant Captain to bring it to the fore. Yes, that really was what she had in mind. It must have been, all along. A young woman could not live alone, unchaperoned, however rich she was. Yes, she knew that, whatever society might have to say about it, she had wanted the Baillie Street house to live in with her mother.

Enter Mr. Chipworth, genial and avuncular, Rigby trailing nervously. "Well met, well met!" said perhaps a little too forcefully. Sitting behind his great desk, the lawyer placed his elbows on the top and rested his chin on his folded hands. "Well, here we are, all of us together." He looked at them brightly. Neither Mariana nor Brion Seymour fulfilled his expectations by replying.

"I know," he said, "you wonder why I have asked you here, and I will not be so unkind as to keep you in suspense. I have been doing a great deal of thinking recently about the many odd complications arising from your late uncle's will." He beamed, then went on deprecatorily. "We all know how eccentric a document it is."

Brion eyed him warily. "You had nothing to do with the composition of the will?"

Chipworth unfolded his hands, shrugged, then clasped his hands again. "Ah, well, as to that, I . . . ah . . . I must confess that I was, you understand, serving my client to the best of my ability."

"And now you are on the other side of the fence?" asked Mariana. "To undo what you have done?"

"Er . . . something like that. You see, the law is a curious thing, Miss Porter. At times it becomes a challenge in the abstract, as it were. A puzzle to be solved."

"Rather like playing chess against oneself?" Brion asked. He seemed serious in saying it. Mr. Chipworth appeared to acquiesce for the sake of moving on. "Let me make my point, sir. We are all friends here. We can speak between ourselves without formality, eh? Eh, Miss Porter?"

"I presume so, Mr. Chipworth. But what is your point?"

He drew himself up and, for all his talk of informality, he struck a distinctly judicial pose. "My point, miss . . . and sir (with a nod to Brion) . . . is this. I propose a merger."

"A merger of what sort?" Brion asked, frowning. "Do you propose to pool our personal difficulties? I assure you, Miss Porter would not find mine particularly fascinating."

"How can you be so sure, Captain Seymour?" Mariana murmured with a touch of malice in her tone. "I daresay they would be instructive, at the very least."

Brion cast his eyes sideways to her. Under hooded lids they shot sparks. "That is not the point, I think."

"Ah, but what is the point?" asked Chipworth sententiously. "Is it not, sir, that Captain Seymour needs a wife and Miss Porter is in need of a husband?"

"Am I?" asked Mariana. "I did not know that. Somehow I fancied I had rather a good bit of time to find myself a partner."

Captain Seymour's face was turkey-red. "Your want of tact, lawyer, is lamentable. You are not above proposing something dastardly, I don't doubt. First you talked me into running that disastrous advertisement, then insisted that I interview each and every one of the young women myself, and now you seem to have something new up your sleeve. I will tell *you* something, sir, of which you may not be aware. I have tendered my advances to Miss Porter, and she, quite within her rights, has seen fit to reject them."

Chipworth looked toward Mariana. "Is that true, miss?"

Mariana found that she was quite as annoyed with him as Brion was. She had intended, nay resolved, that in all dealings with Mr. Chipworth, especially in the matter of marriage, she would keep her demeanour cool and amusedly detached. Such she perceived the properly ladylike attitude—but, really, he was beyond patience!

"I believe you would have advertised me as well, sir, like a heifer at a county fair! I can see that it would please your tidy mind to have all the loose ends of this business caught up in a nice, legal fashion, but that is not the way the world goes, sir! It seems to me you have passed all bounds of propriety. Advertisements, indeed! If Captain Seymour was as discomfited as I should be, my heart quite goes out to him."

Brion swivelled in his chair and smiled wryly. "If you had but seen them, Miss Porter! One more opportunistic than the other. No thought of happiness, nor companionship, nor common bonds of affection. I never knew there were so many marriage-hungry women in the world, let alone claiming kinship. Such far-fetched and inveigled genealogies were never seen!" He subsided somewhat. "Only one of them . . . one, mind you, of close to a score . . . had any heart at all."

Mariana had a quick vision of a pretty gamine with hair the colour of a new-minted penny. "And what happened there, sir?"

He scowled. "She had the deuced taste to prefer someone else."

Archly, "Over you, Captain, and over money? I can hardly believe it."

But Mr. Chipworth was not to be turned aside. "Well, as to the advertisement, you may indict me not, for it served its purpose in bearing fruit. As to the trouble, young man, what were you asking, that I choose *for* you?"

Truculently Brion said, "Zounds, you could have sorted them out a bit, you know."

"Be that as it may," said the lawyer, "you chose none of 'em, what? And you, miss, have you found your own true love, then?"

Mariana's ire rose quickly. "I have scarcely had time, and, I may say, there will be no advertisements for me. Let nature take its course, Mr. Chipworth, if you please. I think we want no marriage-makers here."

He nodded sagely. "Very well, if that is what you insist. For all I know there are hundreds of Forrester males out there in the dark who will come clamouring for your hand. At present I know of but three, and to my mind, Captain Seymour is by far the best of 'em, if I do say so to his face."

She knew the three: Brion, dear Jeremy, and the Tyger. And none of them could she see in the little house in Baillie Street. Tyger was too wild by far, Jeremy, for all his sweetness, far too tame, and Captain Seymour, of course, was out of the question.

"After all," said Chipworth, spreading his hands innocently, "I am merely proposing a merger, not an abomination."

Brion was sharp and to the point. "Idiots may place their trust in you, sir, but I shall not do again. No, by Jove, though I go penniless for it!"

"What do you imply by a merger?" Mariana asked. The term was unfamiliar to her.

"A merger, Miss Porter, is simply this: consolidation. The putting together of two or more individual advantages for the common good of all concerned." He quite beamed upon her, and she realised that she had fallen into the trap of his rhetoric.

"How will it affect me, if you please?"

"You are in an unfortuitous circumstance, Miss Porter. You will be aware that the control of your fortune cannot exactly be your own. By the terms of your uncle's will it cannot pass into the hands of your father. It follows, then, that you must marry."

"Because my uncle believed no woman could manage money? How unfair!"

"I do not dispute that," Chipworth answered, and she felt a certain current of sympathy from him. "Nevertheless, it is so. When you marry, the control of your fortune passes into the hands of your spouse. And marry you must, or lose it altogether. There is no way around that."

"And what of me?" Brion asked. "Is my fortune to pass into the hands of my spouse as well?"

"You jest, sir," said the benevolent Jove across the desk, "but the late Mr. Forrester was not unaware of the singular freedom in such matters as entertainment and pastime enjoyed by military men."

"And have I ever been known as a libertine?" asked the captain.

"Have you ever been *rich*?" asked Chipworth bluntly. The point was a good one. "Your uncle was well aware of the settling power of a good woman, a woman whose worth, I believe the good book says, is beyond rubies."

Both his clients were silent. Perhaps he had stunned them into acquiescence for a moment. He moved to seize the momentary advantage.

"What I am proposing . . . and I use the term seriously . . . is a *mariage de convenance*, as the Frenchies say. A marriage that would fulfill the letter of the will but leave each of you to go your chosen way without let or hindrance."

Mariana's brows knit. "You are saying a legal fiction, Mr. Chipworth? A marriage in name only?"

He nodded complacently. "A mutually advantageous arrangement, don't you agree?"

"A demmed ungentlemanly suggestion," Brion snapped, springing up from his chair with such energy that Rigby shrank in alarm. "It is insulting to Miss Porter and offensive to me! If you *were* a gentleman, sir, I would call you out!"

"Oh, pish!" said Mariana.

Brion stared at her unbelievingly. "You astound me, Miss Porter. Do you mean that you would even consider . . ."

"It seems to me at least worth considering," she said with a calm she did not altogether feel. "We have a year of time to mull it over, after all, in case the 'unknown beloved' should suddenly appear upon the horizon. And I daresay we can assume that Lawyer Chipworth has at his fingertips the necessary legal expertise to safeguard each of us from the other."

Brion slapped his hand down on the desktop full force. "Well, if that don't tear it! Safeguard you against me, is it? Let me tell you something, miss; I have met more scheming, avaricious females in the last month than I ever knew existed. And I don't mean they all came from the advertisement, either. Give me a bully-boyo anytime for honesty and straightforward behaviour. Marry for convenience, is it? Turn our backs on each other once the ceremony was done? I suppose you'd find yourself some accommodating cicisbeo in no time at all, eh? And I find a complaisant female?" His building wrath was wonderful to behold. "No, by God, I'll not give up my manhood on a legal quirk! Much as I would like to accommodate Miss Porter, I hardly think that a contented future could be built on a marriage where the parties turn their backs on each other once the knot is tied."

"But the fortune, sir?" asked Chipworth.

"With all due respect, both to you and to my late uncle," Brion said with the hint of a gambler's grin, "I can always go back to my regiment. War is not an overly particular mistress, and there is always a battle raging somewhere."

And with a bow, he was gone out of the door.

"Ah," said the lawyer with seeming satisfaction, "there you see, Miss Porter, a self-sufficient man." Her amused smile agreed. "However, I should not worry. I daresay he could be persuaded if you want him to be?" The statement ended as an enquiry.

"I confess, I am not sure," Mariana said musingly. "It is certainly an interesting notion, I allow, to be rich, protected by the conventions, and only legally encumbered. I promise that I shall give it my attention."

"Serious attention?" asked the legal mind at work.

"Oh, very serious. Very serious indeed."

—16—

"BUT WHAT I cannot fathom," said Lucy, "is your attitude."

Bridie, bustling about the suite of rooms, sniffed audibly. Like every proper maid, she knew exactly the subject of the conversation and was quick to express her opinion. "Will there be anythin' else, miss?" she asked slyly. "I know all there is to know," she seemed to be saying, "and I can afford to be about my business."

"No, Bridie, you are free to go. Spend your afternoon as you will. I shall not be requiring you until dinnertime."

When she had gone Lucy continued her interrogation. "I mean to say, my dear, that Brion is still the same man you have been avoiding, been turning your back on, been freezing with every syllable you utter. And yet you will consider him for a husband?"

"It would be a matter of convenience merely," Mariana patiently explained. "It would serve the purpose of securing both my fortune and his, without prejudice on either side."

"What do you mean by 'without prejudice?'"

"I should go my way and he should go his. The will is most specific that we must each marry within the family."

"But, my dear," said Lucy, quite scandalised, "what on earth would you do if you fell in love?"

"I have a year, haven't I? The relative of my dreams may yet arrive."

"But," said Lucy, "you mistake me. I meant to say, what if you should fall in love with Brion?"

Mariana all but laughed in her face. "What an absurd thought!"

"Why is it?"

"Why, because Captain Seymour is no more to my taste than I am to his. He is a stick, my pet. Stiff, upright, and humourless. If I should ever fall in love it would not be with a man like that."

Lucy hooted. "But he would be all right to marry? How cynical you have become in your mature years!"

"But those are the very qualities I should value most in a *husband*. Convenience and companionship, that's the ticket. You are awfully lucky, you know. You and Lord Robert suit each other down to the ground, but look where love led my mama. No, I'll have no more of it than I must." She was obstinately silent for a few moments, then she brightened. "And I have a year to make up my mind. Dear me, a year is practically forever!"

Lucy was at once contrite. "Oh, puss, I *am* sorry. I shouldn't have at you so when you have already as good as warned me off. Try to remember that I care for you, and lay it to my concern."

Mariana was instantly mollified, and in a little while they were agitatedly discussing the new white silk they had seen worn by the Dowager Countess of Ravenspur. "She is quite old, you know," confided Lucy with the air of sharing a state secret, "but still very handsome. Somehow you don't think of a lady in her fifties as being a great beauty, but *she* still is. My father says she is as beautiful now as when Lord Mordaunt married her. He says they used to stand on chairs to see her when she entered a ballroom."

"I can well believe it. They say that Lady Blanche was quite put out at the attention the Countess received at the opera."

Lucy giggled. "My pet, Lady Blanche is quite put out at any attention diverted from herself. She is quite the goddess in her own eyes. As you have reason to know."

Mariana was all open face and wide eyes. "Whatever do you mean by that?"

"I hear you bent her nose at Strawberry Hill."

"Stuff!" Mariana drifted to the window and looked out. Lucy kept her silence. She knew her friend well enough not to disturb one of her brown moods. She was rewarded presently when Mariana asked, "Do you suppose he would be faithful as a husband? He seems to be on the town a good deal."

"I presume you refer to Captain Seymour?"

"Of course there are also Jeremy and the Tyger."

"Mariana, you'd never marry the Tyger?"

"Why on earth not? Two could certainly live on my money, and he *is* family."

Cautiously, Lucy broached another name. "Do you know I believe Jeremy is just a bit in love with you. He came for chocolate on Monday and talked of no one else. With notes, you know."

"So that is what you knew of Strawberry Hill? Dear Jeremy. If I had had a brother, I would want him to have the same dear heart and gentle nature."

"A brother; I see."

The door was flung open. "Here, Mariana! Wake up, gel! Whatever are you thinking of? Are you going to change your frock?"

"Change, Aunt? For what reason?" She smoothed the fabric of her skirt. "This is a favourite of mine."

"It is well enough for an afternoon at home among friends, but do you think it suitable in which to meet a princess of the blood?" Before her niece could answer Lady Battledore seemed to reconsider.

"Oh, tush, come as you are. Princess Augusta has seen many a dull dress in her life, I'll be bound. You've never seen such economics as they practise at Kew. Prinny gets all the money and the rest daren't ask the nation for more than they had ten years ago. It is a scandal!"

She looked Lucy up and down. "And you'll do. Ten minutes, mind you, in the drawing room. Don't dawdle!"

"Something I have always wondered, Lucy," Mariana mentioned when Lady Emilia had gone. "Why is only the Princess Charlotte married? Could not the rest fall in love like other girls?"

Lucy was rather taken aback. "Oh, you have become so forward! I hope you will not ask that to the Princess's face?" Her voice assumed a conspiratorial tone. "The fact is, they say, that the king's girls are as romantic as anyone. More so, perhaps, since they have been kept away from men altogether."

"What on earth for?"

"Who is to read the mind of kings? I expect Farmer George remembers the days of his youth and vows no man is good enough for his five virgins still at home. God knows, they say Charlotte's is no love match."

158

Mariana considered that the poor Princess would be too pale and sad for much amusement. She was unprepared for the actuality. The king's second daughter turned out to be lively, cheerful, and full of humour. Her first words to Mariana were, "Such a pity, dear girl, to have had such a short career. I understand that Lady Blanche is a crack shot. Do wear something dark so the stains won't show."

"I beg Your Royal Highness's pardon?" asked Mariana in consternation. "Have you confused me with someone else?"

But the joke was not done. "Do you mean to say she has not yet called you out? Well, perhaps I am mistaken, but I hear you put her nose quite out of joint, and she lays her jilting at your feet."

It was Lucy who voiced their question. "Her jilting, ma'am?" Then realised she had not even been introduced.

Lady Battledore rescued her. "Miss Lucy . . ." she began, but Princess Augusta waved her aside. "I know, I know. She's marrying Lord Robert, eh? Good catch. One expects *you* to do as well, girl," she said to Mariana.

"But please, ma'am, the jilting?"

"Oh, lud, the girl believes me. I daresay you will not be challenged, though the jilting, they say, is real. She had her heart set on young Seymour, who has all Forrester's money. Now there's a man to set your cap for."

So that was it? The scene in the library at Strawberry Hill was explained. But not the Captain's involvement in it. Unless, of course, by some mad chance Lady Blanche was part of the Forrester connection, which seemed to grow by leaps and bounds.

She realised that the Princess was studying her face intently.

"Turn your face, my darling . . . No, no, to the light. The likeness is amazing. Lady Emilia, didn't you see it? I am surprised that Prinny said nothing."

"Likeness, Your Royal Highness?"

"Why, bless me, she's the living image of Grannie. My, my, my. You couldn't be more like if you were one of the family."

The silence lay heavily upon them. Mariana felt quite calm but she could see that Aunt Emilia was visibly trembling. Lucy had her hand to her mouth and her colour had quite gone off. Only the Princess Augusta seemed quite calm.

"They told me, you know, but I had to see for myself. Especially as you are my godchild. Well, it is time I did something in the godmotherly vein, eh? In any case, I am here at the behest of the Regent."

Oh, dear, thought Mariana, does the whole world know of my mother's friendship with Prince Ernest? But what was it her aunt had said to her? Ah, yes, "no one would believe it who could count." But this lady, was she then another aunt, as was Lady Battledore? Could she be *Aunt* Augusta?

"The Regent, ma'am?"

The ruddy-faced Princess nodded vigorously. "He was much taken with you at your coming-out. He plans to entertain once again.

"As you know," she went on, her voice saddening a little for a moment, "my dear sister Amelia has been gone for a year now. He feels, does Prinny, that it is high time the court came out of mourning. Not that he is heartless, you know, but he is not the sort who can grieve forever."

Lady Battledore looked as if she might have something to say on the subject, but she wisely held her tongue. Mariana was glad of it, for she had had quite enough controversy for one day.

"This will be your official entrée into society, Miss Porter. You will be the *pièce de résistance*, the cynosure of two hundred pair of eyes, at Carlton House. Your name will be made."

"But . . . but what is it I am to do?" asked Mariana worriedly.

"Whatever your pleasure," said the Princess Augusta. "Mostly you are simply to be."

"But, ma'am . . ."

"It is the Regent's pleasure." Her homely face was kind but firm. "You are a beautiful young woman. The new court society is sorely in need of beauty. We have lived with frumpishness far too long. Please consider carefully. It will be the great event of the season, for the world is waiting to see what the Prince has done with Carlton House. He is so looking forward to a splendid evening. I hope you will not disappoint the dear boy."

"Your Royal Highess is very kind," Mariana said. "I shall certainly be reluctant to cause the Prince Regent any discomfort."

Princess Augusta remained genial, but her next point was well taken. "Your position will be unassailable, you know, once you have appeared in the Regent's company. No one would dare question your antecedents." She smiled again, but there was no accompanying reflexion in her eyes. "No matter what they might be."

When she had gone there was a peculiar atmosphere among the other three. Lucy looked almost frightened, Lady Battledore was near rage, and only Mariana felt quite calm. Some drama was about to be played out for which she felt herself unprepared but confident. Of no account now were any of the lessons in polite deportment so strongly schooled by the descendants of Miss Pecksniff. It was not unease that so discomfited her, but a kind of surprise that something so grand, so elevated, as the opening of Carlton House should have, by the mere expression on the middle-aged princess's face, become a trial rather than a joy.

"What did she mean, Aunt, when she said I looked like one of her family?"

Lucy murmured incoherently. "What, Lucy?" Mariana prompted.

"Mama said the same thing, but Papa told her not to be silly." Her friendly face crumbled almost into tears. "Oh, Mariana, I don't understand what is happening!"

Mariana pressed her friend's hand. "Nor do I, dearest. Aunt, can you offer a solution? Whom did the Princess mean by 'Grannie?'"

Lady Emilia had not weathered forty-odd years of society in vain. She had seen favourites rise and fall at the whim of fashion, just as she had seen more futures blighted by over-familiarity and ennui than misdemeanour. Mariana was not to be among the casualties if it could be avoided. Dismissing the servants, she led the girls to the Long Gallery at the top of the house, where portraits of persons known and unknown to Mariana struck attitudes of joy, delight, amiability, or indifference to the eye of the beholder. Her ladyship paused before one that Mariana had often remarked but never recognised.

"This is the Princess-Dowager Augusta," she said, "the mother of the poor, mad King. She was treated very cruelly when her husband was alive. Not by him, you understand, but certainly because of him. He was not popular."

To Mariana, who knew her history tolerably well, this seemed a vast understatement. The popular press, when Prince Frederick came to an untimely end, all but yawned. She remembered the strange epitaph which had seemingly characterised his life.

> . . . 'tis only Fred
> *Who was alive and is dead.*
> *There's no more to be said.*

But after his death the Princess Dowager had more or less come into her own. She and her friend, Lord Bute had been of great influence in the life of the young George III. However, to Mariana's unwilling eye the portrait conveyed nothing.

With Lucy it was another thing. She quite goggled.

"Why, puss, it might almost be *you* grown old. Badly painted, of course, and in fancy dress, but, my dear, it is uncanny!"

Mariana remained practical. "I certainly can't see it, myself." She refused to be overcome by painted glory. "What do you think, Aunt?" But the older woman had slipped away, as if to leave the girls to their own conclusions in the matter. It was so out of character that Mariana began actually to believe that something disturbing might be afoot.

"It'd be the eyes, I think, that do it," Lucy was saying critically. Her passing fear seemed to have quite dissolved. "Your neck is better, but if you'll forgive me, love, her mouth is smaller." She stepped back and surveyed the canvas from a middle distance. "I can only hope that you will make as good an effect at Carlton House."

She had no notion why Mariana gave her such a withering look.

But, later, even Bridie was quick to sense the unusual mood of her mistress. Since coming from Dublin she had been somewhat overawed by the grandeur of her new surroundings and it had subdued her, but now she spoke with the familiarity of an old friend.

"If you ask me, miss, it's no good, really it isn't. I think you know it. Why, you're scarcely the same girl that come with me from the old sod."

For Bridie the impetus to come, as well as the final decision, had been all her own, not Lady Battledore's, much less that of Mariana. Why, Lord knew, if it hadn't been for herself the girl would have been all alone in this great place, a stranger in a strange land, just as it was said in the good book. Nevertheless she took a tittle of warning from the look Mariana threw her. "I daresay I may be speakin' out of turn, miss, but you have begun to change something fierce, you know."

In fact, Mariana hadn't known it. "Have I, Bridie?" she asked in surprise. "In what way?"

The maidservant considered. "I don't know exactly, but you see, in Dublin you seemed quite a different person. Don't you remember how you and me and Cook used to sit in the kitchen and have a good gossip over a cuppa tea? You knew who you was then, like, and it showed. We each did our bit and let the others get on with theirs. And don't you remember how we were all friendly and nice back then?"

It struck Mariana that she had perhaps been more than a little unfair to her old friend. She had brought her here to this country, this new life, and then, wrapped up in her own concerns, had more or less abandoned her.

"You know, miss," the maid went on, "p'raps I shouldn't be sayin' it, but in for a penny, in for a pound, as they say." Then she paused, touched her nose, and seemed to think better of it after all.

But Mariana pushed her on. "What is it? What do you want to say? You can, you know. I shan't be angry."

"Very well, then," said Bridie a little defiantly. "I daresay it's because of meeting dukes and princes and princesses and the like, but you know, miss, you mustn't let it go to your head that you a bit take after the old lady in the picture upstairs."

It caught her mistress by surprise. "Good heavens, you too? Does everybody see it but me?"

Her point established, Bridie went back to folding the linens. "Oh, yes, miss. All the servants talk about it. They took me up to see the first week we was here."

"And you saw the resemblance they say is there?"

"Oh, yes, it's there, all right." She sniffed. "I must say I think you're prettier by a long way. *Such* a long neck she had, my word— like a camel! I knew a woman like her in Dublin, neck like a camel, breath like a cow. Mrs. Sheridan; you knew her."

"Bridie, are you happy here? I know you came because you believed I shouldn't be alone, but if you would rather go back to Dublin, I can arrange it."

She took Bridie quite off guard. Her breath all went out in a startled gasp. "Why, Lord love you, miss, what have I done to deserve such treatment? Just when things is getting interesting? And how would *you* manage, I'd like ter know? I daresay you think that tweeny, Lily, could do for you? Well, I ain't a-goin'. You can't in all conscience ask me to! No, I ain't a-goin', an' that's that!" She stomped grandly to the door of the dressing room and turned for a final volley.

"And don't you be thinkin' otherwise, Miss Mariana!" She shook her finger. "The like of it! Just when I've got these clothes all properly done up!" As she closed the door behind her Mariana heard a final, explosive, "Lily! Hah!"

Bridie would not be going home to Dublin.

Lily herself came to the door of the chamber not three minutes later. Would Miss Mariana please to come to the library as soon as she was able? And of course she would. But she sighed about it. Social protocol left her no time to herself whatsoever.

She went downstairs quietly, though resigned. Her aunt was not to be seen. There was only one person in the library.

Mariana had seen a great many beautiful women since she had returned to London. The streets, the theatres, the assemblies, and especially the ballrooms were full of them. So much so that mere comeliness was garden-plain by comparison. It took more to capture the eye of the Londoner these days. Charm counted for a great deal, vivacity added a crucial point or two, and breeding was, as always, worth a good half of the final reckoning, but beyond all that, sheer beauty carried the day. Mariana knew pretty well where she stood along the scale. Her primary fault, she had been informed both by Lady Battledore and by Lucy, and at different times, was that she allowed her keen intelligence to lead her into serious conversation. No man with a lovely girl in his arms, they assured her, wants conversation. Alas, if conversation is all she has to offer at such a moment, something has gone awry.

But the woman Mariana found in her aunt's library that afternoon could have said what she liked, danced how she would and where. No man in his right mind would have cared a whit, no matter what his age. For she was not a girl by any means and yet her great beauty was only a little dimmed by age, some might have said even enhanced by time. Her hair was a blue-black cloud that artfully floated about a face so perfectly proportioned, so absolute in its symmetry that one knew how goddesses must once have been. Add to this enchantment a pair of violet eyes ringed round by lashes as an evening pool is set by rushes and a tender mouth at once sweetly humourous and ironic with remembered pain.

Mariana knew her at once, but she did not know how to begin.

"How do you do?" she said at last. "I am Mariana Porter and you, I believe, must be my mother."

Lady Spurrell said nothing at all. Only opened her arms in a wide, welcoming gesture and drew her daughter in.

=17=

"MY LIFE," SAID Lady Spurrell in answer to Mariana's questions, "has not been exemplary. I fear, my darling, that I am incurably light-minded, and that has led me into a number of extremely difficult situations.

"You must know," she continued, "that I did not stay away from you from choice, but I knew that in the long run it would undoubtedly be best for you. No well-brought-up girl can afford to have a raffish mother, and that is what I have sadly become over the years. Well, a woman must live and have friends, must she not? I very foolishly exempted myself from the great world and had to content myself with the crumbs to be found on the fringes. Really, my dearest, you were better off without me."

"I had no mother," said Mariana, "and I needed a mother."

"Tush, you had your father and any number of well-intentioned school mistresses. How many girls do you think have better? Why, I scarcely saw my mother until I had my coming-out. After that, you know, we met on all sorts of occasions. But until that time I was, like you, in the care of a series of nurses, nannies, and school mistresses. You, at least, had the advantage of being placed with the Pecksniff Academy. I remember that old place as housing my happiest years."

"But I still do not understand why you had to go away," said Mariana. "Why, I thought you were dead."

"Your papa never spoke of me?"

"Hardly ever. And then only as a memory. He kept your picture beside his bed, but he never talked about you. I am sure he would have welcomed you back."

"Ah, would he indeed?" said her mother rather tartly. "Never fear, I lived up to my part of the bargain."

Something in her tone provoked her daughter's curiosity. "What bargain, Mother? With whom? Did Father pay you to stay away? Is that what you are saying?"

Lady Spurrell's partridge-plump figure went almost stiff with indignation. "No, not your wool-gathering father, bless his soul. It was his uncle. I really had no choice, you know. Your father gambled away everything he could lay his hands on, Ernest was too proud to marry me, and Spurrell had not come along yet. I had to live on something! Air is a Spartan diet, I am afraid."

"Are you saying that Uncle Forrester gave you money? Did he settle an annuity on you?"

The sparks in the depths of the violet eyes snapped angrily. "If only he had done! No, my dear, I was paid by the quarter. So long as I kept my distance I had my living, you see. It was not much, even so. It barely kept me alive. He was a cruel man to use me so."

Almost without volition Mariana began to piece together the disparate fragments: what she knew of her uncle and his passion for family respectability; what she knew of her mother's association with Prince Ernest; what she knew of her father's nature; and, oh, a hundred feelings and impressions collected all through her childhood. She remembered a game, a memory, that her mother would one day suddenly appear at the Pecksniff school to sweep her away, to take her into that enchanted world outside the dull confines of the schoolroom and dormitory. But her mother had never come. And now she knew why.

"But afterward, when you had married Lord Spurrell?"

"Spurrell? What a joke! My love, he was poorer than I. We married only to pool our resources so that we should not starve."

Looking at her mother's well-rounded figure Mariana strove against and mastered her inclination to smile.

"But why did he pay to keep you away from Papa, especially after you and Lord Spurrell were married?"

Her mother's well-defined eyebrows rose in surprise. "Your father? How absurd! Once he cast Lynval off, he couldn't have had the slightest interest in his companions. Oh, no, my sweet, it was *you* he paid me to stay away from!"

It came as such a surprise that Mariana felt quite weak. So it had not been either Papa or her mother, really, who had kept her to herself, it was not Papa to whom the inheritance was ceded, it was Uncle Forrester all the time, standing in the shadows, pulling the strings like the French marionette-men who made their little dolls dance. Had he done it for her? He hardly knew her. Had he done it for his idea of family? How could that be, when he had paid to keep hers apart? Why then, for his own self? To give himself the satisfaction of leaving his fortune in respectably proper hands? How odious. And yet, and yet, how easily one could be persuaded to understand.

"Of course, I kept away from your coming-out. Even I hadn't the face for that. It would have ruined everything. I daresay they all would have stayed away in droves." She smiled her perfectly enchanting smile. "Ah, but it will all come right now. We shall be together again."

From then on, Battledore House was enlivened by a constant stream of callers. Between the young men, related and unrelated, who came to lay siege to Mariana and the older, established gentlemen, and even highly respectable matrons, who came to gaze upon the legendary Lady Spurrell, to say nothing of the usual intimates of Lady Battledore's own set, the servants rarely had a quiet moment. Their lips were primly sealed, but their ears were open and their eyes missed nothing.

Bridie kept her mistress well informed. "And that little gold comfit box that yer aunt set such store by? Marasham knows who took it, but he wouldn't say a word."

"He knows who stole something from my aunt and yet will not tell?"

"As good as his position, miss. Accuse one of her ladyship's cronies? Not likely. She'd have to dismiss him out of hand. She couldn't turn her friend away, could she? And yet she couldn't have Marasham overlooking it all, could she?"

And Mariana, her hair in papillotes, would sit as still as a doll while Bridie ministered to her. Her skin was bleached with lemon, her eyes (a trick she learned from Lady Spurrell) were enhanced by belladonna, and the slightest touch of ratafia paper enlivened her lips. One never spoke of such things, but every clever woman did it.

The gossip was well worth hearing, for Bridie was of that inquisitive nature that can add a paltry two and two into an admirable sum. "And did you hear, miss, about Lady Strang? They say it was the butler did it, but from what I can conceive it were more like one of the grooms. The butler, after all, miss, is very nearly a gentleman."

"And we all know what gentlemen are, don't we, Bridie?" asked her mistress drolly.

"Exactly, miss. No butler would jeopardise his place by taking up with a lady, now would he?"

"Not unless he were Malvolio," Mariana answered.

Bridie had to think about that. "I don't believe I've heard that name mentioned, miss. Is he here in London?"

Mariana smiled. "No, he was from another country, but quite well known, I believe."

"Oh," said Bridie with all the scorn of the well placed, "a foreign gentleman."

But Lady Strang was not the only slightly questionable visitor to Battledore House of late. There were a number of men and women of impeccable appearance, superbly mannered in a way that seemed somehow to underscore the slight raffishness of their reputations. To be honest, a good many of Mama's associates seemed to have about them just the slightest whiff of rapscality. And oddly enough, they all seemed to be cronies of the Regent. It made for an interesting leavening on the evenings of large affairs, although inevitably, isolated instances were sometimes less exemplary. There had been, on those crowded occasions, one or two times when the going had been a little sticky, when even Mariana had been forced to freeze gentlemen who had become too full of ardour. No nice girl likes to be placed in such a position.

And yet no one seemed to suffer from it. They were in Vauxhall Gardens on the evening that "the ethereal Saqui" gave her première performance. Mariana, who had quite expected to be ravished by novelty and excitement, found the acrobat to be just the faintest disappointment. Perhaps the work in which she was engaged *was* very daring—the mast of the fire-work tower was some sixty feet high and the tightrope descent a little sticky—but the lady herself was so very corporeal and of such a masculine aspect, what with her old Roman helmet and classical tunic, that the nankeen trousers tied about the ankles like a schoolgirl gave an effect somewhat lacking in spice, despite the presence of the shooting blue flames and the Chinese fire.

Lady Blanche chided her for her lack of wonder. "I daresay they have better in Dublin, Miss Porter? Or perhaps you yourself could demonstrate to us just what she *should* have done."

"Oh, I am sorry, Lady Blanche. I had no idea she was such a favourite of yours. I daresay I am too critical. Perhaps one should not speak at all of how well it was done, but marvel that it could be done at all." She was determined not to put Lady Blanche's nose a second time out of joint, as they said she had already. "But it is a matter of such small moment, and the gardens are so pleasing, that I shall go away the happier for just having been here."

But Blanche was not to be mollified. "And will that be soon, Miss Porter?"

Mariana's laughter was at the ready. "They say there are twelve acres, Lady Blanche. Surely that is large enough to harbour both of us?"

In truth Mariana did not want her evening spoiled, for she had only been there once or twice before and she was still enchanted with these gardens, which offered both elegant festivity and a reputation for daring seclusion for those who chose to take advantage of it.

And elegant it was. Although the dining was certainly al fresco, let it not be thought that it in any way resembled the simple joys of bucolic picnicking, for what picnic could be supplied with the likes of Madame Sestina warbling from the front balcony of the Rotunda or the edifying spectacle of fashionable London disporting itself in the soft evening, ogling each other as avidly as the men of fashion had eyed the original Countess Ogle a century and a quarter before.

"But come along, my pet, we must find our places. This is the evening that the Prince Regent may come to be seen. And they say that Mrs. Fitz is coming. And the two haven't met since you-know!"

We don't want to miss that encounter, do we? Shan't we promenade a little?"

Handsome Bob, to whom this exhortation was addressed, merely went on with his repast, chewing placidly. "There's time, there's time. The Prince don't come out until after he has dined. I say, Marquis, have you ever seen such elegant victuals as these? Why, this ham has a thinness quite past belief. I swear you could read the *Postboy* or *Chronicle* through it with perfect ease!"

Tyger, who was there because of Lady Blanche, perhaps to take advantage of his cousin's recent defection, laughingly agreed that the carver here was famous. "Don't you know, Bob, they say he can cover the whole of the gardens with the slices from a single joint?"

"Twelve acres, sirrah!" cried Lady Battledore. "And I believe it!"

Certainly the famous Vauxhall chickens were no bigger than sparrows, and happy feasters must order again and again, cheerfully throwing into the wind what would have kept a poor family for a month. But no denizen of the Gardens was likely to know those poorer families, and thus was not likely to think of them.

Throughout all this Lady Spurrell was the calm center. Mariana found that her mother's trick was to be still and let the interesting things of the world come to her, rather than chase after them. All things considered, there was much to be said in favour of such a point of view. It required only composure and a supreme confidence that the world *would* come. So far, it seemed to do so. She was the cynosure of all eyes.

Curiously—perhaps it was that very encroachment of the fashionable world that always seemed to be at the door—Mariana and her mama had found hardly any time to talk to one another. It seemed unlikely that they would discover much opportunity in the near future. Lady Spurrell always rose late, usually appearing only when Mariana was embarking upon her busy day. She had not yet told her mother of her plans for the house, but went about them in secret. The element of surprise was a savoury one. Papa had come round, at least, and was helping a good deal. He had not yet seen his former wife. Mariana did not know if this was by accident or design. He had promised to join the party this evening, but so far he was not here.

"Mariana, my dear . . ." It was as if Mama had read her mind. "Shall we walk a little? The evening is so fine."

"What, Mama, alone?"

Lady Spurrell waved a somewhat languid hand. "Oh, certainly not. I daresay one or two of the gentlemen will accompany us. At a discreet distance, of course. Now, who shall it be?"

The offers were luxurious in their plentitude. Lady Spurrell made an occasion of it. You would have thought they were to be wearing her colours. "Let it be . . . ah, yes, the Marquis and . . . dear, dear Jeremy."

Mariana had a fleeting pity for "dear, dear Jeremy," since the Marquis, whatever his virtues, was at times a nonstop talker. In Jeremy he would find no resistance whatsoever.

The evening was indeed a fine one. Only a little distance away from the rotunda one might almost fancy oneself deep in the country, so complete was the quiet. This was an enticement for lovers whose cooing tones emitted intermittently from the shadows, but for most it was a balm, the great healing after the abrasions of city noise and discomfort.

The four walked in silence, too, for the most part. The men stayed a discreet distance behind, the Marquis only occasionally murmuring some unresponsive comment. Lady Spurrell sighed once or twice, and cleared her throat. Then at last she said bluntly, "Do you think I am a bad woman, Mariana?"

The girl hardly knew what to answer. It was not that she had ever permitted herself to ask the question in the silence of her heart. She had chosen, rather, to quiet it, to smother it under a number of less pressing enquiries.

"I don't know, Mother. We know so little about one another that I can hardly judge. I am not sure that I am capable of judging in any case."

Her mother understood what she meant. "Yes, you *are* young and your life has been lived on the quiet, so to speak." They walked along a little further. Then, "Well, I am *not* bad. I have often been foolish, and careless and light, but not ever bad. Will you try to believe that of me?"

The rush of affection Mariana felt would have washed away any lingering doubts. She pressed her parent's arm in silence. Behind them the Marquis was lecturing poor Jeremy on the value of a Grand Tour. "Not that you can indulge in such things at the moment! Damn the little Corsican upstart! Damn him, I say!" Jeremy made a few tentative throat-clearing sounds as if to concur.

"They will tell you all sorts of things if they can," Lady Spurrell said bitterly. "Lord, if I had had affairs with half the men they have named, I'd either be as rich as Croesus or a worn-out husk.

"Maybe both," she giggled. Mariana could begin to see that what had been called light-mindedness was more likely an inborn vivacity. It would explain a great deal of what she had heard, even account for much of what she merely surmised.

The pathway, while not dark, was shadowy and subdued, their party of friends far away from this enchanted spot. Even the Marquis had fallen silent. The moonlight struck against the walk ahead just enough to illuminate the face of the man approaching them.

He was not alone—at least two companions were sheltered in the dark—but his presence and the strength of his personage were enough to have put any accosters to flight after one look from those piercing eyes.

He and Lady Spurrell faced each other with no aura of surprise about them whatsoever. The Duke spoke first. His voice was as cool as new silk. "Well met, my lady. I wondered if it might not be soon."

Lady Spurrell allowed him the courtesy of a slight inclination of her head. "Your Grace." She drew Mariana closer to her side. "May I present, sir, my daughter."

The shadows and the softening of the moonlight erased much of the shock of his scarred face. It left him almost handsome and his expression amiable.

"Ah, yes. Miss . . . Porter, is it?" Mariana wondered why he gave the question such an odd inflection. It seemed to conceal rather than seek information. A tension out of all proportion seemed to envelop the small group. Mariana was glad Jeremy and the Marquis were just there beside them. But the Duke of Cumberland chose to display only his social graces. Now to Mariana's mother he said winningly,

"I hope, madam, that we shall see you in society now that you have returned to your home."

"I have no home at the moment, Your Grace. I have come only for a flying visit with my daughter."

The Duke peered into Mariana's face. "Curious, you know, my brother and sister are quite right. The gel does show a marked resemblance to the old Princess, what? Coincidence, eh?"

There seemed to be a half-concealed snicker in the darkness behind him, which was rewarded by a quick but icy-cold shot from his good eye. No one laughed at the Duke's sallies until he had indicated that he wished them to be appreciated.

Lady Spurrell's lovely face was still. She seemed to be reflecting upon some private knowledge of her own. "There are a great many coincidences in the world, sir. One more or less should not amaze you." The words were unaccented but the tinge of genteel dismissal was not lost upon His Grace, though he chose to pass it over.

"I have never had a daughter among all my bastards, you know. Or, I should say, none I could claim. Odd, ain't it, that the King sired a quiverful, and all I have running about are little Hanoverian gallants. Fine enough, one or two of 'em, but hardly first quality. It takes breeding on both sides for that.

"Eh, my lady?" he interrogated, as if Lady Spurrell were in a witness box and he hoped to trap her into an untoward admission. "Eh, what do you say to that?"

The lady summoned up the ghost of a patrician smile that never reached her violet eyes. "What I say to it, sir, is that I have no knowledge of your attainments. For all I know, you might have filled a nunnery."

He took it in good part. "Depleted one, more like!" he guffawed, and this time his henchmen were allowed to join in his coarse laughter. Mariana felt her mother's body grow rigid. Really, for all his lineage the man was proving himself to be an insensitive and boorish double-ganger of that fallen angel she thought she had perceived that night at the opera. The Duke seemed to sense her revulsion.

"Well, Miss Priss, have they made you into a bluestocking or have you learned to move with the music, as your mother always used to do? Lynnie Porter was no great barrier to your education, I'll be bound!"

At this seemingly slighting reference to his friend, the Marquis moved a little closer to the conversation. He and Jeremy had been keeping a discreet distance, but now their presence seemed justified. The Duke took note of them at once. His demeanour changed only slightly, but it was evident that the presence of even nominal protectors restrained his conversational excesses. Mariana, however, was not about to let the implied slight pass unnoticed.

"Are you well accquainted with my father, Your Grace?"

Cumberland shot a vaguely uncomfortable look at Lady Spurrell as if asking her intervention. Something that had begun as a light jest might have more serious consequences if the girl chose to make an issue of it with the Regent, who was obviously taken with her, if reports were true. He backtracked. Not because he was afraid of the girl, but because he and the Regent were just at this moment not the best of friends. However, he could not prevent his arrogance from showing through a bit at the edges.

"I gave your father his first wager, I believe, Miss Porter. It was on the leaping abilities of two frogs. He lost . . . which I believe became a pattern of sorts, eh?" He peered at her through his glass. "Zounds! What a scowl! Will you call me out, then, to defend a gambler's honour?"

But another voice interposed a mocking note. "What need has she to do that, Your Grace, when he is present to defend his own honour if need be?"

Mariana peered into the darkness. "Papa?"

He made a little half-bow. "Your servant, my dear. And yours, Lady Spurrell."

It was something of a personally historic moment for these two, who had not spoken for over fifteen years. The drama was not lost on the Duke. Nor the fact that Papa was not alone, as Mariana realised when she saw that two familiar figures had joined the group, Brion and Tyger, the cousins of Jeremy.

"Lady Battledore was beginning to worry a bit about you, Miss Porter," said Seymour, moving closer. The Duke's companions shifted uncertainly.

"Jeremy and the Marquis were with us," Mariana pointed out. "I am sure we were in no danger."

"You shame me, Miss Porter," laughed Cumberland heavily. "Am I such an ogre even to you?" He said to the men, "I would gladly have seen the ladies back to their pavillion, even if they had been alone. Besides, the ways about here are quite safe, you know. The Gardens would hardly be the Gardens if one had to fret about such things, eh?"

Lynval offered his arm to his former wife. "May I escort you, ma'am?" he asked, oblivious of the Duke's tightening jaw.

She allowed her fingers to rest lightly upon his arm. If she trembled a little, it was not obvious in the darkness. She stood very straight and was very gracious when the Duke swept into a low and exaggeratedly courtly bow.

"May I hope, madame, to have the honour of calling upon you one day very soon?" He hardly expected her reply.

"I regret, Your Grace, that I am not quite recovered from my recent illness. I shall be receiving only my closest and oldest friends." Her smile was serene but her eyes dared him to make something of her words. He chose the better part.

"You wound me. I had thought I belonged by right upon that sacred roster. What must I do to atone?"

"Nothing, sir," she answered. It was a plain answer. Nothing. Nothing to be done, for nothing *could* be done.

The irony returned to the Duke's eyes, his fallen-angel visage intact once more. Silently he, with his followers—had he implied that they were his sons?—faded into the shadows. The Marquis heaved a sigh of relief.

"Don't mind sayin', Lynnie, that I was deuced happy to hear your voice. It was a bit of a sticky situation."

Lynval Porter clasped his old friend's arm. "I know you would have defended the ladies, old man."

The Marquis laughed. "Ah, yes, but who would have defended *me*?"

Captain Seymour walked along beside Miss Porter. They said nothing to each other, but their silence was companionable and relaxed. It was odd, Mariana thought, that just now, when they *might* talk to each other without rancour, they needn't. How very odd it was. Should she ask him about Lady Blanche? No, perhaps not. There seemed to be no need. Suddenly a thought came to her that quite surprised her. She no longer disliked him. She wondered if she ever really had. Mariana knew that she, like most people, occasionally struck attitudes to herself that were sometimes difficult to abandon. Had she done this with Brion Seymour? He had certainly done nothing to change her mind, but now she liked him. It was rather like the puzzle of the hanging boxes. Dear me, she thought, am I to say like Mama that I have an incurably light mind?

It was not until the evening was quite over that she realised that neither the Prince Regent nor Mrs. Fitzherbert had ever appeared.

═══**18**═══

SISTERS AT BREAKFAST; aristocratic, reserved, and aloof. Before the servants. Sisters alone; like sisters everywhere.

"And you are not going to tell me a thing?" Lady Battledore complained.

Lady Spurrell remained calm. "There is really nothing to tell. Ernest proclaimed and Lynval reclaimed. At least for the moment."

Lady Emilia seized on this avidly. "There, you see! You never change. You drop these little interesting . . . *fascinating* . . . bits of information, and then you simply seal your lips with that stupid little self-congratulatory smile. You've done it since we were girls, and it infuriates me!"

The smile became a trifle more pronounced and crept upward into the violet eyes. But no further confidences were imparted. Instead, Lady Spurrell sipped her *café-au-lait* meditatively before asking the very thing to which she had slowly been leading.

"What do you think of that dashing young Tyger as a prospect for Mariana?"

Lady Battledore sniffed derisively. "You can't be serious? Not suitable at all. She's a great heiress. Money needs looking after."

"She is also a woman," observed her sister, "and deserves a woman's happiness."

"Happiness is of more long-range importance than a mere tumble," said Lady Battledore severely. "Look at the two of us, if you doubt it. Where might we be if we had been wiser?"

Lady Spurrell's smile faded. The truth was too, too obvious. Both she and her sister had conducted their emotional lives with very little eye for the morrow. She herself had spent, it seemed, a lifetime regretting a year's thoughtlessness. And yet there had been happiness too. That was all she craved for her child, a chance at happiness.

"What about the dear Captain?" counter-questioned Lady Battledore. "Think of the combined fortunes. They would be among the richest couples in London."

"He struck me as rather a stick," Lady Spurrell answered. "And yet I saw her walking with him last evening. Can she really care for him? He is too like old Josiah for my taste."

"Well, what would you? She *must* marry within the family, and who is left but poor little Jeremy?"

"There are absolutely no others?"

"Not unless Chipworth turns one over in the good country earth. Forrester had distant relations near Bristol, they say, but ones that even he avoided."

Lady Spurrell shuddered. "Untenable." Then she asked after Jeremy as if his name had not been mentioned. He was a poet, was he? And a gentleman, one could tell. How did it happen that he lost his speech?

"An accident at school, I believe. I really do not know the details."

"I do," said Lynval Porter coming in unannounced. "If I tell you, will you ring for fresh tea, my dear sister?"

"You make yourself free in my house, sir," Lady Emilia protested amiably. "What business have you here at this hour?"

"I've come to see Mariana upon a matter of business."

Lady Battledore looked at him askance. "Lud, you're not going to be touching her for money, I hope?"

Porter tried to seem outraged, but failed. "Not at all, dear one. I have my own money now, you know. Not much, but honestly come by."

"What, then, is the business?"

"Must I perforce disclose my concerns to all and sundry, madam?" asked Porter. "It is a family matter."

"And amn't I a part of the family?"

"Not so close," said Lynval, "as others in this room. Good morning, dear Lady Spurrell."

Lady Spurrell's smile, hardly gone, had now returned to add a glow of youthfulness to her face. The thick, rushlike lashes hid the violet eyes, but could not conceal the welcome she extended to her former husband. "Good morning, sir. I trust you slept well?"

"Why," Lady Battledore asked the air, "is it that I feel an intruder in my own morning room? You are both far too old for such mooning. Brother, what is it you have to say of Jeremy?"

"Well," said Lynval, settling down, "I had it straight from Seymour, you know, and since it concerns him, I suppose he can be counted upon to have the truth of it."

"Something dread," said Lady Battledore. "I can feel it in my bones."

"Do hush, Emilia," her sister said. "Let him get on with the story. It isn't sad, is it, Lynval?"

"No, it isn't sad. And it's not long. Quite the reverse. Seems there was a fire at the school and Jeremy saved all their lives. Actually went back into the flames to help Seymour."

"Went back into a burning building to help his cousin?" asked Lady Spurrell. "What a heroic gesture. Is that how he lost his voice?"

"Yes. Irreparably damaged his vocal cords, they say. Had a promising career as a barrister, but that is all gone now."

"Still," said Lady Spurrell, "I shouldn't like Mariana to wed a man who couldn't speak. Such a lonely life, don't you think?"

Mr. Porter's glance upon his former wife was both exasperated and fond. "I should hope, my dear, that she marries for love, not conversation, what?" Slyly he added, "Too much talk could wreck a marriage, I should think."

Lady Battledore snorted. "Just listen to us! Each has decided to champion a different suitor for the dear gel's hand! I hope she has the wisdom to make her own choice and stick to it."

"Perhaps she could marry all three," said Lady Spurrell frivolously. She flashed an enchanting smile at Porter, but he seemed not to respond.

"Let us hope she has the wisdom to learn from our mistakes."

On the evening of the great event, Mariana attended the Regent's affair with none of her suitors, but in the company of her father and

Lady Battledore. Lady Spurrell, as a friend of the Princess Augusta, came in that lady's party. Certainly she was reentering society under fortuitous shelter. Few would dare brave the wrath of the blunt and outspoken princess.

Any sort of arrival was not easy. Although none of the guests were invited before nine of the clock, the streets leading to Carlton House were blocked with carriages much earlier. Pall Mall, the Haymarket, and St. James's Street were virtually impassable and the din was beyond description. Coachmen, footmen, and the packed crowds of onlookers vilified each other with good-humoured abandon, and one enterprising equipage even utilized a posting horn to make way. Through it all the band of the Coldstream Guards could sometimes be heard above the din, playing robustly in the courtyard of the Prince's residence.

Although this party was nowhere nearly as large as the fête Prinny had given in honour of the exiled Bourbons, when some fifteen hundred invitations had been accepted, even these greatly reduced numbers could not all hope to sit down *with* His Highness. To accommodate the overflow, straw matting had been laid down over the lawns and galleries and promenades created in which guests might sup or dally as they chose. Many simply wandered about the grandiose rooms in a kind of stunned astonishment, staring open-mouthed at the conspicuous extravagance, while members of the household in their dull-blue liveries picked out with gold lace hurried about attending to the comfort of the visitors. It was as if they considered themselves surrogate hosts, anxious to please.

There was no doubt in Mariana's mind that one should be impressed—but not seduced. It was all overdone, overdecorated, and opulent to the point that a sensible mind no longer boggled, but merely accepted what it observed as a tenable, though novel, mode of living. Carlton House suited the Prince Regent exactly by mirroring his mind and providing him a theatre in which to play out his fantasies.

Lady Battledore was soon captured and swept off by the Marquis, who was as affable as ever to his old friend. Lynval, too, seemed friendlier. When the couple had gone, Mariana said to him, "Isn't it time, Papa, that you and the Marquis mended your break? You must certainly miss his companionship as much as he does yours. Now that there is no question of money, I am sure that you can return to your old ways."

"Money?" huffed Lynval. "What the devil do you mean by that? D'ye think I'd let money stand in the way of friendship? Why, if a friend were in need I'd give everything I had!"

"Ah, but would you accept it? The dear Marquis wanted to marry me more to provide for us than for any other reason, and yet you scorned him for it."

"Did I, Mariana? Yes, I suppose I did. Silly old fool, amn't I?" He considered. "I say, d'ye think he's interested in Emilia? It seems to me he's around her a great deal."

"You may be right," Mariana agreed. "How nice it would be to have him in the family."

"Hmph," said her father. "Yes, I suppose so."

They wandered about the great house and gardens. Mariana was content to be introduced to her father's old friends and to sip lightly of the iced champagne that flowed so freely. It amazed her that despite all the confusion outside, within the house everything was well ordered. No crowding, none of the bustle, only a sort of efficient graciousness.

They had just left off a brief conversation with the great Brummell and were ambling through a picture gallery when Lynval introduced a subject he had not mentioned to her before.

"I say, Mariana . . . about your house . . ."

"My new house, Papa?"

"The Baillie Street house."

"Yes, Papa, the house I have just furnished in Baillie Street."

"Attached to it, are you?"

His tone was peculiarly diffident. He seemed to be saying far more than the weight of the mere words conveyed.

"I've been thinking about that house, you know. A man needs a house in town."

"You will certainly be welcome there any time you come to London, Papa. You shall have your own rooms."

He seemed a little flustered by that. "Well, the fact is, you see, I imagine you'll be wanting something grander before long."

"Will I, Papa? Why is that?"

"When you marry, you know. You'll need a larger house in which to entertain."

"Perhaps I shall. I never thought of it. It is such a dear little house."

"It *is* a nice little house. I must say I've missed it." He cleared his throat. "Ah, you see . . . if ever you decide to sell, I might be in the market."

She smiled secretly to herself. "Would you, Papa?"

"Yes, I might. A man needs a house in town."

They encountered another old crony of his just as she heard familiar laughter from a nearby room. She kissed him on the cheek and went to find Lucy. Just before she left him, she finished their conversation. "Yes, I think that house suits you, Papa."

"It does, my dear, it does. A man needs a house in town."

Her blood-sister (they had once taken vows with cut fingertips) seemed to be having the time of her life in the midst of an admiring masculine circle. Despite the fact that her wedding day was very near—or perhaps because of it—half the bucks of London were finding Lucy very nearly irresistible. Well, thought Mariana, she is going to go out in style. But Lord Bob was standing at the outer edge, trying very hard to remain composed. It was clear that he was wanting not to be a beast and spoil Lucy's fun, but all the same, he was looking more than a little vexed, and Mariana remembered that theirs was to be a modern marriage. Perhaps he had not thought to be fending off rivals quite so soon. Mariana, taking pity, glided to his rescue.

"Ah, Bob, my dearest," she trilled in a deceptively ardent tone. "I won't let that naughty Lucy monopolise you until you are safely at the altar! Lauk, she will soon have enough of you to satisfy both of you. You must promise to give the rest of us poor mortals a look from time to time." She tapped him lightly on the cheek and murmured in his ear, "Smile, wretch, and look as if you cannot resist me."

He looked quite blank at first, then smiled engagingly and made as though to draw her aside. "Shall we find a quiet corner, Miss Porter?"

The sea of bachelors parted immediately as Lucy hurried to claim her property. One of the young men called out, "See here, old chap, you've already hooked one beauty, you can't have 'em all!"

The fascinating Miss Porter was still uncaught, her cash reserve still untapped. They surged around her, but she brushed them off with her furled fan.

"Ah, no, gentlemen, you shall not trifle with me. I want no fickle hearts hanging about my door, and I swear Miss Lucy does not either." And to her friend, "Come, dear heart, we shall explore this enchanted cavern together and let these boobies do as they will."

"What, all of us?" asked Tyger Dobyn, coming out of the crowd. He looked deucedly handsome, and she relented.

"Well, you and Lord Bob, perhaps, may trail along behind us a step or two, but mind you tell us all the scandalous things you know about everyone we meet." Linking her arm in Lucy's she said to her, "Now, my girl, we must see everything before Aladdin's magical wishes wear away!"

"So, Miss Porter, you think my palace a cave of wonders, what?" asked a richly rotund voice. She spun into a curtsey that swept the floor.

"Good evening, Your Royal Highness. You are very kind to allow so many the opportunity of viewing your treasures."

The Prince Regent insinuated himself between the two ladies, quite shutting out the Tyger and Lord Robert, who smiled cheerfully. For all the manipulation, Bob found himself in essentially the same situation as ten minutes before, and no closer to his bride. The Prince Regent swept them off through the great rooms, keeping up a running commentary on both his possessions and the social stream as it passed.

"That is a lovely bit, eh? Gainsborough, you know. The Lady Sarah Lennox. Might 'a been my mam if the P.M. hadn't interfered. My papa never got over it, you know, poor old fellah."

Then, nodding and bowing: "Good evening Lady Marchpane, Lady Bessborough. Charming evening, what?" And when they had passed: "Tell me that I have aged well, my dears. Those two ladies, who look as if they might be my aunts, are exactly a year younger than I am."

"Oh, sire," cooed Lucy, "you must, I know, be jesting. I have no idea how old you are, but . . ."

Regent took bait. "Yes, yes, tell me, miss, how old am I?"

Lucy pretended to ponder the question. "More than thirty, I think?"

He sighed. "Much more," he agreed in a lugubrious tone. "Pray, make me laugh, don't throw me into the slough of despond."

". . . But less than fifty?"

The Prince snorted. "Well, bless me! *Certainly* less than fifty, gel! Egad, what use is that? Don't be afraid. Convince me I look thirty-five, and Lord Bob shall be a peer!" He swung round to Mariana. "You, Miss Porter, what do you say?" He giggled a little. "I have already promised my sister Augusta to look to your advancement." He bowed graciously and serenely to a passing couple. "Shall I be invited to dance at your wedding this season?"

"Certainly I should be honoured, sir, but the question of the groom remains in doubt."

This seemed to confuse the Prince immeasurably. "Does it, by Jove?" He turned back to the Tyger. "Here, you wretch, I thought you had it all set up, what?"

"The lady has not done me the honour, sire."

"Asked you, did he?" Prinny inquired of Mariana.

"In a way, sir, but not very conventionally. In any case, my heart is not engaged at the moment, and though it is dreadfully old-fashioned, I hope to marry for love."

"Do you, by gad? More power to you, I say! Don't love Tyger, eh? What if we made *him* a peer?"

Mariana smiled. She was not certain how serious the Prince was, nor did she think he knew himself.

He sighed romantically. "Marry for love, if you can, Miss Porter. Convenience is much over-rated." He looked a little startled when he heard what he had said. "Is that a epigram, do you think? Demmed clever, at any rate. Fitzie would have loved it." He grew nostalgically confidential. "You know, Miss Porter, I never loved Mrs. Fitzherbert in time, nor appreciated her so much as when she was gone, poor dear . . . Poor *me*, for that matter. It is a poor thing for *all* when a man cannot even choose his own wife." His eyes mis-

185

tily sought Mariana's. "And so you see, my dear, you *must* marry for love, if you can at all afford it!"

Presently the Regent was detained by guests and Mariana found herself unconsciously scanning the crowd in hopes of seeing Captain Seymour amongst the promenade. It occurred to her how pleasant it might be to rest upon his arm rather than that of this beruffled partridge whose nest had been made upon the throne of England.

Taking advantage of the diversion, Lord Robert affixed himself to Lucy as quickly as possible and Tyger offered himself to Mariana as a replacement for the Prince. And then, horrors, she recognised among the crowd the familiar ice-beauty of Lady Blanche, who was dressed in an oddly becoming gown that almost resembled a *robe de chambre*, with a corded gathering at the waist and long, full sleeves that all but covered her hands. Exceptional it might be, but by tomorrow, doubtless, it would be the height of fashion.

Lady Blanche was on the arm of her cousin, Mr. Parmalee Phipps, a snuff-coloured man in snuffy garb. He raised his handkerchief delicately to his nose as they approached, sneezed affectedly, then pointed his toe and made his leg. Tyger was civil but quite cool. Mariana wondered if it was because he had tried his luck with Lady Blanche and failed. She was her usual glacial self, but Mr. Phipps seemed determined to make an impression by babbling nonstop about the Prince Regent's residence.

"Prinny changes these gauds by the week, you know," he confided. "He is such an insatiable—quite, quite in*sa*tiable—collector that one thing is no sooner in place than something else must be shifted. It is a house in flux, you know, a house in flux! One can scarcely get used to one arrangement before it is turned out for another." He snickered at what he supposed to be his own wit. "I suppose he must find *something* to fill his time, for God knows he does not reign, no matter what his title." But he looked about furtively to be sure no one had overheard him.

Mariana privately thought there was something awfully strong about denigrating a man in his own house while preparing to feed at his table. "You must have visited here often, Mr. Phipps?" she asked.

"Oh . . . I . . . ah . . . actually, this is my first time, but I have my sources! Yes, I daresay I know things that go on here that even the Regent has no knowledge of."

"Is that a fact?" asked Prinny, who had caught up to them. They were standing under Cutler's great portrait of Queen Anne, and that lady had the faintest smile about her lips. The Prince Regent chummily placed his heavy arm about the shoulders of Mr. Phipps. "Come along, old chap. You'll tell me *everything*, what? No one ever does, you know, and you can't imagine what a bore it is! So glad I found you."

Lady Blanche was left unescorted and had no choice but to take the Tyger's offered arm. They walked along in silence in the long lines of sightseers moving in orderly fashion, conversing quietly behind their handkerchiefs and fans. It occurred to Mariana how like this promenade was to the rituals of the Vauxhall Gardens, where the couples and clusters of the *ton* met and regrouped in much the same way.

One of the Prince's dull-blue minions approached and discreetly drew the Tyger aside. Presently Dobyn asked the ladies to excuse him. "I have a message from a certain Personage," he told them in an undertone. "I hope you will forgive my desertion, Lady Blanche, and you, Miss Porter."

He was scarcely gone when Lady Blanche bowed distantly, hardly more than an inclination, really, and made her own excuses. "For I believe, Miss Porter, that neither of us should run the risk of compromise by being seen in the other's company."

Startled, Mariana watched her move away. Was it possible that her ladyship, after all, possessed a shred of humour?

By some chance she was left alone for the next few moments and was examining the rosy glow of the marble Carelli group when the Tyger returned. He seemed more than a little discomfited.

"Miss Porter, thank heaven you are still here. Would you be so good as to accompany me? Your presence has been requested by a member of the family."

"The family, Mr. Dobyn? Who on earth can you mean?"

He lowered his voice. "For heaven's sake, Miss Mariana, please do not embarrass me. A certain highly placed person has asked me to escort you. You will be quite safe; you are in the house of the Prince Regent, after all!" She allowed herself to be drawn along.

The next thing he said as they walked briskly along the halls did not surprise her, although she had thought the subject had been discussed and abandoned. It was almost as if it were being opened a final time, as if he was reassuring himself.

"You have definitely decided, Miss Porter, that you could not marry me?"

She looked at him. Certainly he was as fine-looking a man as any woman could choose for a husband; tall, well built, and graceful. And certainly he had demonstrated on several occasions a sensitivity that his profession belied, a delicacy of feeling one would not expect in a pugilist. And certainly he *was* one of the Forrester family. But, no, she could not marry him.

"Very well." He took it without question and nodded as if her answer confirmed a decision of his own.

"It is a fine evening," he said, and began to lightly whistle under his breath.

"Who is it we are going to meet?" Mariana asked him.

"You'll see soon enough," he answered with a conspiratorial smile. "I declare, Miss Porter, I believed that you thought better of me than to distrust me so."

What an odd thing for him to say, when she had not mentioned distrust at all. Really, she had not even thought it.

"This way," he directed. They turned into a narrower corridor, not mean by any description, but certainly less designed to impress. He paused before a closed door and knocked. He listened, then knocked again, and at last opened the door himself. "Your friend seems not yet to have arrived," he observed.

"My *friend?*" asked Mariana. "Who is it?"

He ushered her inside and stood waiting by the door. The room was tastefully done in white enamel and blue velvet. The windows looked into the private park. Over the mantel was a painting of the Princess Dowager Augusta, younger, more vibrant than in the painting in the Long Gallery at Battledore House. Otherwise the room was empty.

"You have but to wait a moment or two," the Tyger said. He closed the door softly behind him. With a look at her apprehensive face he added kindly, "There is nothing to be afraid of, you know."

Mariana looked him straight in the eye. "Who is it wishes to see me, Tyger? If you do not tell me, I shan't stay."

Dobyn looked distinctly uncomfortable, far too much like a young boy caught, not with his paw in the jam jar, but at something a bit more reprehensible. It made her uneasy. "Well, if you must know it is . . . it is the Queen!"

"The Queen? She is here in Carlton House? Whatever for?"

"She wishes to see you, actually," Tyger said glibly. "She has heard the rumours and wants to examine you for herself." He edged toward the door. "I mustn't wait. You'll be expected to see her alone." He turned back as he went out. "Everything will be all right, Mariana. You'll see."

—19—

MARIANA AWOKE WITH a start. She did not know how long she had been dozing. Not very long, surely, for the fire still burned as brightly as before, but she was not alone in the room. The other was a young girl in the Carlton House dull blue setting down a laden tea tray. Mariana wondered how long she had been there.

"Will the Queen be much longer, do you think?" The maid must know something about it or she would not have known to bring the refreshment. But the girl only looked at her blankly.

"The Queen," repeated Mariana. "I have been summoned to an audience with her here."

The girl's brows knit in concentration. Then she touched her lips with her fingertips and shook her head. It was obvious to Mariana that she was, like Jeremy, a mute. But the girl wanted to communicate. She circled her head with a finger to indicate a band or coronet, then extended spread fingers on either side of her brow. Ah, yes, Mariana understood, a crown . . . the Queen. But the head was shaken. No, it was *not* the Queen who was expected, but someone else. Hopefully, Mariana fluttered her fingers in the rudimentary sign sequence she had learnt from Jeremy, and the girl's eyes lit up. She began to gesticulate rapidly, so rapidly that Mariana had not a hope of following her. Frantically she waved her hands to slow the girl down, but it was too late. The door of the chamber opened and a man stood there. It was the same individual Mariana had seen skulking about the house in Baillie Street. And behind him stood a man with the face of a ruined angel, His Royal Highness, the Duke of Cumberland.

For the first time in her life Mariana felt herself in the presence of danger, and yet the Duke seemed to be at least affecting a semblance of amiability.

"Ah, my dear Miss Porter. I hope you have not been too bored the while you awaited me. I was detained, I fear, by the press of popularity."

Mariana's face must have betrayed some of the astonishment she felt, for he hastened to amplify his statement. "Oh, I know what they say, my dear, that I am the ugliest and most hated man in England, eh?"

"Surely, sir, your misfortune . . ."

"Ah, very kind of you, I am sure; but it is true, you know. No, not *this*," he gestured to the scars, "but what they think they see inside me. By 'they,' of course, I mean all those mollycoddles, those fools and fops who toady about my brother, what? They're all here tonight, every demmed sycophant in London." He sounded so fierce that Mariana stirred uncomfortably in her chair and began to rise. He stilled her with a gesture.

"I am here, Your Royal Highness, under false circumstances. I was led to believe, by a man I thought my friend, that my presence had been requested by your mother, the Queen. Since that is not the case, perhaps you will give me leave to retire?"

"Not so quickly, surely. Since no one knows you are here, your reputation is quite safe. My man, Stephenson, is keeping watch in the passage. No one will get past him."

But Mariana rose purposefully. "I beg you, sir, to let me go."

"Not until we have had an opportunity to talk, to discuss certain things of interest to both of us."

"What things can they be, Your Royal Highness?"

The Duke opened his hands wide in a gesture indicating his disinclination to do her harm. "You shall leave as soon as ever you like, Miss Porter, once you have heard me out. I promise not to detain you over half an hour by the clock." She hesitated. "I cannot command, but I humbly request your acquiescence." It became obvious to Mariana that even though he most often wore a mask of irascibility, he could, when he chose, be as winning as ever his older brother was. He saw how she relaxed, and smiled at her. "Please, do sit down again."

191

He waited until she had resettled in her chair, poured her tea, and even then hesitated a trifle before he began. He sat down near her, carefully positioning himself so that the ruined profile was all but hidden, and at last opened the discussion with a hard question.

"What do you know, Miss Porter, of my relationship with your mother?"

"I know, sir," she answered carefully, "that she does not care to discuss the subject with me."

"And you think it improper to discuss it behind her back?"

"That is right, Your Highness. It would shame me to do so."

He tried another tack. "Well, then, let us speak of Mr. Porter instead. Perhaps I can convince you that I mean no harm. He is good to you, is he? You have never wanted?"

"Never, sir."

"And you have been happy with him?"

"Why, how else should I be, sir, since he is my father?"

The Duke hesitated once more. He asked diffidently, as if it were a matter of no great importance, "And if he were *not* your father?"

She paled. "What are you implying, Your Royal Highness?"

"If he were not your true father, but only a very kindly, very generous man who gave you his name despite much sorrow in doing so?"

Mariana's mouth was quite dry. "Please, sir, do not jest about such things," she managed to whisper.

"Do have more tea, Miss Porter, it will refresh you for what lies ahead."

Mariana's mind whirled, but she remembered one thing Aunt Emilia had told her. "I believe, sir, that I was born a good two years before you knew my mother in Flanders."

His reply was sharp and to the point. "Your mother, miss, was lady companion to my mother, the Queen, a good two years *before* you were born." He touched the scarred side of his face ruefully. "And I was still a pretty lad then. They all loved me, all the young maids." Turning his head so that they looked full face at each other, he concluded, "But I had eyes for only one of them."

The silence hung heavily between them. Mariana raised her eyes to the portrait of the Dowager-Princess Augusta. "Yes," said the Duke, "I can see that they have pointed out your resemblance to your great-grandmother." When she dropped her eyes he asked, "Is it such a terrible thing to be the daughter of a king's son?"

Mariana looked at him coldly. "I am not your daughter, sir," she said, "and nothing will make me believe otherwise."

He seriously seemed not to understand her. "Is it the money? That is it, eh? If I acknowledge you, you lose the Forrester inheritance? Child, do you think I would let you lose by such a thing? I may be *King* someday!"

In a fluid motion Mariana moved swiftly toward the door, but the Duke caught her by the wrist as she passed him and drew her firmly back. "Do you think I would say such things if I could not prove them to you? You foolish child, it matters not what you think of *me* but of your future."

Mariana's face had grown quite taut; her jaw was tight with such a fury as she had never felt before. How dare this man, no matter who he was, say such things to her? "What I think, sir, is that you have gone quite, quite mad!"

Before she suspected what was coming, his fury matched her own and with a stinging blow across her face the Duke of Cumberland silenced the dreadful words that any son of George III least wanted to hear. "How dare you? If I did not love you as my own blood, I would make you pay dearly for your temerity!" Both of them were breathing in short, ragged gasps, each as pale as the other. His grasp on her wrist slackened not at all as he turned his head toward the door, shouting, "Stephenson, come to me!"

Through the doorway burst both the equerry and another of the Duke's servants. "Take her!" snapped their master. To Mariana he said, "They will not harm you if you go with them quietly. You and I shall have opportunity to speak again when our tempers have cooled." He laughed in a sharp bark. "Another inheritance, we all have short fuses, what?"

Adjusting his neckcloth and setting his coat upon his shoulders, he eased out of the room. Mariana watched him go with almost unbearable despair. She began to cry softly. "Please, Miss Porter," Captain Stephenson said quietly, "I should dislike to use force. If you will come with us quietly, I guarantee as I am a gentleman that you will suffer no indignity."

She allowed them to lead her away, holding her head high, but failing to disguise the traces of tears on her cheeks. There was no one to mark them, however, but one of the maids whom everyone believed was simple-minded because she could not speak. Mariana's hand went up to her face as if to brush her eyes and her fingers fluttered. Unobtrusively the little maid nodded in reply. The two men had seen nothing. Only a few steps along the corridor was a door that led into the service quarters and thence into the cool evening air, where a carriage waited in the darkness. Tyger stood beside it. He could not meet her eyes.

"Would you get into the carriage, please, Miss Porter?" said Captain Stephenson.

Mariana paused before Tyger Dobyn and looked into his face. "I believe the words for you are 'consummate villain,' Tyger. It seems that my instincts were correct. I do not think you would have been a likely husband."

"The carriage, please, Miss Porter," said Stephenson again, and when they were inside he added, "Really, you must not think too badly of him. Your father can be a most persuasive man."

"The Duke of Cumberland is *not* my father," replied Mariana icily.

"Be that as it may, he *believes* he is, and he is only acting in a way commensurate with that belief," said Stephenson. "All he really wants is your love and acceptance."

"If he wants my love," said Mariana, "he has chosen the wrong way to obtain it."

—20—

BRION SEYMOUR, ONLY half-listening to the whispered tirade pouring out from Lady Blanche, idly examined the elegant fans in the case before them. One in particular caught his eye. It was an Italian piece and depicted the capture and sacrifice of Iphigenia at Aulis. It seemed to him that the hapless victim pictured bore a remarkable resemblance to Mariana Porter. Poor unfortunate, he thought, does she feel that she is being strapped to the altar of our uncle's legacy?

". . . and, furthermore, sir," his companion hissed into his ear, "there are worthier men than you suing for my hand!"

He raised an eyebrow. "Really, Blanche? Who, for example?"

She was taken aback by the unexpected question. Quickly she ran over the list in her head. So many men had shown marked attention, but then drifted off to ally themselves with lesser, empty-headed chits. Most men really do not care for strong women, she decided, only the exceptional ones. "My cousin Parmalee, for one. His is as pure a strain as my own. Our children would be clear-bred aristocrats."

"Then," said Brion lazily, "I think that you should by all means accept his offer. I believe it would make you both *supremely* happy."

This startled her into a brief silence. Then, "You do?" she asked.

He nodded affirmatively. "And speaking of the devil . . ." Blanche saw that Parmalee Phipps was making his way toward them through the crowd.

"Oh, I say, Seymour . . . that friend of yours, the dummy, you know, seems to be gettin' quite agitated over there."

Brion looked across the gallery to see Jeremy gesticulating in agitation. "Then, perhaps I had better see what it is all about," he said.

195

"By the way, Phipps, let me be the first to congratulate you on your betrothal to Lady Blanche. Lucky dog, you cut us all out and won the prize, eh?" He bowed to Blanche. "Your Ladyship, I truly hope you will be very happy." He kept his eyes down, for he knew he dared not look into either face.

When he reached Jeremy's side he could see that his friend was working himself up into a grand explosion. "Steady, old boy, what's going on, then?" Jeremy was struggling desperately to make a sound, his fingers were twitching spasmodically. "Is he having a fit?" someone in the crowd asked. "Disgraceful! And in the Regent's house, too!"

Brion knew very little of the abbé's finger language and he put his hands over those of his friend, stilling the frantic movements. "Easy, Jemmy, let's get out of this crush," he murmured. Almost at once Jeremy calmed, but continued to pluck at Brion's arm, dragging him away. "M . . . mmm . . . mmm!" he was groaning. People stared and opened a way for them as Brion tried several doors, then drew Jeremy into a small chamber and closed the door. He placed firm hands on his friend's shoulders, willing strength and fortitude into them.

"Steady on, old fellow," he repeated over and over, but Jeremy continued to struggle. "Mmmm!" he anguished. "Mmmm!" His face grew very red with the strain and Brion could feel his body trembling. Whatever it was, it was something of such magnitude that he was like to break under the burden of it.

"MMMM . . . MAR . . . NA . . . MAR . . . NA!"

Under the terrible pressure of needing to communicate, Jeremy was actually forcing himself to regain mastery of his lost speech!

"MA . . . MMMA . . . NNNA . . . MA-NA!" As a result of the horrendous effort tears were springing to Jeremy's eyes; they were matched by the tears of joy in Brion's own eyes as he witnessed his friend overcoming the blockage that had silenced him for so many years. And then, suddenly, he understood.

"Mariana? Are you saying 'Mariana,' Jemmy?"

A great smile, like sunlight, sprang into Jeremy's face and he nodded vigorously. "Ma-na! Ma-na!"

"What of her? Is she in trouble? Where is she?"

In reply Jeremy placed one hand to the side of his face, twisting the flesh into a caricature of humanity.

"Cumberland? Are you saying the Duke of Cumberland has done something to her?" Another avalanche of grunts and nods.

"Where, fellow? Where has he taken her?"

Roughly grabbing at Brion's arm, Jeremy dragged him from the room. Unceremoniously they forced themselves through the promenading crowd, turning at last into an empty corridor, at the end of which Brion saw a slight young girl in the Carlton House dull blue. Frantically she waved them on and pushed them through a doorway into the service courtyard. By some miracle horses were waiting and a young boy holding them. In finger-speech the girl commanded him.

"Good work, lad!" cried Brion.

The boy grinned in return. "Lizzie's me sister, sir. I wager she knows what she's about, for all she's a dummy. Good luck, sir. They can't be far ahead. The carriage'll have a slow time through the crowds." They were already mounted and on their way when the lad called after them, "You want to watch out, sir! 'Ee's a nasty lot, that Tyger!"

The streets leading to Carlton House were still blocked with the arriving and departing carriages, perhaps even more so than they had been at the beginning. Leaning low in his saddle, Brion accosted a burly fellow who looked as if he might be a well-dressed navvy. But he had seen nothing like the equipage of the Duke of Cumberland.

"Be pretty 'ard ter miss, wouldn't it, guvnor? They been nothink like it that I seen!" With a sinking heart Brion realised that, of course, no girl would be abducted in a state coach, but something smaller, lighter, and less obtrusive. Despairingly he surveyed the press of carriages ahead. He could scarcely tell one from the other. He had absolutely no way of knowing in which, if any, Mariana was being carried farther and farther away from him.

Jeremy pressed his mount close to Brion's and caught at his arm. Once having gained his attention, he cupped a hand behind one ear in a listening attitude. Brion strained to hear what his friend was intercepting, but could not. "Ma-ri-aa-nnna!" Jeremy shouted impatiently.

"Lead on!" Brion replied. "I'll follow you!"

They threaded their way through the crowd as swiftly as they were able. From time to time Jeremy would pause, then start off again. Far from having grown deaf, as many mutes do, his hearing seemed to have heightened with his disability. At last, some fifty feet ahead, he turned back toward Brion and pointed across the confusion. Brion, too, could see what he meant. Two coaches had collided, the leathers and harness of the horses becoming entangled, the wheels of the carriages blocking each other. On the box of the nearest carriage a tall figure stood up and brandished a coach-whip menacingly above his head.

"Back off your nags, damn your eyes! I've an urgent errand!"

This was the wrong thing to say to a London coachman, even coming from a toff in fine clothes who chose to sit on the box beside the driver. "Back off, yerself, me fine lad! The fault was yours from the beginning. When will you buckos learn to leave the drivin' to them as knows wot they be doin'? Back off, now, there's the good lad, eh?"

In response the tall man on the box cracked the whip loudly above the other's head in an effort to intimidate him. The result was something quite disastrous. The panicking horses, already distrait because of the unaccustomed tangle, reared up and twisted between the shafts. The Duke's carriage teetered, swayed dangerously under the imbalance, and slowly, with a great screeching whine, toppled to one side. The coach driver was trapped, but the whip-wielding "toff" was thrown quite free. Brion could see now that it was his cousin, Tyger Dobyn. What the devil did *he* have to do with this?

Without paying attention to the driver or the screaming horses, Tyger was wrenching at the uppermost door of the carriage, reaching within and assisting—more nearly hauling out—a bedraggled but seemingly unhurt Mariana Porter. Brion's heart sank as he leapt to an obvious conclusion. Damme, if the gel wasn't eloping with the Tyger!

Two things happened simultaneously. The Tyger, without letting loose of Mariana, put out a hand to assist still another person, a man. Stephenson, by damn! Mariana, seizing the moment, tore her arm from the Tyger's grip and half-stumbling in her haste, clambered down from the upturned equipage and began to struggle through the crowd, who took it as a great joke.

"'Ere, this way, dearie, ol' Bill will pertect yer!" . . ."Ye best look sharp, me luvly, 'ee's gainin' on yer!" One smitten mudlark made sure the Tyger noticed *her* existence by bawdily lifting her skirts and demanding why her goods weren't as fine as those of "them as don't woncher!"

It was as good as a fair-day troupe of mummers, but a silence fell upon them when Tyger caught up with his pretty prey. The young lass fought bravely against him, but she was outweighed and out-classed. The Tyger's swift hand raised and fell in a chopping blow. Mariana fell like a dead weight, straight into his arms.

The merry crowd was far from pleased. "'At's no way ter myke 'er luv'yer, mate!"

To Brion it was a spur that had never before pricked him. Throughout all his military career Seymour had been known for pos-sessing a clear head, whether at the tavern table or in battle. At the siege of Gerona it was this very coolness that had won his honours; even the glory of the battle had not much quickened his pulse. Nerves of steel, they said of him, but this was all in the past. As he saw Tyger's blow fall upon Mariana, a red, blinding fury began to boil up from somewhere deep inside him. Leaping from his horse, he thrust boldly toward the centre of the action. He was completely unarmed and he saw that Stephenson was approaching from the other direction, but it booted nothing. The scarlet rage was now his master, not any reasoning power whatsoever. With a mounting roar he flung himself forward upon the ablest pugilist of the time!

Eventually they dragged him off Tyger's unconscious body. Jeremy was beside him, half-supporting him, and Mariana was staring at him in wide-eyed, open-mouthed wonder. And Stephenson, ever the social diplomat, was trying to smooth over the incident.

"A grave mistake, sir. The fellow shall be thoroughly chastised by the Duke, I assure you. Nothing of this kind was ever intended, I know. His Royal Highness holds Miss Porter in nothing but the highest esteem . . ." His words dried in his mouth as Brion turned his red-rimmed eyes full upon him, and slowly, slowly began to move toward him. Slowly still he raised his hands as if to continue with the equerry the violence he had wreaked upon his cousin Tyger.

Stephenson squeaked and retreated, but the crowd about them, eager for any diversion, closed until it was far too dense to let him go far. Backed up against them, he all but gibbered in fright.

"Please . . . please . . . oh dear, I'll have to shoot, you know!" But undeterred, Brion continued the slow advance. The situation was bizarre in the extreme . . . the silent, red-eyed man seemingly inhabited by some vengeful fury, the urbane equerry reduced to near incontinence by his fear.

"'Ere, lookit!" some wag in the crowd cried out. "'Ee's gonter get yer-r-r!"

Stephenson raised his weapon uncertainly. "Oh, God! Stop! Please stop!"

Brion reached out implacably. The firearm exploded as Stephenson sobbed in terror, rooted to the spot.

Jeremy half-carried Brion back to his horse, leaving the befuddled object of the pursuit standing uncertainly where she was. Then Jeremy turned back to her and commanded in the clearest tones he could muster, "Ma-ri-aa-nnna, come!"

—21—

WHEN BRION SEYMOUR awoke it was in his own rooms, but he was not alone. The woman sitting in a chair by the window with the early morning light full on her was not unfamiliar to him (though faded, her beauty was unmistakable), but he wondered at her presence here.

"Lady Spurrell," he whispered, "is it really you?"

"Yes, Captain Seymour. Pray do not think of arising, the doctor has advised a good rest."

He tried to move his head, but it ached abominably. "Forgive me, madam, but why are you here? I mean, why you?"

His visitor smiled a little at his question. "It was that or give leave for my daughter's reputation to be torn to shreds. She insisted on coming here with you."

"Mariana is here?" He stretched his neck and shoulders. They ached too.

"Yes, she is asleep on the chaise longue in your dressing room. She was quite exhausted by her adventure. I owe you a great debt for saving her from that madman."

"Do you mean my cousin Tyger? I thought they were eloping."

Her amusement was evident. "Forgive me for laughing, Captain, but you seem to need a recital of the events over which you triumphed. My daughter was indeed being abducted, perhaps even by your cousin, but not for the purposes of matrimony."

With an oath, he half-rose from bed, then settled back as the pain in his shoulder engulfed him. Lady Spurrell sprang to his side. "No, you must not try to move." Gently she pressed his forehead. "The fever seems to have abated." She returned to her chair and continued,

"It was not *that* sort of abduction at all, you see. There is a man who has the peculiar idea that I cannot determine the father of my own child."

"The Duke?" he asked. He found himself eager to hear the tale of this past history.

"Yes," she acknowledged, "the Duke. Quite ridiculous, of course. I may be light-minded but I am not such an imbecile as all that. No, Mariana is Porter's child, well enough. I am sorry if that inconveniences you."

"How can it do that?"

She gave him a sharp look. "If she were *not* Porter's child, she could not inherit, I should think. It would revert to you and that charity of Forrester's."

"The City Merchant's Benevolent Fund, yes; but I had not thought about that." He stirred again. "She *is* all right? I saw that bloody b . . . that scoundrel strike her. She took no harm of it?"

"No, nothing of note. Although there is an ugly bruise, she will outlive it. I hope she may never have worse." It seemed to Brion that she said this with the spirit of one who has seen a great deal worse. For all her beauty, it was said she had lived a difficult life. He studied the still-delicate profile. He reflected how unlike her Mariana was. Although the daughter was beautiful in her own way, perhaps it was a more satisfying way. Mariana's was the sort of beauty that has its source within.

The bedroom door opened a crack and Jeremy's gentle face looked in. "You are awake, cousin?"

"Jeremy, I didn't dream it, then? You can speak again? How did it happen?"

"I don't think I understand it myself," Jeremy said. "The doctor puts it down to shock all the way around; that is, that I lost it in the fear of the fire at school, and the shock of Mariana's abduction brought it back. I don't suppose I shall ever know."

"But you are speaking so fluently now, when before you were barely able to get the words out."

Lady Spurrell's laugh brightened the room. "Perhaps that is because he has been talking nonstop for two days. He has had time for practice."

"Two days? What do you mean? How long have I been here?" He tried to rise again and this time managed to remain in a sitting position.

"Well, if you must sit up, let us at least put pillows behind you."

"How long, please?"

"It has been three days since the Prince Regent's great affair. Mariana's great escapade, however, has all but put that in the shade. They say it is likely she will never be welcome again at court." She looked out of the window as though she saw something of great interest there. "I hope she will not mind too much. But then, she is a sensible girl. I daresay she will marry happily and live quietly. A good life."

Brion frowned. "But how should she suffer when it was the Duke who was at fault?"

"What an innocent you are, to think that the King's son could come to grass in such a situation. No, it is the woman who will suffer, as is usually the case."

"What of the Tyger? Certainly he can be punished."

"No, he was only following his master's orders. The Duke has taken him up, I believe. His future is assured."

"But he won't be in a state to enjoy the patronage quite yet," said Jeremy. "You did quite a job on him, old chap. He'll be laid up for some time to come. Where did that sudden strength come from? He's no puling boy, after all."

"I don't know," said Brion. "All I can remember is that when I saw him strike Mariana I started toward him. I think I may have gone a little mad."

"Well, I believe he'll be avoiding you for some time to come. Pity, I rather had a soft spot for the old Tyger. I daresay the Duke will ship him off to Hanover for the time."

"Or discard him, now that his usefulness is at an end," said Lady Spurrell acidly. "The Duke is rather good at that." She rose again from her chair. "I will go and see to Mariana. I imagine you will want Jeremy to help you freshen yourself."

"You do smell a bit high, cousin," Jeremy agreed. "Will you be wanting to shave as well?"

When Mariana's mother was gone, Jeremy put on a serious face.

"You'll be marrying her, I suppose. Mariana, I mean. She's not left your side for more than an hour or two all this time. I think it is evidently more than gratitude."

Brion was thoughtful. "We shall see," he said after a moment. "Now as to that bath and shave? You'll have my man heat up the water?"

Jeremy smiled. "Nothing like a military man for giving orders."

When he emerged, bright and shining, an hour later, he found that Mariana was no longer in his quarters. "Well, she *has* a home, old chap," Jeremy protested. "I daresay she wanted freshening, too."

At precisely three of the clock that afternoon, Captain Brion Seymour, late of the Irish Ultonia, presented himself at Battledore House and was ushered by Marasham into the drawing room, where he surprised Mariana Porter diligently working over an embroidery hoop. They were, at first, very reserved with each other, she having no idea of his intentions, but thrilled at the memory of his fury vented upon the man who struck her; he having no idea that she was not the selfsame cool and withdrawn young woman he had always been acquainted with. He could not see that her fingers were trembling as she stabbed nervously at the embroidery. She had, in fact, managed to take only three stitches, having hurriedly picked it up when she heard he was at the door. It was not even her own embroidery.

They stared at each other rather sullenly for a long moment, unsure how to begin to mend their relationship. Then each began to speak at once, saying almost the same thing.

"I am grateful, sir/miss, for your attention and concern."

It truly *was* said almost in unison and with almost the same words. Close enough, in any case, to bring foolish smiles to their faces. Close enough that Seymour felt free to begin his suit with a rough jest.

"What is this of marriage, then, Miss Porter?" he asked without preamble. Nothing could have failed nore dismally, or startled her more, but she masked it.

"And what marriage is that, sir?"

"Why, ours, to be sure. It has been reported to me that you spent so much time in my quarters that your reputation is quite in tatters and can only be repaired by a good proposal."

"And do you think that that is what you are making, Captain? A good proposal?"

She listened to the bantering tone in her own voice and was astonished. A week ago she would have cut him down for presumption, but now he seemed to radiate a new magnetism that drew her to him in spite of herself. She found herself studying the lean, decidedly masculine figure with new eyes, and she knew as well from the glow in his face as he looked at her that something paramount had changed between them. She tried to keep her voice light, but failed miserably.

"You have recovered from your swoon, then, Captain? I have never seen a man go berserk before."

"Did you find it instructive?" he asked huskily. It was not the surface conversation that mattered, but the subtext, which was declaring true and changeless things.

Clumsily she stabbed herself with the needle and raised her finger to her lips. "You've hurt yourself," he said unnecessarily. She waved away his concern. She felt suddenly ill-equipped to take on the task of facing down this man.

"I thought you . . ." She gave up, knowing she could not pretend. "Oh, Captain Seymour, I was so worried. The doctor kept saying it was brain fever, and I had no idea what to expect." She shuddered. "Thank heaven my mother was there to keep me from going mad!"

He crossed the room and drew her up into his arms. He could see the pulse beating in her throat like a little frightened bird; he bent his head and kissed her, and she made an astounding discovery. This man whom she had so fought against both soothed and excited her. On the one hand she felt so safe, so protected, and on the other she seemed on the brink of new discovery.

"Must I do it all properly?" he murmured, "or may I chance sweeping you off your feet while remaining on mine?"

He could feel rather than hear the little chuckle that began in her chest and issued from between half-parted lips. "Do you mean on bended knee, sir? I think that would be delicious."

He groaned, drawing himself away from her. "You're serious?" Her eyes twinkled and she tried to keep her lips from curving in a smile. "Amn't I worth a serious proposal, Captain?"

And then he became very serious himself. "You are worth anything in the world, Miss Porter, no matter how foolish others might take it to be." Quickly he went down on one knee with a resolution she found oddly touching. He looked up at her and asked, "Will you marry me, Miss Porter?" The door opened.

"Oh, dear," said Lady Spurrell, "am I interrupting? I shan't be long. I've only come to find my embroidery. Why, there it is! How did it get here on the floor? Mariana, have you been toying with my needlework? How very vexing!"

She blithely crossed the room and paused, effectively, in the library door, bestowing a warm smile on them. "Oh, do get on with it, Captain Seymour. I'm sure we all know she is going to answer 'yes,' don't we?"

Brion stood up and took her hands in his. "Are you going to say 'yes?'" he asked.

"Of course," said Mariana. "Did you ever doubt it?"

— 22 —

ST. JAMES'S CHURCH in Jermyn Street was designed by the great Christopher Wren. It has an altarpiece and font by Gibbons and an organ by Renatus Harris upon which the incomparable Handel used to play. It was on this day to be the setting for a double wedding ceremony. All of the *ton* were in attendance; most, it is true, properly to wish the happy couples well, but some, unworthily, to catch their first glimpse of the notorious Miss Mariana Porter, who had, in a most suspect escapade, allowed herself to be abducted by the Duke of Cumberland. Or so it was said by some; others attributed the Duke's banishment to his estates in Hanover to the direct intervention of this same Miss Porter, who had inherited such an immense fortune from her great-uncle, a city merchant, that she could affect the fate of kings' sons. Some said she was the Duke's mistress and should not be in a Christian church at all, others that she was his unacknowledged daughter. It was hard to think of such an adventuress settling down to a private life, what?

But all was forgotten when Harris's pipe-organ began to roll out the resounding chords of the bridal chorus from *Penthe* and the two wives-to-be made their appearance at the end of the aisle. They say that all brides are beautiful, each in her own way, but Lucy and Mariana were beautiful by any standard. Lucy was in white satin and silver lace, which gave her an ethereal quality quite at odds with her true nature, while Mariana's old ivory silk and the ivory veil worn by her Aunt Emilia at her first marriage softened the girl's sometimes severe beauty and lent her the air of a medieval Madonna. But the deep love that shone out of their eyes, when they knelt with their grooms upon velvet cushions to take their vows, could be misinterpreted by no one. Even the Prince Regent, seated with his sister Augusta in a place of honour, was observed to wipe away a sentimental tear. His presence satisfied many and set the stamp of respectability upon the nuptials.

The vows exchanged in fervent tones, the rings given, the kisses taken, the brides and grooms moved up the aisle to an organ fanfare, eyes alight, faces suffused with happiness. Mariana's eyes roved amongst the spectators: her own mother, lovely in dove grey; Lucy's parents, staid and upright, she in pale carnation and he in silk cord; Mrs. Damer, elegant in a deep blue that heightened the colour of her eyes; and, resplendent in watered silk, Lady Blanche Westring. Their eyes met and passed over each other, sliding smoothly on to the next countenance.

Only her father was missing. He had presented her at the altar, but then he had gone—where? She sensed rather than heard Brion's exclamation at her side. "What the devil is *he* doing here?" She looked past him toward the door and her eyes met a pair cornflower blue. He was quite tall, perhaps past six foot, and masterfully tailored so that his extremely broad shoulders and powerful chest did not appear at all grotesque. His hair was cut in the fashionable Corinthian mode that set off his hawklike profile to perfection. Her father was angrily turning him away from the door.

Was there a look of longing in those blue eyes, or only the chagrin of a missed opportunity? Tyger Dobyn raised the fingertips of his right hand to his forehead in a mocking salute to cousin and bride. Mariana looked up into the face of her new husband adoringly. When she looked toward the door again, the Tyger was gone.

If you have enjoyed this book and would like to receive details of other
Walker Regency romances, please write to:

Regency Editor
Walker and Company
720 Fifth Avenue
New York N.Y. 10019